Richard Harding Davis

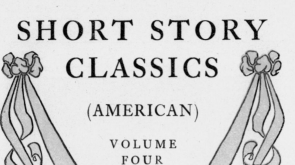

SHORT STORY CLASSICS

(AMERICAN)

VOLUME FOUR

EDITED BY

William Patten

WITH
AN INTRODUCTION
AND NOTES

P. F. COLLIER & SON
NEW YORK

CONTENTS—VOLUME IV

AFTER THE BATTLE

BY JOSEPH A. ALTSHELER

Joseph Alexander Altsheler (born at Three Springs, Ky., April 29, 1862), one of the leading writers of American historical fiction, is here represented by a story only generally historic in its scene—any battlefield in the Civil War—but thoroughly localized in its psychology. Only the author's native State, and the primitive mountain region of that, could have supplied the two characters of the story, in one of whom rages a conflict between two primal impulses of his nature, beside which the clash of Union and Rebel arms seems a mimic strife.

AFTER THE BATTLE

BY JOSEPH A. ALTSHELER

THE falling dusk quenched the fury of the battle. The cannon glimmered but feebly on the dim horizon like the sputter of a dying fire. The shouts of combatants were unheard, and Dave Joyce concluded that the fighting was over for that day at least. In his soul he was glad of it.

"Pardner," he said to the wounded man, "the battle has passed on an' left us here like a canoe stuck on a sand bank. I think the fightin' is over, but if it ain't we're out of it anyhow, an' I don't know any law why we shouldn't make ourselves as comf'table as things will allow."

"If there's anythin' done," said the wounded man, "you'll have to do it, for I can't walk, an' I can't move, except when there's a bush for me to grab hold of and pull myself along by."

"That's mighty bad," said Joyce, sympathetically. "Where did you say that bullet took you?"

"I got it in my right leg here," the other replied, "an' I think it broke the bone. Leastways the leg ain't any more use to me than if it was dead, though it hurts like tarnation sometimes. I guess it'll be weeks before I walk again."

"Maybe I could do somethin' for you," said Joyce,

"if there was a little more light. I guess I'll take a look, anyhow. I haven't been two years in the army not to know anythin' about bullet wounds."

He bent down and with his pocket-knife cut away a patch of the faded blue cloth from the wounded man's leg.

"I guess I'd better not fool with that," he said, looking critically at the wound. "The bullet's gone all the way through, but the blood's clotted up so thick over the places that the bleedin' has stopped. You won't die if you don't move too much an' start that wound to bleedin' again."

"That's consolin'," said the wounded man; "but, since I can't move, I don't know what's to become of me but to lay here on the field an' die anyway."

"Don't you fret," said Joyce, cheerfully. "I'll take care of you. You're Fed. an' I'm Confed., but you're hurt an' I ain't, an' if the case was the other way I'd expect you to do as much for me. Besides, I've lost my regiment in the shuffle, and the chances are if I tried to find it again to-night I'd run right into the middle of the Yankee army, and that would mean Camp Chase for your humble servant, which is a bunk he ain't covetin' very bad just now. So I guess it'll be the safe as well as the right thing for me to do to stick by you. Jerusalem! listen to that! Just hear them crickets chirpin', will you!"

There was a blaze of light in the west, followed by a crash which seemed to roll around the horizon and set all the trees of the forest to trembling. When the echoes were lost beyond the hills the silence became heavy and portentous. The night was hot and sticky, and the powdery vapor that still hung over the field crept into Joyce's throat and made him cough for breath.

"Thunderation!" he said at length, still looking in the direction in which the light had blazed up. "I guess at least a dozen of the big cannon must have been fired at once then. Can't some fellows get enough fightin' in the daytime, without pluggin' away in the night-time too? Now I come of fightin' stock myself— I'm from Kentucky—but twelve hours out of the twenty-four always 'peared to me to be enough for that sort of thing. Besides, it's so infernal hot to-night, too."

"It was hotter than this for me a while ago," said the wounded man.

"So it was, so it was," said Joyce, apologetically, "an' I mustn't forget you, either. Let 'em fight over there if they want to, an' if they're big enough fools to spile a night that way when they might be restin'. What you need just now is water. I think there's a spring runnin' out of the side of that hill there. If you'll listen you'll hear it tricklin' away, so cool and refreshin' like. I guess it was tricklin' that same way, just as calm an' peaceful as Sunday mornin', while the battle was goin' on round here. Don't you feel as if a little water would help you mightily, pardner?"

" 'Twould so," said the wounded man. "I'm burnin' up inside, an' if you'd get me a big drink of it I'd think you were mighty nigh good enough to be one of the twelve apostles."

"It's easy enough for me to do it," said Joyce. "I'll be back in a minute."

He took off his big slouch hat and walked toward the source of the trickling sound. From beneath an overhanging rock in the side of the hill near by a tiny stream of water flowed. After a fall of five feet it plunged into a little basin which it had hollowed out for itself in the rock, and formed a deep and cool little pool. Around the edge of the pool the tender green grass grew. The overflow from it wandered away in a little rill through the woods.

"Thunder, but ain't this purty?" exclaimed Joyce, forgetting that the wounded man was out of hearing. "It's just like our springhouse back in old Kentuck. I've put our butter-crocks an' milk-buckets a hundred times to cool in our pool when I was a boy. Wish I had some of them things now!"

The stirring of peaceful memories caused Joyce to linger a little, in forgetfulness of the wounded man. It was cool in the shadow of the hill, and the gay little stream tinkled merrily in his ears. He would have liked to remain there, but he pulled himself together with an impatient jerk, filled the crown of his hat with the limpid water, and started back to the relief of the wounded man.

He followed the channel of the stream for a little way, and as he turned to step across it he noticed the increasing depth of its waters.

"It's dammed up," he muttered. "I wonder what's done that."

Then he started back shuddering and spilled half the

water from his hat, for he had almost stepped on the body of a man that had fallen across the channel of the poor little rivulet, checking the flow of its waters and deepening the stream.

The body lay face downward, and Joyce could not see the wound that had caused death. But as he stooped down he saw again the broad red flash in the west, and heard the heavy crash of the cannon.

"Will them cannon always be hungry?" he muttered. "But I guess I must give this poor little stream which 'ain't done no harm to anybody the right of way again."

He stooped and pulled the body to one side. With a thankful rush and gurgle the waters of the recent pool sped on in their natural channel, and Joyce returned to the fountain-head to fill his hat again.

He found the wounded man waiting with patience.

"I was gone longer than I ought to have been. Did you think I had left you, pardner?" asked Joyce.

"No," said the man. "I didn't believe you'd play that kind of a trick on me."

"An' so I haven't," said Joyce, "an' for your faith in me I've brought you a hatful of the nicest an' freshest an' coolest water you ever put your lips to in all your born days. Raise your head up, there, an' drink."

The wounded man drank and drank, and then when the hat was emptied he laid his head back in the grass and sighed as if he were in heaven.

"I must say that you 'pear to like water, pardner," said Joyce.

"Like it?" said the wounded man. "Wait till you've been wounded, an' then you'll know what it is to want water. Why, till you brought it I felt as if my inside was full of hot coals an' I'd burn all up if I didn't get something mighty quick to put the fire out."

"Then I reckon I've stopped a whole conflagration," said Joyce, "an' with mighty little trouble to myself, too. But I don't wonder that you get thirsty on a night like this. Thunderation, but ain't it clammy!"

He sat down on a fallen tree and drew his coat-sleeve across his brow. Then he held up the sleeve: it was wet with sweat. There was no wind. The night had brought no coolness. The thick and heavy atmosphere hung close to the earth and coiled around and embraced everything. Through it came the faint gunpowdery vapor that crept into the throats and nostrils of the two men.

"I wish I was at home sleepin' on the hall floor," said Joyce. "I'll bet it would be cool there."

The wounded man made no answer, but turned his face up to the sky and drew in great mouthfuls of the warm air.

"Them tarnation fools over yonder 'pear to have their dander up yet," said Joyce, pointing to the west, where the alternate flashing and rumbling showed that the battle still lingered. "I thought the battle was over long ago, but I guess it ain't. I've knowed some all-fired fools in my time, but the fellows that would keep on fightin' on a hot night like this must be the all-firedest."

Then the two lay quite still for a while, watching

the uneasy rising and falling of the night battle. Had
they not known so much of war, they might have per-
suaded themselves that the flashes they saw were
flashes of heat-lightning and the rumbling but the
rumbling of summer thunder. But they knew better.
They knew it was men and not the elements that
fought.

"It's mighty curious," said Joyce, "how the sand's
all gone out of me for the time. To-day I felt as if
I could whip the whole Yankee army all by myself.
To-night I don't want to fight anythin'. I'm as peaceful in temper as a little lamb friskin' about in our old
field at home. I hope that there fightin' won't come
our way; at least not to-night. How are you feelin',
pardner?"

"Pretty well for a wounded man," replied the other;
"but I'd like to have some more water."

"Then I'm the man to get it for you," said Joyce,
springing up. "An' I'm goin' to see if I can't get
somethin' to eat, too, for my innards are cryin' cup-
board mighty loud. There's dead men layin' aroun'
here, an' there may be somethin' in their haversacks.
I hate to rob the dead, but if they've got grub we need
it more'n they do."

He returned with another hatful of water, which
the wounded man drank eagerly, gratefully. Then
he went back and searched in the grass and bushes for
the fallen. Presently he came in great glee, and
triumphantly held up two haversacks.

"Luck, pardner!" he exclaimed. "Great luck!
Bully luck! One of these I got off a dead Fed. and

t'other off a dead Confed., and both must have been boss foragers, for in one haversack there's a roast chicken an' in t'other there's half a b'iled ham, an' in both there's plenty of bread. I haven't had such luck before in six months. You're a Yank, pardner, and a Northerner, an' maybe you don't know much about the vanities of roast chicken an' cold b'iled ham. But it's time you did know. I've come from the field at home when I'd been plowin' all day, an' my appetite was as sharp as a razor an' as big as our barn. I'd put up old Pete, our black mule that I'd been plowin' with, an' feed him; then I'd go to the house an' kinder loosen my waist-ban', an' mother would say to me, 'Come in the kitchen, Dave; your supper's ready for you.' Say, pardner, you ought to see me then. There'd be a pitcher of cold buttermilk from the spring-house, and one dish of roast chicken, an' another of cold ham, an' all for me, too. 'An' say, pardner, I can taste that ham now. When you eat one piece you want another, an' then another, an' you keep on till there ain't any left on the dish, an' then you lean back in your chair an' wish that when you come to die you'd feel as happy as you do then. Pardner, I wish them times was back again."

"I wish so too," said the wounded man.

"We can't have 'em back, at least not now," said Joyce, cheerily, "but we can make believe, an' it'll be mighty good make-believe, too, for we've got the ham an' the chicken, an' we can get cold water to take the place of cold milk. I guess you can use your arms all right; so you can spread this ham an' chicken out

on the grass, an' I'll see if I can't find a canteen to keep
the water in. Say, pardner, we'll have a banquet, you
an' me, that's what we'll have."

The stalwart young fellow, full of boyish delight at
the idea that the thought of home had suggested to
him, swung off in search of the canteen. He found
not one alone, but two. Then he returned clanking
them together to indicate his success. As he came up
he called out, in his hearty voice:

"Pardner, is the supper-table ready? Have you
got the knives an' forks? You needn't min' about the
napkins. I guess we can get along without 'em just
this once."

"All ready," said the wounded man; "an' I guess
I can keep you company at this ham an' chicken an'
bread, for I'm gettin' a mighty sharp edge on my
appetite too."

"So much the better," said Joyce. "There's plenty
for both, an' it wouldn't be good manners for me to
eat by myself."

He sat down on the grass in front of the impro-
vised repast, and placed one canteen beside the
wounded man and the other beside himself.

"Now, pardner," he said, "we'll drink to each
other's health, an' then we'll charge the ham an'
chicken with more vim than either of us ever charged
a breastwork."

They drank from the canteens; and then they made
onslaught upon the provisions. Joyce ate for a while
in deep and silent content, forgetting the heat and the
battle which still lowered in the west. But presently,

when his appetite was dulled, he remembered the cannonade.

"There they go again!" he said. "Boom! Boom! Boom! Won't them fellows ever get enough? I thought I was hungry, but the cannon over there 'pear to be hungrier. I suppose there ain't men enough in all this country to stop up their iron throats. But bang away! They don't bother us, do they, pardner? They can't spile this supper, for all their boomin' an' flashin'."

The wounded man bowed assent and took another piece of the ham.

Joyce leaned back on the grass, held up a chicken leg in his hand, and looked contemplatively at it.

"Ain't it funny, pardner," he said, "that you, a Tommy Yank, an' me, a Johnny Reb, are sittin' here, eatin' grub together, as friendly as two brothers, when we ought to be killin' each other? I don't know what Jeff Davis an' old Abe Lincoln will say about it when they hear of the way you an' me are doin'."

The wounded man laughed.

"You can say that I was your prisoner," he said, "when they summon you before the court-martial. An' so I am, if you choose to make me. I can't resist."

"I'm thinkin' more about gettin' back safe to our army than makin' prisoners," said Joyce, as he flung the chicken bone, now bare, into the bushes.

"That may be hard to do," said the wounded man; "for neither you nor me can tell which way the armies will go. Listen to that boomin'! Wasn't it louder than before? That fightin' must be movin' round nearer to us."

"Let it move," said Joyce. "I tell you I've had enough of fightin' for one day. That battle can take care of itself. I won't let it bother me. I don't want to shoot anybody."

"Is that the way you feel when you go into battle?" asked the wounded man.

"I can't say exactly," replied Joyce. "Of course when I go out in a charge with my regiment I want to beat the other fellows, but I don't hate 'em, no, not a bit. I've got nothin' against the Yanks. I've knowed some of 'em that was mighty good fellows. There ain't any of 'em that I want to kill. No, I'll take that back; there is one, just one, a bloody villain that I'd like to draw a bead on an' send a bullet through his skulkin' body."

"Who is that?" asked the wounded man; "an' why do you make an exception of him?"

Joyce remained silent for a moment or two and drew a long blade of grass restlessly through his fingers.

"It's not a pleasant story," he said at last, "an' it hurts me now to tell it, but I made you ask the question, an' I guess I might as well tell you, 'cause I feel friendly toward you, pardner, bein' as we are together in distress, like two Robinson Crusoes, so to speak."

The wounded man settled himself in the grass like one who is going to listen comfortably to a story.

"It's just a yarn of the Kentuck hills," said Joyce, "an' a bad enough one, too. We're a good sort of people up there, but we're hot-blooded, an' when we get into trouble, as we sometimes do, kinfolks stan' together. I guess you're from Maine, or York State, or somewhere away up North, an' you can't understand us. But it's just as I say. Sometimes two men up in our hills fight, an' one kills the other. Then the dead man's brothers, an' sons if he's got any old enough, an' cousins, an' so on, take up their guns an' go huntin' for the man that killed him. An' the livin' man's brothers an' sons an' cousins an' so on take up their guns an come out to help him. An' there you've got your feud, an' there's no tellin' how many years it'll run on, an' how many people will get killed in it. —Thunderation, but wasn't them cannon loud that time! The battle is movin' round toward us sure!"

Joyce listened a moment, but heard nothing more except the echoes.

"Our family got into one of them feuds," he said. "It was the Joyces and the Ryders. I'm Dave Joyce, the son of Henry Joyce. I don't remember how the feud started; about nothin' much, I guess; but it was a red-hot one, I can tell you, pardner. It was fought fair for a long time, but at last Bill Ryder shot father from ambush and killed him. Father hadn't had much to do with the feud, either; he didn't like that sort of thing—didn't think it was right. I said right then that if I ever found the chance when I got big enough I'd kill Bill Ryder."

"Did you get the chance?" asked the wounded man.

"No," replied Joyce. "Country got too hot for

Ryder, and he went away. He came back after a
while, an' I was big enough to go gunnin' for him
then, but the war broke out, an' off he went into the
Union army before I could get a chance to draw a
bead on him. I ain't heard of him since. Maybe he's
been killed in battle an' his bones are bleachin' somewhere in the woods."

"Most likely," said the wounded man.

"There's no tellin'," said Joyce. "Still, some day
when we're comin' up against the Yanks face to face
I may see him before me, an' then I'll hold my gun
steady an' shoot straight at him, instead of whoopin'
like mad an' firin' lickety-split into the crowd, aimin'
at nothin,' as I generally do."

"It's a sad story, very sad for you," said the
wounded man.

"Yes," said Joyce. "You don't have such things as
feuds up North, do you?"

"No," replied the other, "an' we're well off without
'em. Hark, there's the cannon again!"

"Yes, an' they keep creepin' round toward us with
their infernal racket," said Joyce. "Cannon love to
chaw up people an' then brag about it. But if them
fellows are bent on fightin' all night I guess we'll have
to give 'em room for it. What do you say to movin'?
I've eat all I want, an' I guess you have too, an' we
can take what's left with us."

"I don't know," said the wounded man. "My leg's
painin' me a good deal, an' the grass is soft an' long
here where I'm layin'. It makes a good bed, an' maybe I'd better stay where I am."

"I think not," said Joyce, decidedly. "That night fight's still swingin' down on us, an' if we stay too long them cannon'll feed on us too. We'd better move, pardner. Let me take a look at your wound. It's gettin' lighter, an' I can see better now. The moon's up, an' she's shinin' for all she's worth through them trees. Besides, them cannon-flashes help. Raise up your head, pardner, an' we'll take a look at your wound together."

"I don't think you can do any good," said the wounded man. "It would be better not to disturb it."

"But we must be movin', pardner," said Joyce, a little impatiently. "See, the fight's warmin' up, an' it's still creepin' down on us. Seems to me I can almost hear the tramp of the men an' the rollin' of the cannon-wheels. Jerusalem! what a blaze that was! I say, it's time for us to be goin'. If we stay here we're likely to be ground to death under the cannon-wheels, if we ain't shot first. Just let me get a grip under your shoulders, pardner, an' I'll take you out of this."

The cannon flamed up again, and the deep thunder filled all the night.

"Listen how them old iron throats are growlin' an' mutterin'," said Joyce; "an' they're sayin' it's time for us to be travelin'."

"I believe," said the wounded man, "that I would rather stay where I am an' take my chances. If I move I'm afraid I'll break open my wound. Besides, I think you're mistaken. It seems to me that the fight's passin' round to the right of us."

"Passin' to the right of us nothin'," said Joyce. "It's coming straight this way, with no more respect for our feelin's than if you an' me was a couple of field-mice."

The wounded man made no answer.

"Do you think, pardner," asked Joyce, slight offence showing in his voice, "that the Yanks may come this way an' pick you up an' then you won't be a prisoner? Is that your game?"

As his companion made no answer, Joyce continued:

"You don't think, pardner, that I want to hold you a prisoner, do you? an' you a wounded man, too, that I picked up on the battle-field and that I've eat and drank with? Why, that ain't my style."

He waited for an answer, and as none came he was seized with a sudden alarm.

"You ain't dead, pardner?" he cried. "Jerusalem! what if he's died while I've been standin' here talkin' an' wastin' time!"

He bent over to take a look at the other's face, but the wounded man, with a sudden and convulsive movement, writhed away from him and struck at him with his open hand.

"Keep away!" he cried. "Don't touch me! Don't come near me! I won't have it! I won't have it!"

"Thunderation, pardner!" exclaimed Joyce; "what do you mean? I ain't goin' to harm you. I want to help you." Then he added, pityingly, "I guess he's got the fever an' gone out of his head. So I'll take him along whether he wants to go or not."

He bent over again, seized the wounded man by the shoulders, and forcibly raised him up. At the same moment the cannonade burst out afresh and with increased violence. A blaze of light played over the face of the wounded man, revealing and magnifying every feature, every line.

Joyce uttered no exclamation, but he dropped the man as if he had been a coiling serpent in his hands, and looked at him, an expression of hate and loathing creeping over his face.

"So," he said, at last, "this is the way I have found you?"

The wounded man lay as he had fallen, with his face to the earth.

"No wonder," said Joyce, "you wanted to keep your face hid in the grass! No wonder you hide it there now!"

"Oh, Dave! Dave!" exclaimed the man, springing to his knees with sudden energy, "don't kill me! Don't kill me, Dave!"

"Why shouldn't I kill you?" asked Joyce, scornfully. "What reason can you give why I shouldn't do it?"

"There ain't any. There ain't any. Oh, I know there ain't any," cried the wounded man. "But don't do it, Dave! For Christ's sake don't do it!"

"You murderer! You sneakin', ambushin' murderer!" said Joyce. "It's right for you to beg for your life an' then not get it! Hear them cannon! Hear how they growl, an' see the flash from their throats! They'd like to feed on you, but they won't.

That sort of death is too good for the likes of you.
The death for you is to be shot like a ravin' cur."

He drew the loaded pistol from his belt and cocked
it with deliberate motion.

"Dave! Dave!" the man cried, dragging himself to
Joyce's feet, "you won't do that! You can't! It
would be murder, Dave, to shoot me here, me a
wounded man that can't help myself!"

"You done it, an' worse," said Joyce. "Of all the
men unburnt in hell I think the one who deserves to be
there most is the man who hid in ambush and shot
another in the back that had never harmed him."

"I know it, Dave, I know it!" cried the wounded
man, grasping Joyce's feet with both hands. "It was
an awful thing to do, an' I've been sorry a thousand
times that I done it, but all the sorrow in the world
an' everythin' else that's in the world can't undo it
now."

"That's so," said Joyce, "but it don't make any reason why the murderer ought to be kept on livin'."

"It don't, Dave; you're right, I know; but I don't
want to die!" cried the man. "I'm a coward, Dave,
and I don't want to die by myself here in the woods
an' in the dark!"

"You'll soon have light enough," said Joyce, "an'
I won't shoot you."

He let down the hammer of his pistol and replaced
the weapon in his belt.

"Oh, Dave! Dave!" exclaimed the man, kissing
Joyce's foot, "I'm so glad you'll let me have my life.
I know I ain't fit to live, but I want to live anyhow."

"I said I wouldn't shoot you," said Joyce, "but I never said I'd spare your life. See that blaze in the trees up there."

A few hundred yards away the forest had burst into flame. Sparks fell upon a tree and blazed up. Long red spirals coiled themselves around the trunk and boughs until the tree became a mass of fire, and then other tongues of flame leaped forward and seized other trees. There was a steady crackling and roaring, and the wind that had sprung up drove smoke and ashes and fiery particles before it.

"That," said Joyce, "is the wood on fire. Them cannon that's been makin' so much fuss done it. I've seen it often in battle when the cannon have been growlin'. The fire grows an' it grows, an' it burns up everythin' in its way. The army is still busy fightin', an' the wounded, them that's hurt too bad to help theirselves, have to lay there on the ground an' watch the fire comin', an' sure to get 'em. By an' by it sweeps down on 'em, an' they shriek an' shriek, but that don't do no good, for before long the fire goes on, an' there they are, dead an' burnt to a coal. I tell you it's an awful death!"

The wounded man was silent now. He had drawn himself up a little, and was watching the fire as it leaped from tree to tree and devoured them one after another.

"That fire is comin' for us, an' the wind is bringin' it along fast," said Joyce, composedly, "but it's easy enough for me to get out of its way. All I've got to do is to go up the hill, an' the clearin's run for a long

way beyond. I can stay up there an 'watch the fire
pass, an' you'll be down here right in its track."

"Dave!" cried the man, "you ain't goin' to let me
burn to death right before your eyes?"

"That's what I mean to do," said Joyce. "I don't
like to shoot a wounded man that can't help himself,
an' I won't do it, but I ain't got no call to save you
from another death."

"I'd rather be shot than burned to death," cried the
man, in a frenzy.

"It's just the death for you," said Joyce.

Then the wounded man again dragged himself to
the feet of Joyce.

"Don't do it, Dave!" he cried. "Don't leave me
here to burn to death! Oh, I tell you, Dave, I ain't
fit to die!"

"Take your hands off my feet," said Joyce. "I
don't want 'em to touch me. There's too much blood
on 'em."

"Don't leave me to the fire!" continued the man.
"You've been kind to me to-night. Help me a little
more, Dave, an' you'll be glad you done it when you
come to die yourself!"

"I must be goin'," said Joyce, repulsing the man's
detaining hands. "It's gettin' hot here now, an' that
fire will soon be near enough to scorch my face.
Good-by."

"For the sake of your own soul, Dave Joyce," cried
the man, beating the ground with his hands, "don't
leave me to be burned to a coal! Think, Dave, how
we eat an' drank together to-night, like two brothers,

an' how you waited on me an' brought the water an' the grub. You'll remember them things, Dave, when you come to die yourself!''

The fire increased in strength and violence. The flames ran up the trees, and whirled far above them in red coils that met and twined with each other, and then whirled triumphantly on in search of fresh fuel. 'A giant oak, burned through at the base and swept of all its young boughs and foliage, fell with a rending crash, a charred and shattered trunk. The flames roared, and the burning trees maintained an incessant crackling like a fire of musketry. The smoke through which the sparks of fire were sown in millions grew stifling.

"God, what a sight!" cried Joyce.

"Dave, you won't leave me to that?" cried Ryder.

Joyce drew down his hat over his eyes to shield them from the smoke. Then he stooped, lifted the wounded man upon his powerful shoulders, and went on over the hill.

ROSEMARY FOR REMEMBRANCE

BY HENRY HARLAND

Henry Harland (born in St. Petersburg, Russia, in March, 1861) has achieved two distinct names for himself in literature. His earlier stories, treating almost exclusively of Hebrew life, were written under the pseudonym of "Sidney Luska," and his later fiction, general in its scope, under his proper name. The styles of the two periods differ as widely as their subject-matter. The "Luska" stories are studies in pure, though refined, realism; the "Harland" ones present an almost fantastic finesse of romance. An example of the latter order is here presented.

ROSEMARY FOR REMEMBRANCE

BY HENRY HARLAND

I

I WONDER why I dreamed last night of Zabetta. It is years since she made her brief little transit through my life, and passed out of it utterly. It is years since the very recollection of her—which for years, like an accusing spirit, had haunted me too often—like a spirit was laid. It is long enough, in all conscience, since I have even thought of her, casually, for an instant. And then, last night, after a perfectly usual London day and evening, I went to bed and dreamed of her vividly. What had happened to bring her to my mind? Or is it simply that the god of dreams is a capricious god?

The influence of my dream, at any rate—the bitter-sweet savor of it—has pursued me through my waking hours. All day long to-day Zabetta has been my phantom guest. She has walked with me in the streets; she has waited at my elbow while I wrote or talked or read. Now, at tea-time, she is present with me by my study fireside, in the twilight. Her voice sounds faintly, plaintively, in my ears; her eyes gaze at me sadly from a pale, reproachful face. . . . She bids me to the theatre of memory, where my youth is rehearsed before me in mimic show. There was one—no, there were two little scenes in which Zabetta played the part of leading lady.

II

I do not care to specify the year in which it happened; it happened a terrible number of years ago; it happened when I was twenty. I had passed the winter in Naples—oh, it had been a golden winter!—and now April had come, and my last Neapolitan day. To-morrow I was to take ship for Marseilles, on the way to join my mother in Paris.

It was in the afternoon; and I was climbing one of those crooked staircase alleys that scale the hillsides behind the town, the salita—is there, in Naples, a Salita Santa Margherita? I had lunched (for the last time!) at the Café d'Europe, and had then set forth upon a last haphazard ramble through the streets. It was tremulous spring weather, with blue skies, soft breezes, and a tender sun; the sort of weather that kindles perilous ardors even in the blood of middle age, and turns the blood of youth to wildfire.

Women sat combing their hair, and singing, and gossiping, before the doorways of their pink and yellow houses; children sprawled, and laughed, and quarreled in the dirt. Pifferari, in sheepskins and sandals, followed by prowling, gaunt-limbed dogs, droned monotonous nasal melodies from their bagpipes. Priests picked their way gingerly over the muddy cobblestones, sleek, black-a-vised priests, with exaggerated hats, like Don Basilio's in the "Barbière." Now and then one passed a fat brown monk; or a soldier; or a white-robed penitent, whose eyes glimmered uncannily from the peep-holes of the hood that hid his face; or

a comely contadina, in her smart costume, with a
pomegranate blossom flaming behind her ear, and red
lips that curved defiantly as she met the covetous
glances wildfire-and-twenty no doubt bestowed upon
her—whereat, perhaps, wildfire-and-twenty halted and
hesitated for an instant, debating whether to accept the
challenge and turn and follow her. A flock of milk-
purveying goats jangled their bells a few yards below
me. Hawkers screamed their merchandise, fish, and
vegetables, and early fruit—apricots, figs, green al-
monds. Brown-skinned, bare-legged boys shouted at
long-suffering donkeys, and whacked their flanks with
sticks. And everybody, more or less, importuned you
for coppers. *"Mossou, mossou! Un piccolo soldo, per
l'amor di Dio!"* The air was vibrant with southern
human noises and dense with southern human smells
—among which, here and there, wandered strangely
a lost waft of perfume from some neighboring garden,
a scent of jasmine or of orange flowers.

And then, suddenly, the salita took a turn, and
broadened into a small piazza. At one hand there was
a sheer terrace, dropping to tiled roofs twenty feet
below; and hence one got a splendid view, over the
town, of the blue bay, with its shipping, and of Capri,
all rose and purple in the distance, and of Vesuvius
with its silver wreath of smoke. At the other hand
loomed a vast, discolored, pink-stuccoed palace, with
grated windows, and a porte-cochère black as the
mouth of a cavern; and the upper stories of the palace
were in ruins, and out of one corner of their crumbling walls a palm-tree grew. The third side of the

piazza was inevitably occupied by a church, a little pearl-gray rococo edifice, with a bell, no deeper toned than a common dinner-bell, which was now frantically ringing. About the doors of the church countless written notices were pasted, advertising indulgences; beggars clung to the steps, like monster snails; and the greasy leathern portière was constantly being drawn aside to let some one enter or come out.

III

It was here that I met Zabetta.

The heavy portière swung open, and a young girl stepped from the darkness behind it into the sunshine.

I saw a soft face, with brown eyes; a plain black frock, with a little green nosegay stuck in its belt; and a small round scarlet hat.

A hideous old beggar woman stretched a claw toward this apparition, mumbling something. The apparition smiled, and sought in its pocket, and made the beggar woman the richer by a soldo.

I was twenty, and the April wind was magical. I thought I had never seen so beautiful a smile, a smile so radiant, so tender.

I watched the young girl as she tripped down the church steps, and crossed the piazza, coming toward me. Her smile lingered, fading slowly, slowly, from her face.

As she neared me, her eyes met mine. For a second we looked straight into each other's eyes. . . .

Oh, there was nothing bold, nothing sophisticated or immodest, in the momentary gaze she gave me. It

was a natural, spontaneous gaze of perfectly frank, of
perfectly innocent and impulsive interest, in exchange
for mine of open admiration. But it touched the wildfire in my veins, and made it leap tumultuously.

IV

Happiness often passes close to us without our sus-
pecting it, the proverb says.

The young girl moved on; and I stood still, feeling
dimly that something precious had passed close to me.
I had not turned back to follow any of the brazenly
provocative contadine. But now I could not help it.
Something precious had passed within arm's reach of
me. I must not let it go, without at least a semblance
of pursuing it. If I waited there passive till she was
out of sight, my regrets would be imbittered by the
recollection that I had not even tried.

I followed her eagerly, but vaguely, in a tremor of
unformulated hopes and fears. I had no definite in-
tentions, no designs. Presently, doubtless, she would
come to her journey's end—she would disappear in a
house or shop—and I should have my labor for my
pains. Nevertheless, I followed. What would you?
She was young, she was pretty, she was neatly
dressed. She had big bright brown eyes, and a
slender waist, and a little round scarlet hat set jauntily
upon a mass of waving soft brown hair. And she
walked gracefully, with delicious undulations, as if to
music, lifting her skirts up from the pavement, and so
disclosing the daintiest of feet, in trim buttoned boots
of glazed leather, with high Italian heels. And her

smile was lovely—and I was twenty—and it was April. I must not let her escape me, without at least a semblance of pursuit.

She led me down the salita that I had just ascended. She could scarcely know that she was being followed, for she had not once glanced behind her.

V

At first I followed meekly, unperceived, and contented to remain so.

But little by little a desire for more aggressive measures grew within me. I said, "Why not—instead of following meekly—why not overtake and outdistance her, then turn round, and come face to face with her again? And if again her eyes should meet mine as frankly as they met them in the piazza. . . ."

The mere imagination of their doing so made my heart stop beating.

I quickened my pace. I drew nearer and nearer to her. I came abreast of her—oh, how the wildfire trembled! I pressed on for a bit, and then, true to my resolution, turned back.

Her eyes did meet mine again quite frankly. What was more, they brightened with a little light of surprise, I might almost have fancied a little light of pleasure.

If the mere imagination of the thing had made my heart stop beating, the thing itself set it to pounding, racing, uncontrollably, so that I felt all but suffocated and had to catch my breath.

She knew now that the young man she had passed

in the piazza had followed her of set purpose; and she was surprised, but, seemingly, not displeased. They were wonderfully gentle, wonderfully winning eyes, those eyes she raised so frankly to my desirous ones; and innocent, innocent, with all the unsuspecting innocence of childhood. In years she might be seventeen, older perhaps; but there was a child's fearless unconsciousness of evil in her wide brown eyes. She had not yet been taught (or, anyhow, she clearly didn't believe) that it was dangerous and unbecoming to exchange glances with a stranger in the streets.

She was as good as smiling on me. Might I dare the utmost? Might I venture to speak to her? . . . My heart was throbbing too violently. I could not have found an articulate human word, nor a shred of voice, nor a pennyweight of self-assurance, in my body.

So, thrilling with excitement, quailing in panic, I passed her again.

I passed her, and kept on up the narrow alley for half a dozen steps, when again I turned.

She was standing where I had left her, looking after me. There was the expression of unabashed disappointment in her dark eyes now, which, in a minute, melted to an expression of appeal.

"Oh, aren't you going to speak to me, after all?" they pleaded.

Wooed by those soft monitors, I plucked up a sort of desperate courage. Hot coals burned in my cheeks, something fluttered terribly in my breast; I was literally quaking in every limb. My spirit was exultant, but my flesh was faint. Her eyes drew me, drew me.

. . . I fancy myself awkwardly raising my hat;
I hear myself accomplish a half-smothered salutation.
"Buon' giorno, Signorina."
Her face lighted up with that celestial smile of hers,
and in a voice that was like ivory and white velvet,
she returned, *"Buon' giorno, Signorino."*

VI

And then I don't know how long we stood together
in silence.

This would never do, I recognized. I must not
stand before her in silence, like a guilty schoolboy. I
must feign composure. I must carry off the situation
lightly like a man of the world, a man of experience.
I groped anxiously in the confusion of my wits for
something that might pass for an apposite remark.

At last I had a flash of inspiration. "What—
what fine weather," I gasped. *"Che bel tempo!"*

"Oh, molto bello," she responded. It was like a
cadenza on a flute.

"You—you are going into the town?" I questioned.
"Yes," said she.

"May I—may I have the pleasure—" I faltered.

"But yes," she consented, with an inflection that
wondered. "What else have you spoken to me for?"

And we set off down the salita, side by side.

VII

She had exquisite little white ears, with little coral
earrings, like drops of blood; and a perfect rosebud
mouth, a mouth that matched her eyes for innocence

and sweetness. Her scarlet hat burned in the sun, and her brown hair shook gently under it. She had plump little soft white hands.

Presently, when I had begun to feel more at my ease, I hazarded a question. "You are a republican, Signorina?"

"No," she assured me, with a puzzled elevation of the brows.

"Ah, well, then you are a cardinal," I concluded.

She gave a silvery trill of laughter, and asked, "Why must I be either a republican or a cardinal?"

"You wear a scarlet hat—a *bonnet rouge*," I explained.

At which she laughed again, crisply, merrily.

"You are French," she said.

"Oh, am I?"

"Aren't you?"

"As you wish, Signorina; but I had never thought so."

And still again she laughed.

"You have come from church," said I.

"Già," she assented; "from confession."

"Really? And did you have a great many wickednesses to confess?"

"Oh, yes; many, many," she answered, simply.

"And now have you got a heavy penance to perform?"

"No; only twenty *aves*. And I must turn my tongue seven times in my mouth before I speak, whenever I am angry."

"Ah, then you are given to being angry? You have a bad temper?"

"Oh, dreadful, dreadful," she cried, nodding her head.

It was my turn to laugh now. "Then I must be careful not to vex you."

"Yes. But I will turn my tongue seven times before I speak, if you do," she promised.

"Are you going far?" I asked.

"I am going nowhere. I am taking a walk."

"Shall we go to the Villa Nazionale, and watch the driving?"

"Or to the Toledo, and look at the shop windows?"

"We can do both. We will begin at the Toledo, and end in the Villa."

"Bene," she acquiesced.

After a little silence, "I am so glad I met you," I informed her, looking into her eyes.

Her eyes softened adorably. "I am so glad too," she said.

"You are lovely, you are sweet," I vowed, with enthusiasm.

"Oh, no!" she protested. "I am as God made me."

"You are lovely, you are sweet. I thought—when I first saw you, above there, in the piazza—when you came out of church, and gave the soldo to the old beggar woman—I thought you had the loveliest smile I had ever seen."

A beautiful blush suffused her face, and her eyes swam in a mist of pleasure. *"E vero?"* she questioned.

"Oh, vero, vero. That is why I followed you. You don't mind my having followed you?"

"Oh, no; I am glad."

'After another interval of silence, "You are not Neapolitan?" I said. "You don't speak like a Neapolitan."

"No; I am Florentine. We live in Naples for my father's health. He is not strong. He can not endure the cold winters of the north."

I murmured something sympathetic; and she went on, "My father is a violinist. To-day he has gone to Capri, to play at a festival. He will not be back until to-morrow. So I was very lonesome."

"You have no mother?"

"My mother is dead," she said, crossing herself. In a moment she added, with a touch of pride, "During the season my father plays in the orchestra of the San Carlo."

"I am sure I know what your name is," said I.

"Oh? How can you know? What is it?"

"I think your name is Rosabella."

"Ah, then you are wrong. My name is Elisabetta. But in Naples everybody says Zabetta. And yours?"

"Guess."

"Oh, I can not guess. Not—not Federico?"

"Do I look as if my name were Federico?"

She surveyed me gravely for a minute, then shook her head pensively. "No; I do not think your name is Federico."

'And therewith I told her my name, and made her repeat it till she could pronounce it without a struggle. It sounded very pretty, coming from her pretty lips, quite southern and romantic, with its r's tremendously enriched.

"Anyhow, I know your age," said I.

"What is it?"

'You are seventeen."

"No—ever so much older."

"Eighteen then."

"I shall be nineteen in July."

VIII

Before the brilliant shop windows of the Toledo we dallied for an hour or more, Zabetta's eyes sparkling with delight as they rested on the bright-hued silks, the tortoise-shell and coral, the gold and silver filagree work, that were there displayed. But when she admired some one particular object above another, and I besought her to let me buy it for her, she refused austerely. "But no, no, no! It is impossible." Then we went on to the Villa, and strolled by the sea-wall, between the blue-green water and the multi-colored procession of people in carriages. And by and by Zabetta confessed that she was tired, and proposed that we should sit down on one of the benches. "A café would be better fun," submitted her companion. And we placed ourselves at one of the out-of-door tables of the café in the garden, where, after some urging, I prevailed upon Zabetta to drink a cup of chocolate. Meanwhile, with the ready confidence of youth, we had each been desultorily autobiographical; and if our actual acquaintance was only the affair of an afternoon, I doubt if in a year we could have felt that we knew each other better.

"I must go home," Zabetta said at last.

"Oh, not yet, not yet," cried I.

"It will be dinner-time. I must go home to dinner."

"But your father is at Capri. You will have to dine alone."

"Yes."

"Then don't. Come with me instead, and dine at a restaurant."

Her eyes glowed wistfully for an instant; but she replied, "Oh, no; I can not."

"Yes, you can. Come."

"Oh, no; impossible."

"Why?"

"Oh, because."

"Because what?"

"There is my cat. She will have nothing to eat."

"Your cook will give her something."

"My cook!" laughed Zabetta. "My cook is here before you."

"Well, you must be a kind mistress. You must give your cook an evening out."

"But my poor cat?"

"Your cat can catch a mouse."

"There are no mice in our house. She has frightened them all away."

"Then she can wait. A little fast will be good for her soul."

Zabetta laughed, and I said, *"Andiamo!"*

At the restaurant we climbed to the first floor, and they gave us a table near the window, whence we could look out over the villa to the sea beyond. The sun was sinking, and the sky was gay with rainbow tints, like mother-of-pearl.

Zabetta's face shone joyfully. "This is only the second time in my life that I have dined in a restaurant," she told me. "And the other time was very long ago, when I was quite young. And it wasn't nearly so grand a restaurant as this, either."

"And now what would you like to eat?" I asked, picking up the bill of fare.

"May I look?" said she.

I handed her the document, and she studied it at length. I think, indeed, she read it through. In the end she appeared rather bewildered.

"Oh, there is so much. I don't know. Will you choose, please?"

I made a shift at choosing, and the sympathetic waiter flourished kitchenward with my commands.

"What is that little green nosegay you wear in your belt, Zabetta?" I inquired.

"Oh, this—it is a rosemary. Smell it," she said, breaking off a sprig and offering it to me.

"Rosemary—that's for remembrance," quoted I.

"What does that mean? What language is that?" she asked.

I tried to translate it to her. And then I taught her to say it in English. "Rrosemérri—tsat is forr rremembrrance."

"Will you write it down for me?" she requested. "It is pretty."

And I wrote it for her on the back of one of my cards.

IX

'After dinner we crossed the garden again, and again stood by the sea-wall. Over us the soft spring night was like a dark sapphire. Points of red, green, and yellow fire burned from the ships in the bay, and seemed of the same company as the stars above them. A rosy aureole in the sky, to the eastward, marked the smouldering crater of Vesuvius. Away in the Chiaja a man was singing comic songs to an accompaniment of mandolins and guitars; comic songs that sounded pathetic, as they reached us in the distance.

I asked Zabetta how she wished to finish the evening.

"I don't care," said she.

"Would you like to go to the play?"

"If you wish."

"What do *you* wish?"

"I think I should like to stay here a little longer. It is pleasant."

We leaned on the parapet, close to each other. Her face was very pale in the starlight; her eyes were infinitely deep, and dark, and tender. One of her little hands lay on the stone wall, like a white flower. I took it. It was warm and soft. She did not attempt to withdraw it. I bent over it and kissed it. I kissed it many times. Then I kissed her lips. "Zabetta—I love you—I love you," I murmured fervently. —Don't imagine that I didn't mean it. It was April, and I was twenty.

"I love you, Zabetta. Dearest little Zabetta! I love you so."

"E vero?" she questioned, scarcely above her breath.

"Oh, *si; é vero, vero, vero,*" I asseverated. "And you? And you?"

"Yes, I love you," she whispered.

And then I could say no more. The ecstasy that filled my heart was too poignant. We stood there speechless, hand in hand, and breathed the air of heaven.

By and by Zabetta drew her bunch of rosemary from her belt, and divided it into two parts. One part she gave to me, the other she kept. "Rosemary— it is for constancy," she said. I pressed the cool herb to my face for a moment, inhaling its bitter-sweet fragrance; then I fastened it in my buttonhole. On my watch-chain I wore—what everybody in Naples used to wear—a little coral hand, a little clinched coral hand, holding a little golden dagger. I detached it now, and made Zabetta take it. "Coral—that is also for constancy," I reminded her; "and besides, it protects one from the Evil Eye."

X

At last Zabetta asked me what time it was; and when she learned that it was half-past nine, she insisted that she really must go home. "They shut the outer door of the house we live in at ten o'clock, and I have no key."

"You can ring up the porter."

"Oh, there is no porter."

"But if we had gone to the theatre?"

"I should have had to leave you in the middle of the play."

"Ah, well," I consented; and we left the Villa and took a cab.

"Are you happy, Zabetta?" I asked her, as the cab rattled us toward our parting.

"Oh, so happy, so happy! I have never been so happy before."

"Dearest Zabetta!"

"You will love me always?"

"Always, always."

"We will see each other every day. We will see each other to-morrow?"

"Oh, to-morrow!" I groaned suddenly, the actualities of life rushing all at once upon my mind.

"What is it? What of to-morrow?"

"Oh, to-morrow, to-morrow!"

"What? What?" Her voice was breathless with suspense, with alarm.

"Oh, I had forgotten. You will think I am a beast."

"What is it? For heaven's sake, tell me."

"You will think I am a beast. You will think I have deceived you. To-morrow—I can not help it—I am not my own master—I am summoned by my parents—to-morrow I am going away—I am leaving Naples."

"You are leaving Naples?"

"I am going to Paris."

"To Paris?"

"Yes."

There was a breathing-space of silence. Then,

"Oh, Dio!" sobbed Zabetta; and she began to cry as if her heart would break.

I seized her hands; I drew her to me. I tried to comfort her. But she only cried and cried and cried.

"Zabetta . . . Zabetta. . . . Don't cry. . . . Forgive me. . . . Oh, don't cry like that."

"Oh, Dio! Oh, caro Dio!" she sobbed.

"Zabetta—listen to me," I began. "I have something to say to you. . . ."

"Cosa?" she asked faintly.

"Zabetta—do you really love me?"

"Oh, tanto, tanto!"

"Then listen, Zabbetta. If you really love me—come with me."

"Come with you. How?"

"Come with me to Paris."

"To Paris?"

"Yes, to-morrow."

There was another instant of silence, and then again Zabetta began to cry.

"Will you? Will you? Will you come with me to Paris?" I implored her.

"Oh, I would, I would. But I can't. I can't."

"Why not?"

"Oh, I can't."

"Why? Why can't you?"

"Oh, my father—I can not leave my father."

"Your father? But—if you love me—"

"He is old. He is ill. He has no one but me. I can not leave him."

"Zabetta!"

"No, no. I can not leave him. *Oh, Dio mio!*"

"But Zabetta—"

"No. It would be a sin. Oh, the worst of sins, He is old and ill. I can not leave him. Don't ask me. It would be dreadful."

"But then? Then what? What shall we do?"

"Oh, I don't know. I wish I were dead."

The cab came to a standstill, and Zabetta said, "Here we are." I helped her to descend. We were before a dark porte-cochère, in some dark back street. high up the hillside.

"*Addio,*" said Zabetta, holding out her hand.

"You won't come with me?"

"I can't. I can't. *Addio.*"

"Oh, Zabetta! Do you— Oh, say, say that you forgive me."

"Yes. *Addio.*"

"And, Zabetta, you—you have my address. It is on the card I gave you. If you ever need anything— if you are ever in trouble of any kind—remember you have my address—you will write to me."

"Yes. *Addio.*"

"*Addio.*"

She stood for a second, looking up at me from great brimming eyes, and then she turned away and vanished in the darkness of the porte-cochère. I got into the cab, and was driven to my hotel.

IX

'And here, one might have supposed, was an end of the episode; but no.

I went to Paris, I went to New York, I returned to Paris, I came on to London; and in this journeying more than a year was lost. In the beginning I had suffered as much as you could wish me in the way of contrition, in the way of regret too. I blamed myself and pitied myself with almost equal fervor. I had trifled with a gentle human heart; I had been compelled to let a priceless human treasure slip from my possession. But—I was twenty. And there were other girls in the world. And a year is a long time, when we are twenty. Little by little the image of Zabetta faded, faded. By the year's end, I am afraid it had become very pale indeed. . . .

It was late June, and I was in London, when the post brought me a letter. The letter bore an Italian stamp, and had originally been directed to my old address in Paris. Thence (as the numerous redirections on the big square foreign envelope attested) it had been forwarded to New York; thence back again to Paris; and thence finally to London.

The letter was written in the neatest of tiny copper-plate; and this is a translation of what it said:

"Dear Friend—My poor father died last month in the German Hospital, after an illness of twenty-one days. Pray for his soul.

"I am now alone and free, and if you still wish it, can come to you. It was impossible for me to come when you asked me; but you have not ceased to be my constant thought. I keep your coral hand.—Your ever faithful   Zabetta Collaluce."

Inclosed in the letter there was a sprig of some dried, bitter-sweet smelling herb; and, in pencil, below the signature—laboriously traced, as I could guess, from what I had written for her on my visiting-card —the English phrase: "Rosemary—that's for remembrance."

The letter was dated early in May, which made it six weeks old.

What could I do? What answer could I send?

Of course, you know what I did do. I procrastinated and vacillated, and ended by sending no answer at all. I could not write and say, "Yes, come to me." But how could I write and say, "No, do not come"? Besides, would she not have given up hoping for an answer by this time? It was six weeks since she had written. I tried to think that the worst was over.

But my remorse took a new and a longer and a stronger lease of life. A vision of Zabetta, pale, with anxious eyes, standing at her window, waiting, waiting for a word that never came—for months I could not chase it from my conscience; it was years before it altogether ceased its accusing visits.

XII

And then, last night, after a perfectly usual London day and evening, I went to bed and dreamed of her vividly; and all day long to-day the fragrance of my dream has clung about me—a bitter-sweet fragrance, like that of rosemary itself. Where is Zabetta now? What is her life? How have the years treated her?

. . . In my dream she was still eighteen. In reality
—it is melancholy to think how far from eighteen she
has had leisure, since that April afternoon, to drift.

Youth faces forward, impatient of the present, panting to anticipate the future. But we who have crossed
a certain sad meridian, we turn our gaze backward,
and tell the relentless gods what we would sacrifice
to recover a little of the past, one of those shining
days when to us also it was given to sojourn among the
Fortunate Islands. *Ah, si jeunesse savait!* . . .

A RED-HAIRED CUPID

BY HENRY WALLACE PHILLIPS

Henry Wallace Phillips (born about 1870, in Staten Island) is one of our few younger writers who have gathered really fresh laurels from that favorite stamping ground of American humorists, the Western plains. His picturesque wit is a development, instead of a reminiscence, of the humor of extravaganza which specially characterizes the elder school of Mark Twain. Romance is no less his métier than humor, as the present story bears witness.

A RED-HAIRED CUPID

BY HENRY WALLACE PHILLIPS

"HOW did I come to get myself disliked down at the Chanta Seechee? Well, I'll tell you," said Reddy, the cowpuncher. "The play came up like this. First they made the Chanta Seechee into a stock company, then the stock company put all their brains in one think, and says they, 'We'll make this man Jones superintendent, and the ranch is all right at once.' So out come Jones from Boston, Massachusetts, and what he didn't know about running a ranch was common talk in the country, but what he thought he knew about running a ranch was too much for one man to carry around. He wasn't a bad-hearted feller in some ways, yet on the whole he felt it was an honor to a looking-glass to have the pleasure of reflecting him. Looking-glass? I should say he had! And a bureau, and a boot-blacking jigger, and a feather bed, and curtains, and truck in his room. Strange fellers used to open their eyes when they saw that room. 'Hellooo!' they'd say, 'whose little birdie have we here?' And other remarks that hurt our feelings considerable. Jonesy, he said the fellers were a rank lot of barbarians. He said it to old Neighbor Case's face, and he and the old man came together like a pair of hens, for Jonesy had sand in spite of his faults.   That was a fight worth traveling to see.   They covered at least an acre of ground; they tore the air with upper swats and cross swipes; they hollered, they jumped and they pitched, and when the difficulty was adjusted we found that Jonesy's coat was painfully ripped up the back and Neighbor Case had lost his false teeth.   One crowd of fellers patted Jones on the back and said, 'Never mind your coat, old horse; you've licked a man twice your age,' and the other comforted Neighbor, saying, 'Never mind, Case; you can ease your mind by thinking how you headed up that rooster, and he fifty pounds lighter than you.'

"Jonesy put on airs after that.   He felt he was a hard citizen.   And then he had the misfortune to speak harshly to Arizona Jenkins when Old Dry Belt was in liquor.   Then he got roped and dragged through the slough.   He cried like a baby while I helped him scrape the mud off, but not because he was scared!   No, sir! That little runt was full of blood and murder.

" 'You mark me, now, Red,' says he, the tears making bad-land watercourses through the mud on his cheeks, 'I shall fire upon that man the first time I see him—will you lend me your revolver?'

" 'Lord, Jones, see here,' says I, 'don't you go making any such billy-goat play as that—keep his wages until he apologizes; put something harmful in his grub; but, as you have respect for the Almighty's handiwork as represented by your person, don't pull a gun on Arizona Jenkins—that's the one thing he won't take from nobody.'

" 'D-d-darn him!' snivels Jonesy, 'I ain't afraid o-o-of him'; and the strange fact is that he wasn't. Well, I saw he was in such a taking that he might do something foolish and get hurt, so I goes to Arizona and says I, 'You ought to apologize to Jones.' What Zony replied ain't worth repeating—'and you along with him,' he winds up.

" 'Now ain't that childish?' I says. 'A six-footer like you, that can shoot straight with either hand, and yet ain't got generosity enough to ease the feelings of a poor little devil that's fair busting with shame.'

" 'Well, what did he want to tell me to shut up my mouth for?' cried Old Dry Belt. 'Men have died of less than that.'

" 'Aw, shucks, Zony,' I says, 'a great, big man like you oughtn't to come down on a little cuss who's all thumb-hand-side and left feet.'

" 'That be blowed,' says he—only he says it different. 'I'd like to know what business such a sawed-off has to come and tell a full-grown man like me to shut up his mouth? He'd ought to stay in a little man's place and talk sassy to people his own size. When he comes shooting off his bazoo to a man that could swaller him whole without loosening his collar, its impidence; that's what it is.'

" 'Well, as a favor to me?' I says.

" 'Well, if you put it that way—I don't want to be small about it.'

"So Arizona goes up to Jones and sticks out his hand. 'There's my hand, Jones,' he says. 'I'm mighty sorry you told me to shut up my mouth,' says he.

" 'So am I,' says Jones heartily, not taking in the sense of the words, but feeling that it was all in good intention. So that was all right and I stood in with the management in great shape for fixing up the fuss so pleasant. But it didn't last. They say nothing lasts in this world. There's some pretty solid rocks in the Cœur d'Alêne, however, and I should like to wait around and see if they don't hold out, but I'll never make it. I've been in too much excitement.

"Well, the next thing after Jonesy got established was that his niece must come out during vacation and pay him a visit. 'Jeerusalem!' thinks I, 'Jonesy's niece!' I had visions of a thin, yaller, sour little piece, with mouse-colored hair plastered down on her head, and an unkind word for everybody. Jonesy told me about her being in college, and then I stuck a pair of them nose-grabber specks on the picture. I can stand 'most any kind of a man, but if there's anything that makes the tears come to my eyes it's a botch of a woman. I know they may have good qualities and all that, but I don't like 'em, and that's the whole of it. We gave three loud groans when we got the news in the bull-pen. And I cussed for ten minutes straight, without repeating myself once, when it so fell out that the members of the board rolled out our way the day the girl had to be sent for and Jonesy couldn't break loose, and your Uncle was elected to take the buck-board and drive twenty miles to the railroad. I didn't mind the going out, but that twenty miles back with Jonesy's niece! Say, I foamed like a soda-water bottle when I got into the bull-pen and told the boys my luck.

" 'Well,' says Kyle Lambert, 'that's what you might expect; your sins have found you out.'

" 'No, they ain't; they've caught me at home as usual,' says I. 'Well, I'll give that Eastern blossom an idea of the quality of this country anyhow. So I togs myself up in the awfulest rig I could find; strapped two ca'tridge belts to me, every hole filled, and a gun in every holster; put candle-grease on my mustache and twisted the ends up to my eye-winkers; stuck a knife in my hatband and another in my boot; threw a shotgun and a rifle in the buckboard, and pulled out quick through the colt-pens before Jonesy could get his peeps on to me.

"Well, sir, I was jarred witless when I laid my eyes on that young woman. I'd had my mind made up so thorough as to what she must be that the facts knocked me cold. She was the sweetest, handsomest, healthiest female I ever see. It would make you believe in fairy stories again just to look at her. She was all the things a man ever wanted in this world rolled up in a prize package. Tall, round, and soople, limber and springy in her action as a thoroughbred, and with something modest yet kind of daring in her face that would remind you of a good, honest boy. Red, white, and black were the colors she flew. Hair and eyes black, cheeks and lips red, and the rest of her white. Now, there's a pile of difference in them colors; when you say 'red,' for instance, you ain't cleaned up the subject by a sight. My top-knot's red, but that wasn't the color of Loys's cheeks. No; that was a color I never saw before nor since. A rose would look like a tomater alongside of 'em. Then, too, I've seen black eyes so hard and shiny you could cut glass with 'em. And again that wasn't her style. The only way you could get a notion of what them eyes were like would be to look at 'em; you'd remember 'em all right if you did. Seems like the good Lord was kind of careless when he built Jonesy, but when he turned that girl out he played square with the fambly.

"I ain't what you might call a man that's easily disturbed in his mind, but I know I says to myself that first day, 'If I was ten year younger, young lady, they'd never lug you back East again.' Gee, man! There was a time when I'd have pulled the country up by the roots but I'd have had that girl! I notice I don't fall in love so violent as the years roll on. I can squint my eye over the cards now and say, 'Yes, that's a beautiful hand, but I reckon I'd better stay out,' and lay 'em down without a sigh; whereas, when I was a young feller, if I had three aces in sight I'd raise the rest of the gathering right out of their foot-leather— or get caught at it. Usually I got caught at it, for a man couldn't run the mint long with the kind of luck I have.

"Well, I was plumb disgusted with the fool way I'd rigged myself up, but, fortunately for me, Darragh, the station-man, came out with the girl. 'There's Reddy, from your ranch now, ma'am,' says he, and when he caught sight of me, 'What's the matter, Red; are the Injuns up?'

"Darragh was a serious Irishman, and that's the mournfullest thing on top of the globe; and besides, he believed anything you'd tell him. There ain't any George Washington strain in my stock, so I proceeded to get out of trouble.

" 'They ain't *up* exactly,' says I, 'but it looked as if they were a leetle on the rise, and being as I had a lady to look out for, I thought I'd play safe.'

"The color kind of went out of the girl's cheeks. Eastern folk are scandalous afraid of Injuns.

" 'Perhaps I'd better not start?' says she.

" 'Don't you be scart, miss, says Darragh, 'You're all right as long as you're with Red—he's the toughest proposition we've got in this part of the country.'

" 'I'm obliged to you, Darragh,' says I. He meant well, but hell's full of them people. I'd have given a month's wages for one lick at him. Nice reputation to give me before that girl! She eyed me mighty doubtful.

"I stepped up to her, with my hat in my hand. 'Miss Andree,' says I (she was Jonesy's sister's child), 'if you come along with me I'll guarantee you a safe journey. If any harm reaches you it will be after one of the liveliest times in the history of the territory.'

"At this she laughed. 'Very well,' says she, 'I'll chance it, Mr. Red.'

" 'His name ain't Red,' puts in Darragh, solemn. 'His name's Saunders. We call him Red becus uf his hair.'

" 'I'm sure I beg your pardon,' says Miss Loys, all of a fluster.

" 'That's all right, ma'm; no damage done at all,' says I. 'It's useless for me to try to conceal the fact that my hair is a little on the auburn. You mustn't mind what Darragh says. We've had a good deal of hot weather lately and his brains have gone wrong. Now hop in and we'll touch the breeze.' So I piled her trunk in and away we flew.

"Bud and Dandy were a corking little team. They'd run the whole distance from the railway to the ranch if you'd let 'em—and I never interfered. A straight line and the keen jump hits me all right when I'm going some place, although I can loaf with the next man, on occasion. So we missed most of the gullies.

"The ponies were snorting and pulling grass, the buckboard bouncing behind 'em like a rubber ball, and we were crowding into the teeth of the northwest wind, which made it seem as if we were traveling 100 per cent. better than a Dutch clock would show.

" 'Goodness gracious!' says the girl, 'do you always go like this in this country? And aren't there any roads?'

" 'Why, no,' says I. 'Hike!' and I snapped the blacksnake over the ponies' ears, and they strung themselves out like a brace of coyotes, nearly pulling the buckboard out from under us. 'Sometimes we travel like *this*,' I says. 'And as for roads, I despise 'em. You're not afraid, are you?'

" 'Indeed I'm not. I think it's glorious. Might I drive?'

" 'If I can smoke,' says I, 'then *you* can drive.' I'd heard about young women who'd been brought up so tender that tobacker smoke would ruin their morals or something, and kind of wondered if she was that sort.

" 'That's a bargain,' says she prompt. 'But how you're going to light a cigar in this wind I don't see.'

" 'Cigarette,' says I. 'And if you would kindly hold my hat until I get one rolled I'll take it kind of you.'

" 'But what about the horses?' says she.

" 'Put your foot on the lines and they'll make. That's the main and only art of driving on the prairie —not to let the lines get under the horses' feet—all the rest is just sit still and look at the scenery.'

"She held my hat for a wind-break, and I got my paper pipe together. And then—not a match. I searched every pocket. Not a lucifer. That is more of what I got for being funny and changing my clothes. And then she happened to think of a box she had for traveling, and fished it out of her grip.

" 'Young lady,' I says, 'until it comes to be your bad luck—which I hope won't ever happen—to be very much in love with a man who won't play back, you'll never properly know the pangs of a man that's got all the materials to smoke with except the fire. Now, if I have a chance to do as much for you sometime, I'm there.'

"She laughed and crinkled up her eyes at me. 'All right, Mr. Saunders. When that obdurate man disdains me, I'll call for your help.'

" 'The place for the man that would disdain you is an asylum,' says I. 'And the only help I'd give you would be to put him there.' She blushed real nice. I like to see a woman blush. It's a trick they can't learn!

"But I see she was put out by my easy talk, so I gave her a pat on the back and says, 'Don't mind me, little girl. We fellers see an eighteen-carat woman so seldom that it goes to our heads. There wasn't no offence meant, and you'll be foolish if you put it there. Let's shake hands.'

"So she laughed again and shook. I mean *shook*. It wasn't like handing you so much cold fish—the way some women shake hands. And Loys and me, we were full pards from date.

"I made one more bad break on the home trip.

" 'Jonesy will be powerful glad to see you,' says I.

" 'Jonesy!' says she, surprised. 'Jonesy! Oh, is *that* what you call Uncle Albert?'

" 'Well, it does sometimes happen that way,' says I. And then my anti-George-Washington blood rose again. 'You see, he was kind of lonesome out here at first, and we took to calling him Jonesy to cheer him up and make him feel at home,' I says.

" 'Oh!' says she. And I reckon she didn't feel so horribly awful about it, for after looking straight toward the Gulf of Mexico for a minute, suddenly she bust right out and hollered. It seems that Jones cut a great deal of grass to a swipe when he was back home in his own street. It's astonishing how little of a man it takes to do that in the East. We had an argument once on the subject. 'It's intellect does it,' says Silver Tompkins. 'Oh, that's it, eh?' says Wind-River Smith. 'Well, I'm glad I'm not troubled that way. I'd rather have a forty-four chest than a number eight head any day you can find in the almanac.' And I'm with Smithy. This knowing so much it makes you sick ain't any better than being so healthy you don't know nothing, besides being square miles less fun. Another thing about the Eastern folks is they're so sot in their views, and it don't matter to them whether the facts bear out their idees or not.

" 'Here, take a cigar,' says one of the Board of Directors to me—a little fat old man, who had to draw in his breath before he could cross his legs—'them cigarettes'll ruin your health,' says he. Mind you, he was always kicking and roaring about his liver, or stummick, or some of his works. I'm a little over six-foot-three in my boots when I stand up straight, and I stood up straight as the Lord would let me and gazed down at that little man. 'Pardner,' says I, 'I was raised on cigarettes. When I was two years old I used to have a pull at the bottle, and then my cigarette to aid digestion. It may be conceit on my part,' I says, 'but I'd rather be a wreck like me than a prize-fighter like you.' They're queer; you'd think that little fat man would have noticed the difference without my pointing it out to him.

"Well, I don't have to mention that Loys stirred things up considerable around the Chanta Seechee and vicinity. Gee! What a diving into wannegans and a fetching out of good clothes there was. And trading

of useful coats and things for useless but decorating
silk handkerchers and things.   And what a hair cutting and whisker trimming.

"But Kyle was the man from the go in.   And it
was right it should be so.   If ever two young people
were born to make trouble for each other it was Kyle
and Loys.

"A nice, decent fellow was Kyle.   Nothing remarkable, you could say, and that was one of his best
points.   Howsomever, he had a head that could do
plain thinking, a pair of shoulders that discouraged
frivoling, and he was as square a piece of furniture as
ever came out of a factory.   More'n that; he had
quite a little education, saved his money, never got
more than good-natured loaded, and he could ride
anything that had four legs, from a saw-horse to old
tiger Buck, who would kick your both feet out of the
sturrups and reach around and bite you in the small of
the back so quick that the boys would be pulling his
front hoofs out of your frame before you'd realize
that the canter had begun.   Nice horse, Buck.   He
like to eat Jonesy up one morning before Silver and
me could get to the corral.   Lord!   The sounds made
my blood run cold!   Old Buck squealing like a boar-
pig in a wolf trap, and Jonesy yelling, 'Help! Murder! Police!'   Even that did not cure Jones from
sticking his nose where it wasn't wanted.   Why, once—
but thunder!   It would take me a long while to tell
you all that happened to Jones.

"One thing that didn't hurt Kyle any in the cam-
paign was that he was 'most as good-looking for a

man as she was for a woman. They made a pair to
draw to, I tell you, loping over the prairie, full of
health and youngness! You wouldn't want to see a
prettier sight than they made, and you could see it at
any time, for they were together whenever it was possible. Loys was so happy that it made you feel like
a boy again to see her. She told me in private that
it was wonderful how the air out here agreed with
her, and I said it was considered mighty bracing, and
never let on that they proclaimed their state of mind
every time they looked at each other. I reckon old
smart-Aleck Jonesy was the only party in the town-
ship who didn't understand. Kyle used to put vine-
gar in his coffee and things like that, and if you'd ask
him, 'What's that fellow's name that runs the clothing store in town?' he'd come out of his trance and
say 'Yes,' and smile very amiable, to show that he
thoroughly admitted you were right.

"Well, things went as smooth and easy as bob-sled-
ding until it came time for Loys to be moseying back
to college again.

"Then Kyle took me into his confidence. I never
was less astonished in my whole life, and I didn't tell
him so. 'Well, what are you going to do about it?'
says I.

"He kind of groaned and shook his head. "I dun-
no,' says he. 'Do you think she likes me, Red?' I
felt like saying, 'Well, if you ain't got all the traits
but the long ears, I miss my guess,' but I made allow-
ances, and says I, 'Well, about *that* I don't think I
ought to say anything; still, if I had only one eye left

I could see plain that her education's finished. She don't want any more college, that girl don't.'

" 'Think not?' says he, bracing up. And then, by and by, they went out to ride, for Jonesy was good to the girl, I'll say that for him. He was willing to do anything for her in reason, according to his views. But Kyle wasn't in them views; he was out of the picture as far as husbands went.

"They came back at sunset, when the whole world was glowing red the same as they were. I reached for the field-glasses and took a squint at them. There was no harm in that, for they were well-behaved young folks. One look at their faces was enough. There were three of us in the bull-pen—Bob, and Wind-River Smith, and myself. We'd brought up a herd of calves from Nanley's ranch, and we were taking it easy. 'Boys,' says I, under my breath, 'they've made the riffle.'

" 'No!' says they, and then everybody had to take a pull at the glasses.

" 'Well, I'm glad,' says Smithy. And darn my buttons if that old hardshell's voice didn't shake. 'They're two of as nice kids as you'd find in many a weary day,' says he. 'And I wish 'em all the luck in the world.'

" 'So do I,' says I, 'and I really think the best we could do for 'em would be to shoot Jones.'

" 'Man! Won't he sizz!' says Bob. And you can't blame us old codgers if we had a laugh at that, although it was such a powerful serious matter to the youngsters.

" 'Let's go out and meet 'em,' says I. And away we went. They weren't a particle surprised. I suppose they thought the whole universe had stopped to look on. We pump-handled away and laughed, and Loys she laughed kind of teary, and Kyle he looked red in the face and proud and happy and ashamed of himself, and we all felt loosened up considerable, but I told him on the quiet, 'Take that fool grin off your face, unless you want Uncle Jones to drop the moment he sees you.'

"Now they only had three days left to get an action on them, as that was the time set for Loys to go back to college.

"Next day they held a council behind the big barn, and they called in Uncle Red—otherwise known as Big Red Saunders, or Chanta Seechee Red, which means 'Bad-heart Red' in Sioux language, and doesn't explain me by a durn sight—to get the benefit of his valuable advice.

" 'Skip,' says I. 'Fly for town and get married, and come back and tell Jonesy about it. It's a pesky sight stronger argument to tell him what you have done than what you're going to do.'

"They couldn't quite agree with that. They thought it was sneaky.

" 'So it is,' says I. 'The first art of war is understanding how to make a grand sneak. If you don't want to take my advice you can wait.' That didn't hit 'em just right either.

" 'What will we wait for?' says Kyle.

" 'Exercise—and the kind you won't take when

you get as old and sensible as me. You're taking long chances, both of you; but it's just like playing cards, you might as well put all your money on the first turn, win or lose, as to try and play system. Systems don't work in faro, nor love affairs, nor any other game of chance. Be gone. Put your marker on the grand raffle. In other words, take the first horse to town and get married. Ten chances to one Jonesy will have the laugh on you before the year is out.'

" 'I don't think you're a bit nice to-day, Red,' says Loys.

" 'He's jealous,' says Kyle.

" 'That's what I am, young man,' says I. 'If I had ten years off my shoulders, and a little of the glow off my hair, I'd give you a run for your alley that would leave you breathless at the wind-up.'

" 'I think your hair is a beautiful color, Red,' says Loys. 'Many a woman would like to have it.'

" 'Of course they would,' I answered. 'But they don't get it. I'm foxy, I am.' Still I was touched in a tender spot. That young woman knew just the right thing to say, by nature. 'Well, what are you young folks going to do?' I asked them.

"They decided that they'd think it over until next day, but that turned out to be too late, for what must Kyle do but get chucked from his horse and have his leg broke near the hip. You don't want to take any love affairs onto the back of a bad horse, now you mark me! There was no such thing as downing that boy when he was in his right mind.

"Now here was a hurrah! Loys, she dasn't cry, for fear of uncle, and Kyle, he used the sinfullest language known to the tongue of man. 'Twas the first time I'd ever heard him say anything much, but he made it clear that it wasn't because he couldn't.

" 'What will we do, Red? What will we do?' says he.

" 'Now,' says I, don't bile over like that, because it's bad for your leg.'

"He cussed the leg.

" 'Go on and tell me what we can do,' says he.

" 'When you ask me that, you've pulled the right bell,' says I. 'I'll tell you exactly what we'll do. I go for the doctor. Savvy? Well, I bring back the minister at the same time. Angevine, he loses the Jersey cow over in the cane-break, and uncle and Angevine go hunting her, for not even Loys is ace high in uncle's mind alongside that cow. The rest is easy.'

" 'Red, you're a brick—you're the best fellow alive,' says Kyle, nearly squeezing the hand off me.

" 'I've tried to conceal it all my life, but I knew it would be discovered some day,' says I. 'Well, I suppose I'd better break the news to Loys—'twouldn't be any more than polite."

" 'Oh, Lord! I wonder if she'll be willing?' says he.

" 'No reason I shouldn't turn an honest dollar on the transaction—I'll bet you a month's wages she is,' says I. He wanted to do it, thinking I was in earnest, but I laughed at him.

"She *was* willing, all right—even anxious. There's

some women, and men, too, for that matter, who go
through life like a cat through a back alley, not caring
a cuss for either end or the middle. They would have
been content to wait. Not so Loys. She wanted her
Kyle, her poor Kyle, and she wanted him quick.
That's the kind of people for me! Your cautious folk
are all the time falling down wells because their eyes
are up in the air, keeping tabs so that they can dodge
shooting stars.

"Now, I had a minister friend up in town, Father
Slade by name. No, he was not a Catholic, I think.
They called him 'Father' because it fitted him. His
church had a steeple on it, anyhow, so it was no mave-
rick. Just what particular kind of religion the old
man had I don't know, but I should say he was a
homeopath on a guess. He looked it. 'Twas a comfort to see him coming down the street, his old face
shining in his white hair like a shriveled pink apple
in a snowdrift, God-blessing everything in sight—
good, bad, or indifferent. He had something pleasant
to say to all. We was quite friends, and every once
in a while we'd have a chin about things.

" 'Are you keeping straight, Red?' he'd ask when
we parted.

" 'Um,' I'd say, 'I'm afraid you'd notice a bend here
and there, if you slid your eyes along the edge.'

" 'Well, keep as straight as you can; don't give up
trying, my boy,' he'd tell me, mighty earnest, and I'd
feel ashamed of myself clear around the corner.

"I knew the old man would do me a favor if it could
be done, so I pulled out easy in my mind.

"First place, I stopped at the doctor's, because I felt they might fix up the marrying business some other time, but if a leg that's broke in the upper joint ain't set right, you can see a large dark-complected hunk of trouble over the party's left shoulder for the rest of his days. The doctor was out, so I left word for him what was wanted, and to be ready when I got back, and pulled for Father Slade's. The old gentleman had the rheumatism, and he groaned when I come in. Rheumatism's no disease for people who can't swear.

" 'How are you, my boy?' says he; 'I'm glad to see you. Here am I, an old man, nipped by the leg, and much wanting to talk to somebody.'

"I passed the time of day to him, but felt kind of blue. This didn't look like keeping my word with the kids. I really hated to say anything to the old man, knowing his disposition; still I felt I had to, and I out with my story.

" 'Dear! dear!' says he. 'The hurry and skurry of young folks! How idle it seems when you get fifty years away from it, and see how little anything counts! For all that, I thank God,' says he, 'that there's a little red left in my blood yet, which makes me sympathize with them. But the girl's people object, you say?'

"I made that all clear to him. 'The girl's *always* all right, Father,' says I, 'and as for the man in this case, my word for him.'

"Now it ain't just the right thing for me to say, but seeing as I've never had anything in particular to be modest about, and I'm proud of what the old gentleman told me, I'm going to repeat it.

" 'Your word is good for me, Red,' says he. 'You're a mischievous boy at times, but your heart and your head are both reliable; give me your arm to the wagon.'

"Then I felt mighty sorry to think of lugging that poor old man all that ways.

" 'Here!' says I. 'Now you sit down again; don't you do nothing of the sort—you ain't fit.'

"He put his hand on my shoulder and hobbled his weight off the game leg.

" 'Reddy, I was sitting there thinking when you came in—thinking of how comfortable it was to be in an easy-chair with my foot on a stool, and then I thought, "If the Lord should send me some work to do, would I be willing?" Now, thanks be to Him! I *am* willing, and glad to find myself so, and I do not believe there's any work more acceptable to Him than the union of young folk who love each other. Ouch!' says he, as that foot touched the ground. Perhaps you'd better pick me up and carry me bodily.'

"So I did it, the old housekeeper following us with an armful of things and jawing the both of us—him for a fool and me for a villain. She was a strong-minded old lady, and I wish I could remember some of her talk—it was great.

"We went around and got the doctor.

" 'Hoo!' says he. 'Is it as bad as that?' I winked at Father Slade.

" 'It's a-plenty worse than that,' says I; 'you won't know the half of it till you get down there.'

"But of course we had to tell him, and he was tickled. Funny what an interest everybody takes in these happenings. He wanted all the details.

" 'By Jove!' says he, 'the man whose feelings ain't the least dimmed by a broken leg—horse rolled on him, you said? Splintered it, probably—that man is one of the right sort. He'll do to tie to.'

"When we reached the ranch the boys were lined up to meet us. 'Hurry along!' they called. 'Angey can't keep uncle amused all day!'

"So we hustled. Kyle was for being married first, and then having his leg set, but I put my foot down flat. It had gone long enough now, and I wasn't going to have him cripping it all his life. But the doctor worked like a man who gets paid by the piece, and in less than no time we were able to call Loys in.

"Wind-River Smith spoke to get to give the bride away, and we let him have it.

"We'd just got settled to business when in comes Angevine, puffing like a buffalo. 'For Heaven's sakes! Ain't you finished yet?' says he; 'well, you want to be at it, for the old man ain't over two minutes behind me, coming fast. I took the distance in ten-foot steps. Just my luck! Foot slipped when I was talking to him, and I dropped a remark that made him suspicious—I wouldn't have done it for a ton of money—but it's too late now. I'll down him and hold him out there if you say so.'

"Well, sir, at this old Father Slade stood right up, forgetting that foot entirely.

" 'Children, be ready,' says he, and he went over the line for a record.

" 'Hurry there!' hollers old Bob from the outside, where he was on watch; 'here comes uncle up the long coulee!'

" 'What are your names?' says Father Slade. They told him, both red'ning.

" 'Do you, Kyle, take this woman, Loys, to have and keep track of, come hell or high water, her heirs and assigns forever?'—or such a matter—says he, all in one breath. They both said they did.

"Things flew till we came to the ring. There was a hitch. We had plumb forgotten that important article. For a minute I felt stingy; then I cussed myself for a mean old long-horn, and dived into my box.

" 'Here, take this!' I says. 'It was my mother's!'

" 'Oh, Red! You mustn't part with that!' cried Loys, her eyes filling up.

" 'Don't waste time talking; I put through what I tackle. Hurry, please, Father.'

" 'Has anybody any objections to these proceedings?' says he.

" 'I have,' says I, 'but I won't mention 'em. Give them the verdict.'

" 'I pronounce you man and wife. Let us pray,' says he.

" 'What's that?' screeches Uncle Jonesy from the doorway. And then he gave us the queerest prayer you ever heard in your life. He stood on one toe and clawed chunks out of the air while he delivered it.

"He seemed to have it in for me in particular. 'You villain! You rascal! You red-headed rascal! You did this! I know you did!'

" 'Oh, uncle!' says I, 'forgive me!' With that I hugged him right up to me, and he filled my bosom full of smothered language.

" 'Cheese it, you little cuss!' I whispered in his ear, 'or I'll break every rib in your poor old chest!' I came in on him a trifle, just to show him what I could do if I tried.

" ' 'Nuff!' he wheezes. 'Quit. 'Nuff.'

" 'Go up and congratulate 'em,' I whispered again.

" 'I won't,' says he. 'Ouch! Yes, I will! I will!' So up he goes, grinding his teeth.

" 'I wish you every happiness,' he grunts.

" 'Won't you forgive me, uncle?' begs Loys.

" 'Some other time; some other time!' he hollers, and he pranced out of the house like a hostyle spider, the maddest little man in the territory.

"Loys had a hard time of it until Kyle got so he could travel, and they went up to the Yellowstone with a team for a wedding trip.

"The rest of Loys' folks was in an unpleasant frame of mind, too. They sent out her brother, and while I'd have took most anything from Loys' brother, there comes a place where human nature is human nature, and the upshot of it was I planked that young man gently but firmly across my knees. Suffering Ike! But he was one sassy young man! Howsomever, the

D

whole outfit came round in time—all except uncle and
me. He used to grit his teeth together till the sparks
flew when he saw me. I was afraid he'd bust a blood-
vessel in one of them fits, so I quit. I hated to let
go of the old ranch, but I'm pretty well fixed—I'm
superintendent here. It's Kyle's ranch, you know.
That's his brand—the queer-looking thing on the left
hip of that critter, over the vented hash-knife. Loys'
invention, that is. She says it's a cherublim, but we
call it the 'flying flap-jack.' There's a right smart lot
of beef critters toting that signal around this part of
the country. Kyle's one of the fellers that rises like
a setting of bread—quiet and gentle, but steady and
sure. He's going to the State Legislature next year.
'Twon't do no harm to have one honest man in the
outfit.

"Now, perhaps if I'd married some nice woman I
might have had 1,000 steers of my own, and a chance
to make rules and regulations for my fellow-citizens
—and then again I might have took to gambling and
drinking and raising blazes, and broke my poor wife's
broom-handle with my hard head. So I reckon we'll
let it slide as it is. Now you straddle that cayuse
of yours and come along with me and I'll show you
some rattling colts."

THE WILD HORSE OF TARTARY

BY CLARA MORRIS

*Mrs. Frederick C. Harriott (**born in To-
ronto, Canada, in 1849**) writes, as she has
acted, under her maiden name of Clara
Morris. The same temperamental genius
which won her the reputation of the greatest
emotional actress of the American stage dis-
tinguishes her literary work. The graphic
power of the born story-teller is displayed in
her reminiscences of the stage no less than in
her fiction. Of this "The Wild Horse of
Tartary" is a convincing illustration. The
story appeared first in "McClure's Magazine" and afterward in Miss Morris's book,
"Life on the Stage."*

THE WILD HORSE OF TARTARY

BY CLARA MORRIS

BUT there! Just as I start to speak of my third season, I seem to look into a pair of big, mild eyes that say, "Can it be that you mean to pass *me* by? Do you forget that 'twas I who turned the great-sensation scene of a play into a side-splitting farce?"—and I shake my head and answer truthfully, "I can not forget. I shall never forget your work that night in Columbus, when you appeared as the 'fiery untamed steed' (may Heaven forgive you!) in 'Mazeppa'!"

Mr. Robert E. J. Miles—or "All-the-Alphabet Miles," as he was frequently called—was starring at that time in the "horse" drama, doing such plays as "The Cataract of the Ganges," "Mazeppa," "Sixteen-String Jack," etc. "Mazeppa" was the favorite in Columbus, and both the star and the manager regretted that they had billed the other plays in advance, as there would have been more money in "Mazeppa" alone. Mr. Miles carried with him two horses; one, for "The Wild Horse of Tartary," was an exquisitely formed, satin-coated creature, who looked wickedly at you from the corner of her blazing eye: who bared her teeth savagely, and struck out with her forefeet, as well as with her hind ones. When she came rearing, plunging, biting, snapping, whirling, and kicking her way on to the stage, the scarlet lining of her dilating nostrils and the foam flying from her mouth made our screams very natural ones, and the women in front used to huddle close together, or even cover their faces.

One creature only did this beautiful vixen love— R. E. J. Miles. She fawned upon him like a dog, and did tricks for him like a dog, but she was a terror to the rest of mankind. It was really a thrilling scene when Mazeppa was bound, his head tailward, his feet maneward, to the back of that maddened beast. She seemed to bite and tear at him, and when set free, she stood straight up for a dreadful moment, in which she really endangered his life; then, with a wild neigh, she tore off up the "runs" as if fiends pursued her, with the man stretched helplessly along her inky back. The curtain used to go up again and again, it was so very effective.

The other horse who traveled with Mr. Miles was an entirely different sort. He would have been described—according to the State where he happened to be—as a piebald, a skewbald, a pinto, or a calico horse. He was very large, mostly of a satiny white color, with big absurdly-shaped markings of bright bay. He was one of that breed of horses which in livery stables are always known as "Doctor" or "Judge." Benevolence beamed from his large, clear eyes, and he looked so mildly wise one half expected to see him put on spectacles. The boy at the stable said one day, as he fed him, "I wouldn't wonder if this ol' parson of a hoss asked a blessin' on them there oats—I wouldn't!"

I don't know whether Old Bob, as he was called, had any speed or not, but if he had it was useless to him; for alas! he was never allowed to reach the goal under any circumstances. He was always ridden by the villain, and therefore had to be overtaken. Besides that he generally had to carry double, as the desperado usually fled holding the fainting heroine before him, and though Old Bob successfully leaped chasms thus heavily handicapped—for truly he was a mighty jumper—nevertheless he was compelled to accept defeat. Mr. Miles always came rushing up to the rescue on the black horse, when Bob was very lucky, indeed, if he didn't have to roll about and die; and he was a very impatient dead horse, often amusing the audience by lifting his head to see if the curtain was not down, and then dropping dead again, with a sigh the whole house could hear.

Anyway, being continually pushed back into second place, and compelled to listen to the unearned applause bestowed upon the beautiful black, Old Bob lost all ambition professionally, and he simply became a gourmet and a glutton. He lived to eat. A woman in his eyes was a sort of perambulating storehouse of cake, crackers, apples, sugar, etc.; only his love for children was disinterested. The moment he was loose he went off on a search for children, no matter whose so long as he found some; then down he would go on his knees, and wait to be pulled and patted. His habit of gathering very small people up by their back breadths, and carrying them a little way before dropping them, always filled the air with wild shrieks of laughter. In the theatre he walked sedately about before rehearsal began, and though we knew his attentions were entirely selfish, he was so urbane, so complaisant in his manner of going through us, that we could not resist his advances, and each day and night we packed our pockets and our muffs with such provender as women seldom carry about in their clothes. All our gloves smelled as though we worked at a cider mill.

While the play was going on, Old Bob spent a great part of his time standing on the first of the screened platforms connecting the runs, and as every one of us had to pass him on our way to dress, he demanded toll of all. Fruits, domestic or foreign, he received with gentle eagerness. Cake, crackers, and sugar—the velvety nose snuffed at them approvingly, and if a girl, believing herself late, tried to pass him swiftly by, his look of amazement was comical to behold, and in an instant his iron-shod foot was playing a veritable devil's tattoo on the resounding board platform. If that failed to win attention, following her with his eyes, he lifted up his voice in a full-chested "Neigh-—hay—hay—*haay!*" that brought her back in a hurry with her toll of sugar. And that piebald hypocrite would scrunch it with such a piteously ravenous air that the girl quite forgot the satirical words her landlady had directed against her recently-acquired sweet tooth.

The dreadful night of disaster came late in the week. I don't recall the name of the play, but in that one piece the beautiful, high-spirited black mare had

to carry double up the runs.   John Carroll and Miss
Lucy Cutler were the riders.   Mr. Carroll claimed that
he could ride a little, and though he was afraid, he
was ashamed to own it.   Mr. Miles said in the morning: "Now if you are the least bit timid, Mr. Carroll,
say so, and I will fasten the bridle reins to the saddle
pommel, and Queen will carry you up of her own
accord as true as a die and as safe as a rock; but if
you are going to hold the bridle, for God's sake be
careful!   If it was Old Bob, you could saw him as
much as you liked and he would pay no attention, but
Queen, who has a tender mouth, is half-mad with excitement at night, and a very slight pressure on the
wrong rein will mean a forty or fifty-foot fall for
you all!"

Miss Cutler expressed great fear, when Mr. Miles
surprisedly said: "Why, you have ridden with me
twice this week without a sign of fear?"

"Oh, yes," she answered, "but *you* know what you
are doing—*you* are a horseman!"

It was an unfortunate speech, and in face of it Mr.
Carroll's vanity would not allow him to admit his anxiety.   "He could ride well enough and he would handle
the reins himself," he declared.

During the day his fears grew upon him.   Foolishly and wickedly he resorted to spirits to try to build
up some Dutch courage.   Then when the scene came
on, half-blind with fear and the liquor—which he was
not used to—as he felt the fierce creature beneath him
rushing furiously up the steep incline, a sort of madness came upon him.   Without rhyme or reason he

pulled desperately at the nigh rein, and in the same
breath their three bodies were hurling downward like
thunderbolts. It was an awful sight! I looked at
them as they descended, and for the fraction of a second they seemed to be suspended in the air. They
were all upside down. All, without turning or twisting, fell straight as plummets—the horse, the same
as the man and woman, had its feet straight in the
air. Ugh! the striking. Ugh! never mind details.
The curtain was rushed down. Miss Cutler was
picked up dazed, stunned, but without a mark. Mr.
Carroll crept away unaided amid the confusion, the
sorrow, and the tears, for splendid Queen was doomed.
Though Mr. Miles had risked his own life in an awful
leap to save her from falling through a trap, he could
not save her life, and the almost human groan with
which she dropped her lovely head upon her master's
shoulders, and his streaming eyes as he tenderly wiped
the blood from her velvety nostrils, made even the
scene-shifters rub their eyes upon the backs of their
hands. While Queen was half-carried to the fire-en-
gine house next door (her stable was too far away),
some one went before the curtain and assured the audience that the accident was very slight, and that the
lady and gentleman would both appear presently.
The audience applauded in a rather doubtful manner, for several ladies had fainted, and the carrying
out of a helpless person in a place of amusement
always has a depressing effect upon the lookers-on.
Meantime Mr. Carroll was getting his wrist bandaged
and a cut on his face patched up, while a basket of

sawdust was hurriedly procured that certain cruel stains might be concealed. The orchestra played brisk-ly, and the play went on. That's the one thing we can be sure of in this world—that the play will go on. Late that night, beautiful Queen died, with her head resting on her master's knee.

Now "Mazeppa" was billed for the next night, and there were many consultations held in the office and on the stage. "The Wild Horse of Tartary" was gone. It was impossible to find a new horse in one day. "Change the bill!" said Mr. Miies. "And have an empty house," answered Mr. Ellsler.

"But what can I do for a horse?" asked Mr. Miles. "Use Old Bob," answered Mr. Ellsler.

"Good Lord!" groaned Bob's master. They argued long, but neither wanted to lose the good house, so the bill was allowed to stand, and "Mazeppa" was performed with Old Bob as "The Wild Horse of Tar-tary." Think of it—that ingratiating Old Bob, that follower of women and playmate of children! Why, even the great bay blotches on his white old hide made one think of the circus, of paper hoops, and of *train-ing*, rather than of wildness. With the hope of mak-ing him at least impatient and restless, he had been deprived of his supper, and the result was a settled gloom, an air of melancholy, that made Mr. Miles swear under his breath every time he looked at him.

The play moved along nicely, the house was large, and seemed pleased. Mazeppa fell into his enemy's hands, the sentence was pronounced, and the order fol-lowed, "Bring forth the fiery, untamed steed!"

The women of the audience began to draw close to
their escorts. Many of them remembered the biting,
kicking entrance of the black, and were frightened
beforehand. The orchestra responded with incidental,
creepy music, but that was all. Over in the entrance,
Old Bob, surrounded by the four men who were supposed to restrain him, stood quietly. But those who
sat in the left box heard "get-ups!" and "go-ons!"
and the cluckings of many tongues. The mighty
Khan of Tartary (who could not see that entrance)
thought he had not been heard, and he roared again,
"Bring forth the fiery, untamed steed!" Another
pause; the house tittered; then some one hit Old Bob
a crack across the rump with a whip, at which he gave
a switch of his tail, and gently ambled on to the stage.
He stopped of his own accord at the centre, and, lowering his head, stretched out his neck and sniffed at
the leader of the orchestra, precisely as a dog sniffs
at a stranger. It was deliciously ridiculous. We
girls were supposed to scream with fear of the "wild
horse," and alas! we were only too obedient; crowding down at the right, clinging together in attitudes
of extremest fright, we shrieked and screeched until
Old Bob pricked up his ears, and looked so astonished at our conduct that the audience simply rocked
back and forth with laughter. And all the time Mazeppa was saying things that did not seem at all like
prayers. Finally he gave orders for the men to sur-
round Bob, which they did, and then a sharp little
spike was used—that was to make him dance about
pretty lively. It pricked him on the shoulder, and the

"wild horse" stood and switched his tail. It pricked him again; he switched his tail again. The men had by this time grown careless, and when the spike was finally used at his mane, he suddenly kicked one of them clear of the stage, and then resumed his unruffled calm. The public thought it was having fun all this time, but pretty soon it knew it. Nothing under heaven could disturb the gentle serenity of that doglike old horse. When Mazeppa was brought forward to be bound upon Old Bob's back, instead of pulling away, and rearing and fighting against the burden, his one and only quick movement was his violent effort to break away from his tormentors and welcome his master joyously.

"Oh!" groaned Miles, "kill him, somebody, before he kills me!"

While Mazeppa was being bound on the "wild horse's" back our instructions were to scream; therefore we screamed as before, and, being on the verge of insanity, Miles lifted his head from the horse's back, and said, "Oh, shut up, do!" The audience heard, and—well, it laughed some more, and then it discovered, when the men sprang away and left the horse free to dash madly up the mountain, that Mazeppa had kept one foot unbound to kick Old Bob with; and truly it did seem that the audience was going into convulsions—such laughter, pierced every now and then by the shrill scream of hysterics. Old Bob ambled up the first run all right, but, alas! for poor Mazeppa, as the "wild horse" reached the first platform, a woman passed on the way to her room, and hungry Bob instantly stopped to negotiate a loan in sugar. Oh, it was dreadful—the wait—and when finally he reappeared, trotting—yes, trotting up the next run—Mr. Miles's foot could be plainly seen kicking with the regularity of a piston-rod, while his remarks were—well, they were irregular in the extreme!

Of course the play was hopelessly ruined. The audience laughed at the slightest mention of the "wild horse," and when the shepherds found horse and man, lying at the foot of the mountain, worn out and exhausted, the building seemed to shake with the laughter.

When the play was over at last, Old Bob walked up to his master and mumbled his hand. Mr. Miles pushed him away with pretended anger, crying: "You infernal old idiot, I'd sell you for a three-cent stamp with gum on it!"

Bob looked hard at him a moment; then he calmly crossed behind him and mumbled his other hand, and Mr. Miles pulled his ears, and said that he, himself, was the idiot for expecting an untrained, unrehearsed horse to play such a part, and Old Bob agreeing with him perfectly, they were, as always, at peace with each other.

A DERELICT

BY RICHARD HARDING DAVIS

Richard Harding Davis (born in Philadelphia in 1864) has a vigorous style of marked individuality which finds expression in two distinct though related forms of literature: special and war correspondence, and fiction dealing with modern types of character and contemporaneous events. No work more typical of his genius could be selected than "A Derelict," a story of journalism in the stress of a war crisis, in which two extreme but thoroughly representative types of newspaper men are brought into vivid contrast.

A DERELICT

BY RICHARD HARDING DAVIS

WHEN the warships of a navy lie cleared for action outside a harbor, and the warships of the country with which they are at war lie cleared for action inside the harbor, there is likely to be trouble. Trouble between warships is news, and wherever there is news there is always a representative of the Consolidated Press.

As long as Sampson blockaded Havana and the army beat time back of the Tampa Bay Hotel, the central office for news was at Key West, but when Cervera slipped into Santiago Harbor and Sampson stationed his battleships at its mouth, Key West lost her only excuse for existence, and the press-boats buried their bows in the waters of the Florida Straits and raced for the cable station at Port Antonio. It was then that Keating, the "star" man of the Consolidated Press Syndicate, was forced to abandon his young bride and the rooms he had engaged for her at the Key West Hotel, and accompany his tug to the distant island of Jamaica.

Keating was a good and faithful servant to the Consolidated Press. He was a correspondent after its own making, an industrious collector of facts. The

This story is reprinted by permission from the book entitled "Ranson's Folly," copyright 1902, by Charles Scribner's Sons.

Consolidated Press did not ask him to comment on what it sent him to see; it did not require nor desire his editorial opinions or impressions. It was no part of his work to go into the motives which led to the event of news interest which he was sent to report, nor to point out what there was of it which was dramatic, pathetic, or outrageous.

The Consolidated Press, being a mighty corporation, which daily fed seven hundred different newspapers, could not hope to please the policy of each, so it compromised by giving the facts of the day fairly set down, without heat, prejudice, or enthusiasm. This was an excellent arrangement for the papers that subscribed for the service of the Consolidated Press, but it was death to the literary strivings of the Consolidated Press correspondent.

"We do not want descriptive writing," was the warning which the manager of the great syndicate was always flashing to its correspondents. "We do not pay you to send us pen-pictures or prose-poems. We want the facts, all the facts, and nothing but the facts."

And so, when at a Presidential convention a theatrical speaker sat down after calling James G. Blaine "a plumed knight," each of the "special" correspondents present wrote two columns in an effort to describe how the people who heard the speech behaved in consequence, but the Consolidated Press man telegraphed, "At the conclusion of these remarks the cheering lasted sixteen minutes."

No event of news value was too insignificant to escape the watchfulness of the Consolidated Press.

none so great that it could not handle it from its inception up to the moment when it ceased to be quoted in the news market of the world. Each night, from thousands of spots all over the surface of the globe, it received thousands of facts, of cold, accomplished facts. It knew that a tidal wave had swept through China, a cabinet had changed in Chili, in Texas an express train had been held up and robbed, "Spike" Kennedy had defeated the "Dutchman" in New Orleans, the "Oregon" had coaled outside of Rio Janeiro Harbor, the Cape Verde fleet had been seen at anchor off Cadiz; it had been located in the harbor of San Juan, Porto Rico; it had been sighted steaming slowly past Fortress Monroe; and the Navy Department reported that the "St. Paul" had discovered the lost squadron of Spain in the harbor of Santiago. This last fact was the one which sent Keating to Jamaica. Where he was sent was a matter of indifference to Keating. He had worn the collar of the Consolidated Press for so long a time that he was callous. A board meeting—a mine disaster—an Indian uprising—it was all one to Keating. He collected facts and his salary. He had no enthusiasms, he held no illusions. The prestige of the mammoth syndicate he represented gained him an audience where men who wrote for one paper only were repulsed on the threshold. Senators, governors, the presidents of great trusts and railroad systems, who fled from the reporter of a local paper as from a leper, would send for Keating and dictate to him whatever it was they wanted the people of the United States to believe, for

when they talked to Keating they talked to many millions of readers.   Keating, in turn, wrote out what they
had said to him and transmitted it, without color or
bias, to the Clearing-house of the Consolidated Press.
His "stories," as all newspaper writings are called by
men who write them, were as picturesque reading as
the quotations of a stock-ticker.   The personal equa-
tion appeared no more offensively than it does in a
page of typewriting in his work.

Consequently, he was dear to the heart of the Consolidated Press, and, as a "safe" man, was sent to the
beautiful harbor of Santiago—to a spot where there
were warships cleared for action, Cubans in ambush,
naked marines fighting for a foothold at Guantanamo,
palm-trees and coral-reefs—in order that he might
look for "facts."

There was not a newspaper man left at Key West
who did not writhe with envy and anger when he
heard of it.   When the wire was closed for the night,
and they had gathered at Josh Kerry's, Keating was
the storm-centre of their indignation.

"What a chance!" they protested.   "What a story!
It's the chance of a lifetime."   They shook their heads
mournfully and lashed themselves with pictures of its
possibilities.

"And just fancy its being wasted on old Keating,"
said the "Journal" man.   "Why, everything's likely
to happen out there, and whatever does happen he'll
make it read like a Congressional Record.   Why, when
I heard of it I cabled the office that if the paper would
send me I'd not ask for any salary for six months."

"And Keating's kicking because he has to go," growled the "Sun" man. "Yes, he is, I saw him last night, and he was sore because he'd just moved his wife down here. He said if he'd known this was coming he'd have let her stay in New York. He says he'll lose money on this assignment, having to support himself and his wife in two different places."

Norris, "the star man" of the "World," howled with indignation.

"Good Lord!" he said, "is that all he sees in it? Why, there never was such a chance. I tell you, some day soon all of those warships will let loose at each other and there will be the best story that ever came over the wire, and if there isn't, it's a regular loaf anyway. It's a picnic, that's what it is, at the expense of the Consolidated Press. Why, he ought to pay them to let him go. Can't you see him, confound him, sitting under a palm-tree in white flannels, with a glass of Jamaica rum in his fist, while we're dodging yellow fever on this coral-reef, and losing our salaries on a crooked roulette wheel?"

"I wonder what Jamaica rum is like as a steady drink," mused the ex-baseball reporter, who had been converted into a war correspondent by the purchase of a white yachting cap.

"It won't be long before Keating finds out," said the "Journal" man.

"Oh, I didn't know that," ventured the new reporter, who had just come South from Boston. "I thought he didn't drink. I never see Keating in here with the rest of the boys."

"You wouldn't," said Norris. "He only comes in here by himself, and he drinks by himself. He's one of those confidential drunkards. You give some men whiskey, and it's like throwing kerosene on a fire, isn't it? It makes them wave their arms about and talk loud and break things, but you give it to another man and it's like throwing kerosene on a cork mat. It just soaks in. That's what Keating is. He's a sort of a cork mat."

"I shouldn't think the C. P. would stand for that," said the Boston man.

"It wouldn't if it ever interfered with his work, but he's never fallen down on a story yet. And the sort of stuff he writes is machine-made; a man can write C. P. stuff in his sleep."

One of the "World" men looked up and laughed.

"I wonder if he'll run across Channing out there," he said. The men at the table smiled, a kindly, indulgent smile. The name seemed to act upon their indignation as a shower upon the close air of a summer day. "That's so," said Norris. "He wrote me last month from Port-au-Prince that he was moving on to Jamaica. He wrote me from that club there at the end of the wharf. He said he was at that moment introducing the President to a new cocktail, and as he had no money to pay his passage to Kingston he was trying to persuade him to send him on there as his Haitian Consul. He said in case he couldn't get appointed Consul, he had an offer to go as cook on a fruit tramp."

The men around the table laughed. It was the

pleased, proud laugh that flutters the family dinner-
table when the infant son and heir says something
precocious and impudent.

"Who is Channing?" asked the Boston man.

There was a pause, and the correspondents looked at
Norris.

"Channing is a sort of a derelict," he said.   "He
drifted into New York last Christmas from the 'Omaha
Bee.'   He's been on pretty nearly every paper in the
country."

"What's he doing in Haiti?"

"He went there on the 'Admiral Decatur' to write
a filibustering story about carrying arms across to
Cuba.   Then the war broke out and he's been trying
to get back to Key West, and now, of course, he'll
make for Kingston.   He cabled me yesterday, at my
expense, to try and get him a job on our paper.   If
the war hadn't come on he had a plan to beat his way
around the world.   And he'd have done it, too.   I
never saw a man who wouldn't help Charlie along, or
lend him a dollar."   He glanced at the faces about him
and winked at the Boston man.   "They all of them
look guilty, don't they?" he said.

"Charlie Channing," murmured the baseball reporter, gently, as though he were pronouncing the
name of a girl.   He raised his glass.   "Here's to Charlie Channing," he repeated.   Norris set down his empty
glass and showed it to the Boston man.

"That's his only enemy," he said.   "Write!
Heavens, how that man can write, and he'd almost
rather do anything else.   There isn't a paper in New

York that wasn't glad to get him, but they couldn't keep him a week. It was no use talking to him. Talk! I've talked to him until three o'clock in the morning. Why, it was I made him send his first Chinatown story to the 'International Magazine,' and they took it like a flash and wrote him for more, but he blew in the check they sent him and didn't even answer their letter. He said after he'd had the fun of writing a story he didn't care whether it was published in a Sunday paper or in white vellum, or never published at all. And so long as he knew he wrote it, he didn't care whether any one else knew it or not. Why, when that English reviewer—what's his name?—that friend of Kipling's—passed through New York, he said to a lot of us at the Press Club, 'You've got a young man here on Park Row—an opium-eater, I should say, by the look of him—who, if he would work and leave whiskey alone, would make us all sweat.' That's just what he said, and he's the best in England!"

"Charlie's a genius," growled the baseball reporter, defiantly. "I say, he's a genius."

The Boston man shook his head. "My boy," he began sententiously, "genius is nothing more than hard work, and a man—"

Norris slapped the table with his hand.

"Oh, no, it's not," he jeered fiercely, "and don't you go off believing it is, neither. I've worked. I've worked twelve hours a day. Keating even has worked eighteen hours a day—all his life—but we never wrote 'The Passing of the Highbinders,' nor the 'Ships that Never Came Home,' nor 'Tales of the Tenderloin,' and we never will. I'm a better news-gatherer than Charlie, I can collect facts and I can put them together well enough too, so that if a man starts to read my story he'll probably follow it to the bottom of the column, and he may turn over the page, too. But I can't say the things because I can't see the things that Charlie sees. Why, one night we sent him out on a big railroad story. It was a beat, we'd got it by accident, and we had it all to ourselves, but Charlie came across a blind beggar on Broadway with a dead dog. The dog had been run over, and the blind beggar couldn't find his way home without him, and was sitting on the curbstone, weeping over the mongrel. Well, when Charlie came back to the office he said he couldn't find out anything about that railroad deal, but that he'd write them a dog story. Of course, they were raging crazy, but he sat down just as though it was no concern of his, and, sure enough, he wrote the dog story. And the next day over five hundred people stopped in at the office on their way downtown and left dimes and dollars to buy that man a new dog. Now, hard work won't do that."

Keating had been taking breakfast in the wardroom of H. M. S. "Indefatigable." As an acquaintance the officers had not found him an undoubted acquisition, but he was the representative of seven hundred papers, and when the "Indefatigable's" ice-machine broke he had loaned the officers' mess a hundred pounds of it from his own boat.

The cruiser's gig carried Keating to the wharf, the crew tossed their oars and the boatswain touched his cap and asked, mechanically, "Shall I return to the ship, sir?"

Channing, stretched on the beach, with his back to a palm-tree, observed the approach of Keating with cheerful approbation.

"It is gratifying to me," he said, "to see the press treated with such consideration. You came in just like Cleopatra in her barge. If the flag had been flying, and you hadn't steered so badly, I should have thought you were at least an admiral. How many guns does the British Navy give a Consolidated Press reporter when he comes over the side?"

Keating dropped to the sand and, crossing his legs under him, began tossing shells at the water.

"They gave this one a damned good breakfast," he said, "and some very excellent white wine. Of course, the ice-machine was broken, it always is, but then Chablis never should be iced if it's the real thing."

"Chablis! Ice! Hah!" snorted Channing. "Listen to him! Do you know what I had for breakfast?"

Keating turned away uncomfortably and looked toward the ships in the harbor.

"Well, never mind," said Channing, yawning luxuriously. "The sun is bright, the sea is blue, and the confidences of this old palm are soothing. He's a great old gossip, this palm." He looked up into the rustling fronds and smiled. "He whispers me to sleep," he went on, "or he talks me awake—talks about all sorts of things—things he has seen—cyclones, wrecks, and strange ships and Cuban refugees and

Spanish spies and lovers that meet here on moonlight
nights. It's always moonlight in Port Antonio, isn't
it?"

"You ought to know, you've been here longer than
I," said Keating.

"And how do you like it, now that you have got to
know it better? Pretty heavenly, eh?"

"Pretty heavenly!" snorted Keating. "Pretty much
the other place! What good am I doing? What's
the sense of keeping me here? Cervera isn't going to come out, and the people at Washington won't
let Sampson go in. Why, those ships have been there
a month now, and they'll be there just where they are
now when you and I are bald. I'm no use here. All
I do is to thrash across there every day and eat up
more coal than the whole squadron burns in a month.
Why, that tug of mine's costing the C. P. six hundred dollars a day, and I'm not sending them news
enough to pay for setting it up. Have you seen 'em
yet?"

"Seen what? Your stories?"

"No, the ships."

"Yes, Scudder took me across once in the 'Iduna.' I
haven't got a paper yet, so I couldn't write anything,
but—"

"Well, you've seen all there is to it, then; you
wouldn't see any more if you went over every day.
It's just the same old harbor-mouth, and the same old
Morro Castle, and the same old ships drifting up and
down; the 'Brooklyn,' full of smoke-stacks, and the
'New York,' with her two bridges, and all the rest of

them looking just as they've looked for the last four weeks. There's nothing in that. Why don't they send me to Tampa with the army and Shafter—that's where the story is."

"Oh, I don't know," said Channing, shaking his head. "I thought it was bully!"

"Bully, what was bully?"

"Oh, the picture," said Channing, doubtfully, "and —and what it meant. What struck me about it was that it was so hot, and lazy, and peaceful, that they seemed to be just drifting about—just what you complain of. I don't know what I expected to see; I think I expected they'd be racing around in circles, tearing up the water and throwing broadsides at Morro Castle as fast as firecrackers.

"But they lay broiling there in the heat just as though they were becalmed. They seemed to be asleep on their anchor-chains. It reminded me of a big bull-dog lying in the sun with his head on his paws and his eyes shut. You think he's asleep, and you try to tip-toe past him, but when you're in reach of his chain— he's at your throat, what? It seemed so funny to think of our being really at war. I mean the United States, and with such an old-established firm as Spain. It seems so presumptuous in a young republic, as though we were strutting around, singing, 'I'm getting a big boy now.' I felt like saying, 'Oh, come off, and stop playing you're a world power, and get back into your red sash and knickerbockers, or you'll get spanked!' It seems as though we must be such a lot of amateurs. But when I went over the side of the

'New York' I felt like kneeling down on her deck and begging every jacky to kick me. I felt about as useless as a fly on a locomotive engine. Amateurs! Why they might have been in the business since the days of the ark; all of them might have been descended from bloody pirates; they twisted those eight-inch guns around for us just as though they were bicycles, and the whole ship moved and breathed and thought, too, like a human being, and all the captains of the other warships about her were watching for her to give the word. All of them stripped and eager and ready—like a lot of jockeys holding in the big race-horses, and each of them with his eyes on the starter. And I liked the way they all talk about Sampson, and the way the ships move over the stations like parts of one machine, just as he had told them to do.

"Scudder introduced me to him, and he listened while we did the talking, but it was easy to see who was the man in the Conning Tower. Keating—my boy!" Channing cried, sitting upright in his enthusiasm, "he's put a combination-lock on that harbor that can't be picked—and it'll work whether Sampson's asleep in his berth, or fifteen miles away, or killed on the bridge. He doesn't have to worry, he knows his trap will work—he ought to, he set it."

Keating shrugged his shoulders, tolerantly.

"Oh, I see that side of it," he assented. "I see all there is in it for *you*, the sort of stuff you write, Sunday-special stuff, but there's no *news* in it. I'm not paid to write mail letters, and I'm not down here to interview palm-trees either."

"Why, you old fraud!" laughed Channing. "You know you're having the time of your life here. You're the pet of Kingston society—you know you are. I only wish I were half as popular. I don't seem to belong, do I? I guess it's my clothes. That English Colonel at Kingston always scowls at me as though he'd like to put me in irons, and whenever I meet our Consul he sees something very peculiar on the horizon-line."

Keating frowned for a moment in silence, and then coughed, consciously.

"Channing," he began, uncomfortably, "you ought to brace up."

"Brace up?" asked Channing.

"Well, it isn't fair to the rest of us," protested Keating, launching into his grievance. "There's only a few of us here, and we—we think you ought to see that and not give the crowd a bad name. All the other correspondents have some regard for—for their position and for the paper, but you loaf around here looking like an old tramp—like any old beachcomber—and it queers the rest of us. Why, those English artillerymen at the Club asked me about you, and when I told them you were a New York correspondent they made all sorts of jokes about American newspapers, and what could I say?"

Channing eyed the other man with keen delight.

"I see, by Jove! I'm sorry," he said. But the next moment he laughed, and then apologized, remorsefully.

"Indeed, I beg your pardon," he begged, "but it

struck me as a sort of—I had no idea you fellows were
such swells—I knew I was a social outcast, but I didn't
know my being a social outcast was hurting any one
else. Tell me some more."

"Well, that's all," said Keating, suspiciously. "The
fellows asked me to speak to you about it and to tell
you to take a brace. Now, for instance, we have a sort
of mess-table at the hotel, and we'd like to ask you to
belong, but—well—you see how it is—we have the
officers to lunch whenever they're on shore, and you're
so disreputable"—Keating scowled at Channing, and
concluded, impotently, "Why don't you get yourself
some decent clothes and—and a new hat?"

Channing removed his hat to his knee and stroked
it with affectionate pity.

"It is a shocking bad hat," he said. "Well, go on."

"Oh, it's none of my business," exclaimed Keating,
impatiently. "I'm just telling you what they're saying. Now, there's the Cuban refugees, for instance.
No one knows what they're doing here, or whether
they're real Cubans or Spaniards."

"Well, what of it?"

"Why, the way you go round with them and visit
them, it's no wonder they say you're a spy."

Channing stared incredulously, and then threw back
his head and laughed with a shout of delight.

"They don't, do they?" he asked.

"Yes, they do, since you think it's so funny. If it
hadn't been for us, the day you went over to Guantanamo the marines would have had you arrested and
court-martialed."

Channing's face clouded with a quick frown. "Oh," he exclaimed, in a hurt voice, "they couldn't have thought that."

"Well, no," Keating admitted grudgingly, "not after the fight, perhaps, but before that, when you were snooping around the camp like a Cuban after rations." Channing recognized the picture with a laugh.

"I do," he said, "I do. But you should have had me court-martialed and shot; it would have made a good story. 'Our reporter shot as a spy, his last words were—' What were my last words, Keating?"

Keating turned upon him with impatience, "But why do you do it?" he demanded. "Why don't you act like the rest of us? Why do you hang out with all those filibusters and runaway Cubans?"

"They have been very kind to me," said Channing, soberly. "They are a very courteous race, and they have ideas of hospitality which make the average New Yorker look like a dog hiding a bone."

"Oh, I suppose you mean that for us," demanded Keating. "That's a slap at me, eh?"

Channing gave a sigh and threw himself back against the trunk of the palm, with his hands clasped behind his head.

"Oh, I wasn't thinking of you at all, Keating," he said. "I don't consider you in the least." He stretched himself and yawned wearily. "I've got troubles of my own."

He sat up suddenly and adjusted the objectionable hat to his head.

"Why don't you wire the C. P.," he asked briskly,

"and see if they don't want an extra man? It won't
cost you anything to wire, and I need the job, and I
haven't the money to cable."

"The Consolidated Press," began Keating, jealously.
"Why—well, you know what the Consolidated Press
is? They don't want descriptive writers—and I've
got all the men I need."

Keating rose and stood hesitating in some embar-
rassment. "I'll tell you what I could do, Channing,"
he said, "I could take you on as a stoker, or steward,
say. They're always deserting and mutinying; I have
to carry a gun on me to make them mind. How would
you like that? Forty dollars a month, and eat with
the crew?"

For a moment Channing stood in silence, smoothing
the sand with the sole of his shoe. When he raised
his head his face was flushing.

"Oh, thank you," he said. "I think I'll keep on trying for a paper—I'll try a little longer. I want to see
something of this war, of course, and if I'm not too
lazy I'd like to write something about it, but—well—
I'm much obliged to you, anyway."

"Of course, if it were my money, I'd take you on
at once," said Keating, hurriedly.

Channing smiled and nodded. "You're very kind,"
he answered. "Well, good-by."

A half-hour later, in the smoking-room of the hotel,
Keating addressed himself to a group of correspondents.

"There is no doing anything with that man Channing," he said, in a tone of offended pride. "I offered

him a good job and he wouldn't take it. Because he got a story in the 'International Magazine' he's stuck on himself, and he won't hustle for news—he wants to write pipe-dreams. What the public wants just now is news."

"That's it," said one of the group, "and we must give it to them—even if we have to fake it."

Great events followed each other with great rapidity. The army ceased beating time, shook itself together, adjusted its armor and moved, and, to the delight of the flotilla of press-boats at Port Antonio, moved, not as it had at first intended, to the north coast of Cuba, but to Santiago, where its transports were within reach of their megaphones.

"Why, everything's coming our way now!" exclaimed the "World" manager in ecstasy. "We've got the transports to starboard at Siboney, and the warships to port at Santiago, and all we'll need to do is to sit on the deck with a field-glass and take down the news with both hands."

Channing followed these events with envy. Once or twice, as a special favor, the press-boats carried him across to Siboney and Daiquiri, and he was able to write stories of what he saw there; of the landing of the army, of the wounded after the Guasimas fight, and of the fever-camp at Siboney. His friends on the press-boat sent this work home by mail on the chance that the Sunday editor might take it at space rates. But mail matter moved slowly and the army moved quickly, and events crowded so closely upon each other that Channing's stories, when they reached New York, were ancient history and were unpublished, and, what was of more importance to him, unpaid for. He had no money now, and he had become a beachcomber in the real sense of the word. He slept the warm nights away among the bananas and cocoanuts on the Fruit Company's wharf, and by calling alternately on his Cuban exiles and the different press-boats, he was able to obtain a meal a day without arousing any suspicions in the minds of his hosts that it was his only one.

He was sitting on the stringer of the pier-head one morning, waiting for a press-boat from the "front," when the "Three Friends" ran in and lowered her dingy, and the "World" manager came ashore, clasping a precious bundle of closely written cable forms. Channing scrambled to his feet and hailed him.

"Have you heard from the chief about me yet?" he asked. The "World" man frowned and stammered, and then, taking Channing by the arm, hurried with him toward the cable office.

"Charlie, I think they're crazy up there," he began, "they think they know it all. Here I am on the spot, but they think—"

"You mean they won't have me," said Channing. "But why?" he asked, patiently. "They used to give me all the space I wanted."

"Yes, I know, confound them, and so they should now," said the "World" man, with sympathetic indignation. "But here's their cable; you can see it's not my fault." He read the message aloud. "Channing, no. Not safe, take reliable man from Siboney." He folded the cablegram around a dozen others and stuck it back in his hip-pocket.

"What queered you, Charlie," he explained, importantly, "was that last break of yours, New Year's, when you didn't turn up for a week. It was once too often, and the chief's had it in for you ever since. You remember?"

Channing screwed up his lips in an effort of recollection.

"Yes, I remember," he answered slowly. "It began on New Year's eve in Perry's drug store, and I woke up a week later in a hack in Boston. So I didn't have such a run for my money, did I? Not good enough to have to pay for it like this. I tell you," he burst out suddenly, "I feel like hell being left out of this war, with all the rest of the boys working so hard. If it weren't playing it low down on the fellows that have been in it from the start, I'd like to enlist. But they enlisted for glory, and I'd only do it because I can't see the war any other way, and it doesn't seem fair to them. What do you think?"

"Oh, don't do that," protested the "World" manager. "You stick to your own trade. We'll get you something to do. Have you tried the Consolidated Press yet?"

Channing smiled grimly at the recollection.

"Yes, I tried it first."

"It would be throwing pearls to swine to have you write for them, I know, but they're using so many men now. I should think you could get on their boat."

"No—I saw Keating," Channing explained. "He said I could come along as a stoker, and I guess I'll take him up, it seems—"

"Keating said—what?" exclaimed the "World" man. "Keating? Why, he stands to lose his own job if he isn't careful. If it wasn't that he's just married, the C. P. boys would have reported him a dozen times."

"Reported him, what for?"

"Why—you know. His old complaint."

"Oh, that," said Channing. "My old complaint?" he added.

"Well, yes, but Keating hasn't been sober for two weeks, and he'd have fallen down on the Guasimas story if those men hadn't pulled him through. They had to because they're in the syndicate. He ought to go shoot himself; he's only been married three months and he's handling the biggest piece of news the country's had in thirty years, and he can't talk straight. There's a time for everything, I say," growled the "World" man.

"It takes it out of a man, this boat-work," Channing ventured, in extenuation. "It's very hard on him."

"You bet it is," agreed the "World" manager, with enthusiasm. "Sloshing about in those waves, seasick mostly, and wet all the time, and with a mutinous crew, and so afraid you'll miss something that you can't write what you have got." Then he added, as an afterthought, "And our cruisers thinking you're a Spanish torpedo boat and chucking shells at you."

"No wonder Keating drinks," Channing said, gravely. "You make it seem almost necessary."

Many thousand American soldiers had lost themselves in a jungle, and had broken out of it at the foot of San Juan Hill. Not wishing to return into the jungle, they took the hill. On the day they did this Channing had the good fortune to be in Siboney. The "World" man had carried him there and asked him to wait around the water-front while he went up to the real front, thirteen miles inland. Channing's duty was to signal the press-boat, when the first despatch-rider rode in with word that the battle was on. The "World" man would have liked to ask Channing to act as his despatch-rider, but he did not do so because the despatch-riders were either Jamaica negroes or newsboys from Park Row—and he remembered that Keating had asked Channing to be his stoker.

Channing tramped through the damp, ill-smelling sand of the beach, sick with self-pity. On the other side of those glaring, inscrutable mountains, a battle, glorious, dramatic, and terrible, was going forward, and he was thirteen miles away. He was at the base, with the supplies, the sick, and the skulkers.

It was cruelly hot. The heat-waves flashed over the sea until the transports in the harbor quivered like pictures on a biograph. From the refuse of company kitchens, from reeking huts, from thousands of empty cans, rose foul, enervating odors, which deadened the senses like a drug. The atmosphere steamed with a heavy, moist humidity. Channing staggered and sank down suddenly on a pile of railroad ties in front of the commissary's depot. There were some Cubans seated near him, dividing their Government rations, and the sight reminded him that he had had nothing to eat. He walked over to the wide door of the freight depot, where a white-haired, kindly-faced, and perspiring officer was, with his own hands, serving out canned beef to a line of Cubans. The officer's flannel shirt was open at the throat. The shoulder-straps of a colonel were fastened to it by safety pins. Channing smiled at him uneasily.

"Could I draw on you for some rations?" he asked. "I'm from the 'Three Friends.' I'm not one of their regular accredited correspondents," he added, conscientiously, "I'm just helping them for to-day."

"Haven't you got a correspondent's pass?" asked the officer. He was busily pouring square hardtack down the throat of a saddle-bag a Cuban soldier held open before him.

"No," said Channing, turning away, "I'm just helping."

The officer looked after him, and what he saw caused him to reach under the counter for a tin cup and a bottle of lime-juice.

"Here," he said, "drink this. What's the matter with you—fever? Come in here out of that sun. You can lie down on my cot, if you like."

Channing took the tin cup and swallowed a warm mixture of boiled water and acrid lime-juice.

"Thank you," he said, "but I must keep watch for the first news from the front."

A man riding a Government mule appeared on the

bridge of the lower trail, and came toward them at a gallop. He was followed and surrounded by a hurrying mob of volunteers, hospital stewards, and Cubans.

The Colonel vaulted the counter and ran to meet him.

"This looks like news from the front now," he cried.

The man on the mule was from civil life. His eyes bulged from their sockets and his face was purple. The sweat ran over it and glistened on the cords of his thick neck.

"They're driving us back!" he shrieked. "Chaffee's killed, an' Roosevelt's killed, an' the whole army's beaten!" He waved his arms wildly toward the glaring, inscrutable mountains. The volunteers and stevedores and Cubans heard him, open-mouthed and with panic-stricken eyes. In the pitiless sunlight he was a hideous and awful spectacle.

"They're driving us into the sea!" he foamed.

"We've got to get out of here, they're just behind me. The army's running for its life. They're running away!"

Channing saw the man dimly, through a cloud that came between him and the yellow sunlight. The man in the saddle swayed, the group about him swayed, like persons on the floor of a vast ballroom. Inside he burned with a mad, fierce hatred for this shrieking figure in the saddle. He raised the tin cup and hurled it so that it hit the man's purple face.

"You lie!" Channing shouted, staggering. "You lie! You're a damned coward. You lie!" He heard his voice repeating this in different places at greater distances. Then the cloud closed about him, shutting out the man in the saddle, and the glaring, inscrutable mountains, and the ground at his feet rose and struck him in the face.

Channing knew he was on a boat because it lifted and sank with him, and he could hear the rush of her engines. When he opened his eyes he was in the wheel-house of the "Three Friends," and her captain was at the wheel, smiling down at him. Channing raised himself on his elbow.

"The despatch rider?" he asked.

"That's all right," said the captain, soothingly. "Don't you worry. He come along same time you fell, and brought you out to us. What ailed you— sunstroke?"

Channing sat up. "I guess so," he said.

When the "Three Friends" reached Port Antonio, Channing sought out the pile of coffee-bags on which he slept at night and dropped upon them. Before this he had been careful to avoid the place in the day-time, so that no one might guess that it was there that he slept at night, but this day he felt that if he should drop in the gutter he would not care whether any one saw him there or not. His limbs were hot and heavy and refused to support him, his bones burned like quicklime.

The next morning, with the fever still upon him, he hurried restlessly between the wharves and the cable office, seeking for news. There was much of it; it was great and trying news, the situation out-

side of Santiago was grim and critical. The men
who had climbed San Juan Hill were clinging to it
like sailors shipwrecked on a reef unwilling to remain, but unable to depart. If they attacked the city
Cervera promised to send it crashing about their ears.
They would enter Santiago only to find it in ruins.
If they abandoned the hill, 2,000 killed and wounded
would have been sacrificed in vain.

The war critics of the press-boats and of the
Twitchell House saw but two courses left open.
Either Sampson must force the harbor and destroy
the squadron, and so make it possible for the army
to enter the city, or the army must be reinforced with
artillery and troops in sufficient numbers to make it
independent of Sampson and indifferent to Cervera.

On the night of July 2, a thousand lies, a thousand
rumors, a thousand prophecies rolled through the
streets of Port Antonio, were filed at the cable office,
and flashed to the bulletin-boards of New York City.

That morning, so they told, the batteries on
Morro Castle had sunk three of Sampson's ships; the
batteries of Morro Castle had surrendered to Sampson; General Miles with 8,000 reinforcements had
sailed from Charleston; eighty guns had started from
Tampa Bay, they would occupy the mountains opposite Santiago and shell the Spanish fleet; the authorities at Washington had at last consented to allow
Sampson to run the forts and mines, and attack the
Spanish fleet; the army had not been fed for two
days, the Spaniards had cut it off from its base at
Siboney; the army would eat its Fourth of July din-

ner in the Governor's Palace; the army was in full retreat; the army was to attack at daybreak.

When Channing turned in under the fruit-shed on the night of July 2, there was but one press-boat remaining in the harbor. That was the Consolidated Press boat, and Keating himself was on the wharf, signaling for his dingy. Channing sprang to his feet and ran toward him, calling him by name. The thought that he must for another day remain so near the march of great events, and yet not see and feel them for himself, was intolerable. He felt if it would pay his passage to the coast of Cuba, there was no sacrifice to which he would not stoop.

Keating watched him approach, but without sign of recognition. His eyes were heavy and bloodshot.

"Keating," Channing begged, as he halted, panting, "won't you take me with you? I'll not be in the way, and I'll stoke or wait on table, or anything you want, if you'll only take me."

Keating's eyes opened and closed, sleepily. He removed an unlighted cigar from his mouth and shook the wet end of it at Channing, as though it were an accusing finger.

"I know your game," he murmured, thickly. "You haven't got a boat and you want to steal a ride on mine—for your paper. You can't do it, you see, you can't do it."

One of the crew of the dingy climbed up the gangway of the wharf and took Keating by the elbow. He looked at him and then at Channing and winked. He was apparently accustomed to this complication.

"I haven't got a paper, Keating," Channing argued soothingly. "Who have you got to help you?" he asked. It came to him that there might be on the boat some Philip sober, to whom he could appeal from Philip drunk.

"I haven't got any one to help me," Keating answered, with dignity. I don't need any one to help me." He placed his hand heavily and familiarly on the shoulder of the deck-hand. "You see that man?" he asked. "You see tha' man, do you? Well, tha' man he's too good for me an' you. Tha' man used to be the best reporter in New York City, an' he was too good to hustle for news, an' now he's—now he can't get a job—see? Nobody'll have him, see? He's got to come and be a stoker."

He stamped his foot with indignation.

"You come an' be a stoker," he commanded. "How long you think I'm going to wait for a stoker? You stoker, come on board and be a stoker."

Channing smiled, guiltily, at his good fortune. He jumped into the bow of the dingy, and Keating fell heavily in the stern.

The captain of the press-boat helped Keating safely to a bunk in the cabin and received his instructions to proceed to Santiago Harbor. Then he joined Channing. "Mr. Keating is feeling bad to-night. That bombardment off Morro," he explained tactfully, "was too exciting. We always let him sleep going across, and when we get there he's fresh as a daisy. What's this he tells me of your doing stoking?"

"I thought there might be another fight to-morrow, so I said I'd come as a stoker."

The captain grinned.

"Our Sam, that deck-hand, was telling me. He said Mr. Keating put it on you, sort of to spite you— is that so?"

"Oh, I wanted to come," said Channing.

The captain laughed comprehendingly. "I guess we'll be in a bad way," he said, "when we need you in the engine-room." He settled himself for conversation, with his feet against the rail and his thumbs in his suspenders. The lamps of Port Antonio were sinking into the water, the moonlight was flooding the deck.

"That was quite something of a bombardment Sampson put up against Morro Castle this morning," he began, critically. He spoke of bombardments from the full experience of a man who had seen shells strike off Coney Island from the proving-grounds at Sandy Hook. But Channing heard him, eagerly. He begged the tugboat captain to tell him what it looked like, and as the captain told him he filled it in and saw it as it really was.

"Perhaps they'll bombard again to-morrow," he hazarded, hopefully.

"We can't tell till we see how they're placed on the station," the captain answered. "If there's any firing we ought to hear it about eight o'clock to-morrow morning. We'll hear 'em before we see 'em."

Channing's conscience began to tweak him. It was time, he thought, that Keating should be aroused and brought up to the reviving air of the sea, but when he reached the foot of the companion ladder he found that Keating was already awake and in the act of drawing the cork from a bottle. His irritation against Channing had evaporated and he greeted him with sleepy good-humor.

"Why, it's ol' Charlie Channing," he exclaimed, drowsily. Channing advanced upon him swiftly.

"Here, you've had enough of that!" he commanded. "We'll be off Morro by breakfast-time. You don't want that."

Keating, giggling foolishly, pushed him from him and retreated with the bottle toward his berth. He lurched into it, rolled over with his face to the ship's side, and began breathing heavily.

"You leave me 'lone," he murmured, from the darkness of the bunk. "You mind your own business, you leave me 'lone."

Channing returned to the bow and placed the situation before the captain. That gentleman did not hesitate. He disappeared down the companionway, and, when an instant later he returned, hurled a bottle over the ship's side.

The next morning when Channing came on deck the land was just in sight, a rampart of dark-green mountains rising in heavy masses against the bright, glaring blue of the sky. He strained his eyes for the first sight of the ships, and his ears for the faintest echoes of distant firing, but there was no sound save the swift rush of the waters at the bow. The sea lay smooth and flat before him, the sun flashed upon it;

the calm and hush of early morning hung over the whole coast of Cuba.

An hour later the captain came forward and stood at his elbow.

"How's Keating?" Channing asked. "I tried to wake him, but I couldn't."

The captain kept his binoculars to his eyes, and shut his lips grimly. "Mr. Keating's very bad," he said. "He had another bottle hidden somewhere, and all last night—" he broke off with a relieved sigh. "It's lucky for him," he added, lowering the glasses, "that there'll be no fight to-day."

Channing gave a gasp of disappointment. "What do you mean?" he protested.

"You can look for yourself," said the captain, handing him the glasses. "They're at their same old stations. There'll be no bombardment to-day. That's the 'Iowa,' nearest us, the 'Oregon' 's to starboard of her, and the next is the 'Indiana.' That little fellow close under the land is the 'Gloucester.'"

He glanced up at the mast to see that the press-boat's signal was conspicuous; they were drawing within range.

With the naked eye, Channing could see the monster, mouse-colored warships, basking in the sun, solemn and motionless in a great crescent, with its one horn resting off the harbor-mouth. They made great blots on the sparkling, glancing surface of the water. Above each superstructure, their fighting-tops, giant davits, funnels, and gibbet-like yards twisted into the air, fantastic and incomprehensible, but the bulk below seemed to rest solidly on the bottom of the ocean, like an island of lead. The muzzles of their guns peered from the turrets as from ramparts of rock.

Channing gave a sigh of admiration.

"Don't tell me they move," he said. "They're not ships, they're fortresses!"

On the shore there was no sign of human life nor of human habitation. Except for the Spanish flag floating over the streaked walls of Morro, and the tiny blockhouse on every mountain-top, the squadron might have been anchored off a deserted coast. The hills rose from the water's edge like a wall, their peaks green and glaring in the sun, their valleys dark with shadows. Nothing moved upon the white beach at their feet, no smoke rose from their ridges, not even a palm stirred. The great range slept in a blue haze of heat. But only a few miles distant, masked by its frowning front, lay a gayly colored, red-roofed city, besieged by encircling regiments, a broad bay holding a squadron of great warships, and gliding catlike through its choked undergrowth and crouched among the fronds of its motionless palms were the ragged patriots of the Cuban army, silent, watchful, waiting. But the great range gave no sign. It frowned in the sunlight, grim and impenetrable.

"It's Sunday," exclaimed the captain. He pointed with his finger at the decks of the battleships, where hundreds of snow-white figures had gone to quarters. "It's church service," he said, "or it's general inspection."

Channing looked at his watch. It was thirty min-

utes past nine. "It's church service," he said. "I can
see them carrying out the chaplain's reading-desk on
the 'Indiana.'" The press-boat pushed her way
nearer into the circle of battleships until their leaden-
hued hulls towered high above her. On the deck of
each, the ship's company stood, ranged in motionless
ranks. The calm of a Sabbath morning hung about
them. The sun fell upon them like a benediction, and
so still was the air that those on the press-boat could
hear, from the stripped and naked decks, the voices
of the men answering the roll-call in rising monotone,
"one, two, three, *four;* one, two, three, *four.*" The
white-clad sailors might have been a chorus of sur-
pliced choir-boys.

But, up above them, the battle-flags, slumbering at
the mast-heads, stirred restlessly, and whimpered in
their sleep.

Out through the crack in the wall of mountains,
where the sea runs in to meet the waters of Santiago harbor, and from behind the shield of Morro
Castle, a great, gray ship, like a great, gray rat, stuck
out her nose and peered about her, and then struck
boldly for the open sea. High before her she bore the
gold and blood-red flag of Spain, and like a fugitive
leaping from behind his prison-walls, she raced forward for her freedom, to give battle, to meet her
death.

A shell from the "Iowa" shrieked its warning in
a shrill crescendo, a flutter of flags painted their message against the sky. "The enemy's ships are coming
out," they signaled, and the ranks of white-clad fig-

ures, which the moment before stood motionless on the decks, broke into thousands of separate beings who flung themselves, panting, down the hatchways, or sprang, cheering, to the fighting-tops.

Heavily, but swiftly, as islands slip into the water when a volcano shakes the ocean-bed, the great battle-ships buried their bows in the sea, their sides ripped apart with flame and smoke, the thunder of their guns roared and beat against the mountains, and, from the shore, the Spanish forts roared back at them, until the air between was split and riven. The Spanish warships were already scudding clouds of smoke, pierced with flashes of red flame, and as they fled, fighting, their batteries rattled with unceasing, fever-ish fury. But the guns of the American ships, strain-ing in pursuit, answered steadily, carefully, with re-lentless accuracy, with cruel persistence. At regular intervals they boomed above the hurricane of sound like great bells tolling for the dead.

It seemed to Channing that he had lived through many years; that the strain of the spectacle would leave its mark upon his nerves forever. He had been buffeted and beaten by a storm of all the great emo-tions; pride of race and country, pity for the dead, agony for the dying, who clung to blistering armor-plates, or sank to suffocation in the sea; the lust of the hunter, when the hunted thing is a fellow-man; the joys of danger and of excitement, when the shells lashed the waves about him, and the triumph of vic-tory, final, overwhelming and complete.

Four of the enemy's squadron had struck their col-

ors, two were on the beach, broken and burning, two
had sunk to the bottom of the sea, two were in abject
flight. Three battleships were hammering them with
thirteen-inch guns. The battle was won.

"It's all over," Channing said. His tone questioned his own words.

The captain of the tugboat was staring at the face
of his silver watch, as though it were a thing be-
witched. He was pale and panting. He looked at
Channing piteously, as though he doubted his own
senses, and turned the face of the watch toward him.

"Twenty minutes!" Channing said. "Good God!
Twenty minutes!"

He had been to hell and back again in twenty
minutes. He had seen an empire, which had begun
with Christopher Columbus and which had spread
over two continents, wiped off the map in twenty
minutes. The captain gave a sudden cry of concern.
"Mr. Keating," he gasped. "Oh, Lord, but I forgot
Mr. Keating. Where is Mr. Keating?"

"I went below twice," Channing answered. "He's
insensible. See what you can do with him, but first
—take me to the 'Iowa.' The Consolidated Press
will want the 'facts.'"

In the dark cabin the captain found Keating on the
floor, where Channing had dragged him, and drip-
ping with the water which Channing had thrown in
his face. He was breathing heavily, comfortably.
He was not concerned with battles.

With a megaphone, Channing gathered his facts
from an officer of the "Iowa," who looked like a

chimney-sweep, and who was surrounded by a crew of half-naked pirates, with bodies streaked with sweat and powder.

Then he ordered all steam for Port Antonio, and, going forward to the chart-room, seated himself at the captain's desk, and, pushing the captain's charts to the floor, spread out his elbows, and began to write the story of his life.

In the joy of creating it, he was lost to all about him. He did not know that the engines, driven to the breaking-point, were filling the ship with their groans and protests, that the deck beneath his feet was quivering like the floor of a planing-mill, nor that his fever was rising again and feeding on his veins. The turmoil of leaping engines and of throbbing pulses was confused with the story he was writing, and while his mind was inflamed with pictures of warring battleships, his body was swept by the fever, which overran him like an army of tiny mice, touching his hot skin with cold, tingling taps of their scampering feet.

From time to time the captain stopped at the door of the chart-room and observed him in silent admiration. To the man who with difficulty composed a letter to his family, the fact that Channing was writing something to be read by millions of people, and more rapidly than he could have spoken the same words, seemed a superhuman effort. He even hesitated to interrupt it by an offer of food.

But the fever would not let Channing taste of the food when they placed it at his elbow, and even as he

pushed it away his mind was still fixed upon the para-
graph before him.   He wrote, sprawling across the
desk, covering page upon page with giant hieroglyph-
ics, lighting cigarette after cigarette at the end of
the last one, but with his thoughts far away, and, as
he performed the act, staring uncomprehendingly at
the captain's colored calendar pinned on the wall before him.   For many months later the battle of Santiago was associated in his mind with a calendar for
the month of July, illuminated by a colored picture
of six white kittens in a basket.

At three o'clock Channing ceased writing and stood
up, shivering and shaking with a violent chill.   He
cursed himself for this weakness, and called aloud for
the captain.

"I can't stop now," he cried.   He seized the rough
fist of the captain as a child clings to the hand of his
nurse.

"Give me something," he begged.   "Medicine, quinine, give me something to keep my head straight until
it's finished.   Go, quick," he commanded.   His teeth
were chattering, and his body jerked with sharp, un-
controllable shudders.   The captain ran, muttering,
to his medicine chest.

"We've got one drunken man on board," he said to
the mate, "and now we've got a crazy one.   You mark
my words, he'll go off his head at sunset."

But at sunset Channing called to him and addressed
him sanely.   He held in his hand a mass of papers carefully numbered and arranged, and he gave them up to
the captain as though it hurt him to part with them.

"There's the story," he said. "You've got to do the rest. I can't—I—I'm going to be very ill."

He was swaying as he spoke. His eyes burned with the fever, and his eyelids closed of themselves. He looked as though he had been heavily drugged.

"You put that on the wire at Port Antonio," he commanded, faintly; "pay the tolls to Kingston. From there they are to send it by way of Panama, you understand, by the Panama wire."

"Panama!" gasped the captain. "Good Lord, that's two dollars a word." He shook out the pages in his hand until he found the last one. "And there's sixty-eight pages here," he expostulated. "Why, the tolls will be five thousand dollars!" Channing dropped feebly to the bench of the chart-room and fell in a heap, shivering and trembling.

"I guess it's worth it," he murmured, drowsily.

The captain was still staring at the last page.

"But—but, look here," he cried, "you've—you've signed Mr. Keating's name to it! 'James R. Keating.' You've signed his name to it!"

Channing raised his head from his folded arms and stared at him dully.

"You don't want to get Keating in trouble, do you?" he asked with patience. "You don't want the C. P. to know why he couldn't write the best story of the war? Do you want him to lose his job? Of course you don't. Well, then, let it go as his story. I won't tell, and see you don't tell, and Keating won't remember."

His head sank back again upon his crossed arms. "It's not a bad story," he murmured.

But the captain shook his head; his loyalty to his employer was still uppermost. "It doesn't seem right!" he protested. "It's a sort of a liberty, isn't it, signing another man's name to it, it's a sort of forgery."

Channing made no answer. His eyes were shut and he was shivering violently, hugging himself in his arms.

A quarter of an hour later, when the captain returned with fresh quinine, Channing sat upright and saluted him.

"Your information, sir," he said, addressing the open door politely, "is of the greatest value. Tell the executive officer to proceed under full steam to Panama. He will first fire a shot across her bows, and then sink her!" He sprang upright and stood for a moment, sustained by the false strength of the fever. "To Panama, you hear me!" he shouted. He beat the floor with his foot. "Faster, faster, faster," he cried. "We've got a great story! We want a clear wire, we want the wire clear from Panama to City Hall. It's the greatest story ever written—full of facts, facts, facts, facts for the Consolidated Press— and Keating wrote it. I tell you, Keating wrote it. I *saw* him write it. I was a stoker on the same ship."

The mate and crew came running forward and stood gaping stupidly through the doors and windows of the chart-room. Channing welcomed them joyously, and then crumpled up in a heap and pitched forward into the arms of the captain. His head swung weakly from shoulder to shoulder.

"I beg your pardon," he muttered, "I beg your pardon, captain, but your engine-room is too hot. I'm only a stoker and I know my place, sir, but I tell you, your engine-room is too hot. It's a burning hell, sir, it's a hell!"

The captain nodded to the crew and they closed in on him, and bore him, struggling feebly, to a bunk in the cabin below. In the berth opposite, Keating was snoring peacefully.

. . . .

After the six weeks' siege the Fruit Company's doctor told Channing he was cured, and that he might walk abroad. In this first walk he found that during his illness Port Antonio had reverted to her original condition of complete isolation from the world, the press-boats had left her wharves, the correspondents had departed from the veranda of her only hotel, the war was over, and the Peace Commissioners had sailed for Paris. Channing expressed his great gratitude to the people of the hotel and to the Fruit Company's doctor. He made it clear to them that if they ever hoped to be paid those lesser debts than that of gratitude which he still owed them, they must return him to New York and Newspaper Row. It was either that, he said, or, if they preferred, he would remain and work out his indebtedness, checking bunches of bananas at twenty dollars a month. The Fruit Company decided it would be paid more quickly if Channing worked at his own trade, and accordingly

sent him North in one of its steamers.   She landed
him in Boston, and he borrowed five dollars from the
chief engineer to pay his way to New York.

It was late in the evening of the same day when
he stepped out of the smoking-car into the roar and
riot of the Grand Central Station.   He had no bag-
gage to detain him, and, as he had no money either,
he made his way to an Italian restaurant where he
knew they would trust him to pay later for what he
ate.   It was a place where the newspaper men were
accustomed to meet, men who knew him, and who,
until he found work, would lend him money to buy a
bath, clean clothes, and a hall bedroom.

Norris, the "World" man, greeted him as he entered the door of the restaurant, and hailed him with
a cry of mingled fright and pleasure.

"Why, we didn't know but you were dead," he
exclaimed.   "The boys said when they left Kingston
you weren't expected to live.   Did you ever get the
money and things we sent you by the Red Cross
boat?"

Channing glanced at himself and laughed.

"Do I look it?" he asked.   He was wearing the
same clothes in which he had slept under the fruit-
sheds at Port Antonio.   They had been soaked and
stained by the night-dews and by the sweat of the
fever.

"Well, it's great luck, your turning up here just
now," Norris assured him heartily.   "That is, if you're
as hungry as the rest of the boys are who had the
fever.   You struck it just right; we're giving a big

dinner here to-night," he explained, "one of Maria's best. You come in with me. It's a celebration for old Keating, a farewell blow-out."

Channing started and laughed.

"Keating?" he asked. "That's funny," he said. "I haven't seen him since—since before I was ill."

"Yes, old Jimmie Keating. You've got nothing against him, have you?"

Channing shook his head vehemently, and Norris glanced back complacently toward the door of the dining-room, from whence came the sound of intimate revelry.

"You might have had, once," Norris said, laughing; "we were all up against him once. But since he's turned out such a wonder, and a war-hero, we're going to recognize it. They're always saying we newspaper men have it in for each other, and so we're just giving him this subscription dinner to show it's not so. He's going abroad, you know. He sails to-morrow morning."

"No, I didn't know," said Channing.

"Of course not, how could you? Well, the Consolidated Press's sending him and his wife to Paris. He's to cover the Peace negotiations there. It's really a honeymoon-trip at the expense of the C. P. It's their reward for his work, for his Santiago story, and the beat and all that—"

Channing's face expressed his bewilderment.

Norris drew back dramatically.

"Don't tell me," he exclaimed, "that you haven't heard about *that!*"

Channing laughed a short, frightened laugh, and moved nearer to the street.

"No," he said. "No, I hadn't."

"Yes, but, good Lord! it was *the* story of the war. You never read such a story! And he got it through by Panama a *day* ahead of all the other stories! And nobody read them, anyway. Why, Captain Mahan said it was 'naval history,' and the 'Evening Post' had an editorial on it, and said it was 'the only piece of literature the war has produced.' We never thought Keating had it in him, did you? The Consolidated Press people felt so good over it that they've promised, when he comes back from Paris, they'll make him their Washington correspondent. He's their 'star' reporter now. It just shows you that the occasion produces the man. Come on in and have a drink with him."

Channing pulled his arm away, and threw a frightened look toward the open door of the dining-room. Through the layers of tobacco-smoke he saw Keating seated at the head of a long, crowded table, smiling, clear-eyed, and alert.

"Oh, no, I couldn't," he said, with sudden panic. "I can't drink; doctor won't let me. I wasn't coming in, I was just passing when I saw you. Goodnight, I'm much obliged. Good-night."

But the hospitable Norris would not be denied.

"Oh, come in and say 'good-by' to him, anyhow," he insisted. "You needn't stay."

"No, I can't," Channing protested. "I—they'd make me drink or eat and the doctor says I can't. You mustn't tempt me. You say 'good-by' to him for me," he urged. "And Norris—tell him—tell him—that I asked you to say to him, 'It's all right,' that's all, just that, 'It's all right.' He'll understand."

There was the sound of men's feet scraping on the floor, and of chairs being moved from their places.

Norris started away eagerly. "I guess they're drinking his health," he said. "I must go. I'll tell him what you said, 'It's all right.' That's enough, is it? There's nothing more?"

Channing shook his head, and moved away from the only place where he was sure to find food and a welcome that night.

"There's nothing more," he said.

As he stepped from the door and stood irresolutely in the twilight of the street, he heard the voices of the men who had gathered in Keating's honor upraised in a joyous chorus.

"For he's a jolly good fellow," they sang, "for he's a jolly good fellow, which nobody can deny!"

THE HAPPIEST TIME

BY MARY STEWART CUTTING

Mrs. Cutting (born Stewart) is the wife of a New Jersey commuter, who was unconscious, when she began writing, that her work had any special suburban character. "I just told the stories that came to me," she said recently, in answer to an inquiry of how she came to conceive the cycle of charming suburban idyls which form her "Little Stories of Married Life." "My own experiences naturally furnished the material, and when it was done I found that it was suburban life and commuters almost exclusively that I had been writing about."

THE HAPPIEST TIME

BY MARY STEWART CUTTING

"AREN'T you coming to church with me this morning?"

"Well—not *this* morning, I think, petty."

"You *said* you would."

"Yes, I know I did, but I have a slight cold. I don't think it would be best for me, really, petty. I've been working pretty hard this week." Mr. Belmore carefully deposited a pile of newspapers beside his armchair upon the floor of the little library, removing and opening the top layer for perusal as he spoke, his eyes already glued to the headlines. "A quiet day will do me lots of good. I'll tell you what it is—I'll promise to go with you next Sunday if you say so."

"You always promise you'll go next Sunday." Mrs. Belmore, a brown-haired, clear-eyed young woman in a blue and white spotted morning gown, looked doubtfully, yet with manifest yielding, at her husband. Mr. Belmore presented the radiantly clean and peaceful aspect of the man who has risen at nine o'clock instead of the customary seven, and bathed and dressed in the sweet unhurried calm that belongs only to the first day of the week, poking dilatorily among chiffonier drawers, discovering hitherto forgotten garments in his

closet, and leisurely fumbling over a change of shirt-
studs before coming down to consume the breakfast
kept waiting for him.

"Of course I know it's your only day at home—"
Mrs. Belmore reverted to her occupation of deftly setting the chairs in their rightful places, and straightening the books on the tables. "I suppose I *ought* to
insist on your going—when you promised—but still—"
She gave a sigh of relinquishment. "I suppose you *do*
need the rest," she added. "We can have a nice afternoon together, anyway. You can finish reading that
story aloud, and we'll go out and take a good look at
the garden. I think the beans were planted too close
under the pear tree last year—that was the reason
they didn't come up right. Edith Barnes and Alan
Wilson are coming out from town after dinner for the
rest of the day, but that won't make any difference
to us."

"What?"

"Now, Herbert, how could I help asking them?
You know the boarding-house she and her mother
live in. Edith never gets a chance to see him alone.
They're saving up now to get married—they've been
engaged a year—so he can't spend any more money
for theatres and things, and they just have to walk and
walk the streets, unless they go visiting, and they've
been almost everywhere, Edith says. She wrote and
asked me to have them for this Sunday; he's been
away for a whole week somewhere up in the State. I
think it's pathetic." In the warmth of explanation Mrs.
Belmore had unwittingly removed the pile of news-

papers from the floor to an ottoman at the further end of the room. "Edith says she knows it's the happiest time of their lives, and she does want to get some of the benefit of it, poor girl."

"What do they want to be engaged for, anyway?"

"*Herbert!* How ridiculous! You are the most unreasonable man at times for a sensible one that I ever laid my eyes on. Why did *we* want to be engaged?"

"That was different." Mr. Belmore's tone conveyed a permanent satisfaction with his own case. "If every woman were like you, petty—I never *could* stand Edith, she's one of your clever girls; there's something about her that always sets my teeth on edge. As for Wilson—oh, Wilson's just a usual kind of a fool, like myself. Hello, where are my newspapers—and what in thunder makes it so cold? You don't mean to say you've got the window open?"

Mrs. Belmore had a habit of airing the rooms in the morning, which her husband approved of theoretically, and combated intensely in practice. After the window was banged shut she could hear him rattling at the furnace below to turn on an extra flow of heat before settling down once more in comfort. Although the April sun was bright, there was still a chill in the air.

She looked in upon him, gowned and bonneted for church, sweet and placid of mien, followed by two little girls, brave in their Sunday best, all big hats and ribboned hair and little starchy ruffles showing below their brown coats. Mrs. Belmore stooped over her husband's chair to kiss him good-by.

"You won't have to talk to Edith and Alan at all," she said, as if continuing the conversation from where they had left off. "All we have to do is to let them have the parlor or the library. They'll entertain each other."

"Oh, don't you bother about that. Now go ahead or you'll be late; and don't forget to say your prayers for me, too. That's right, always go to church with your mother, girlies."

"I *wish* you were going, too." Mrs. Belmore looked at her husband lingeringly.

"I wish I were, petty," said Mr. Belmore with a prompt mendacity so evidently inspired by affection that his wife condoned it at once.

She thought of him more than once during the service with generous satisfaction in his comfortable morning. She wished she had thought it right to remain at home, too, as she did sometimes, but there were the children to be considered. But she and Herbert would have the afternoon together, and take part of it to see about planting the garden, a plot of twenty feet square in the rear of the suburban villa.

The Sunday visit to the garden was almost a sacrament. They might look at it on other days, but it was only on Sunday, beginning with the early spring, that husband and wife strolled around the little patch together, first planning where to start the summer crop of vegetables and afterward watching the green things poking their spikes up through the mould, and growing, growing. He did the planting and working in the long light evenings after he came home, while

she held the papers of seeds for him; but it was only
on Sunday that he could really watch the green things
grow, and learn to know each separate leaf intimately,
and count the blossoms on the beans and the cucum-
bers. From the pure pleasure of the first radish through
all the various wiltings and shrivelings incident to
amateur gardening in summer deluge and drought, to
the triumphant survival of tomato plants and cucumber
vines, running riot over everything in the fall of the
year, the little garden played its old part as paradise
to these two, who became more fully one in the watching of the miracle of growth. When they gathered the
pears from the little tree in the corner of the plot, before the frost, and picked the few little green tomatoes
that remained on the dwindling stems, it was like
garnering a store of peaceful happiness. Every stage
of the garden was a romance. Mrs. Belmore could
go to church without her husband, but to have him
survey the garden without her would have been the
touch beyond.

It must be horrid, anyway, she thought, to have to
go every morning into town in those smoky cars and
crowded ferryboats; just to run into town twice
a week tired her out. Now he would have finished his paper—now little Dorothy would have
come in, red cheeked from her walk, to kiss
daddy before her nap—now he must be pottering
around among his possessions and looking out for
her. She knew so well how he would look when
he came to the door to meet her. The sudden
sight of either one to the other always shed a reflected

light, like the glow of the sun. It was with a feeling of wonder that she marked its disappearance, after a brief gleam, as he not only opened the door, but came out on the piazza to greet her, and closed it behind him.

"They're in there—Edith and Alan." He pointed over his shoulder with his thumb. "I thought they weren't coming until after dinner."

"Why, they weren't."

"Well, they're in the parlor, just the same. Came out over an hour ago. Great Scott, I wished I'd gone with you. I'm worn out."

"You don't mean to say you've stayed with them all the time!" Mrs. Belmore looked scandalized.

"I should say I had; I couldn't lose 'em. Whichever room I went to they followed; at least she did and he came after. I went from pillar to post, I give you my word, petty, but Edith had me by the neck; she never let go her grip for an instant. They won't speak to each other, you see; only to me. I haven't had a chance to even finish the paper. I've had the deuce of a time! I don't know what you are going to do about it."

"Never mind; it will be all right now," said Mrs. Belmore reassuringly. She pushed past him into the parlor, where sat a tall, straight girl with straight, light brows, a long straight nose, and a straight mouth with a droop at the corners. In the room beyond, a thickset, dark young man with glasses and a nervous expression was looking at pictures. It did not require a Solomon to discover at a glance how the land lay.

If Mrs. Belmore had counted easily on her powers

of conciliation she was disappointed this time. After the dinner, whereat the conversation was dragged laboriously round four sides of a square, except when the two little girls made some slight diversion, and the several futile attempts when the meal was over to leave the lovers alone together, Mrs. Belmore resigned herself, perforce, to the loss of her cherished afternoon.

"It's no use; we'll have to give up the reading," she said to her husband rapidly, in one of her comings and goings. "Perhaps later, dear. But it's really dreadful; here we've been talking of religion and beet-root sugar and smallpox, when any one can see that her heart is breaking."

"I think he is getting the worst of it," said Mr. Belmore impartially.

"Oh, it won't hurt *him.*"

"Well, you've given them plenty of opportunities to make up."

"Yes; but he doesn't know how."

She added in a louder tone, "You take Mr. Wilson up to your den for a while, Herbert; Ethel and I are going to have a cosey little time with the children; aren't we, dear?"

"Have a cigar?" said Mr. Belmore as the two men seated themselves comfortably in a couple of wooden armchairs in the sunny little apartment hung with a miscellaneous collection of guns, swords, and rods, the drawing of a bloated trout, and a dusty pair of antlers.

"Thank you; I'm not smoking now," said Mr. Wilson with a hungry look at the open box on the table beside him.

"Oh!" said his host genially, "so you're at that stage of the game. Well, I've been there myself. You have my sympathy. But this won't last, you know."

"Does your wife like smoking?"

"Loves it," said Mr. Belmore, sinking the fact of his official limit to four cigars a day. "That is, of course, she thinks it's a dirty habit, and unhealthy, and all that sort of thing, you know; but it doesn't make any *difference* to her—not a pin's worth. Cheer up, old fellow; you'll get to this place, too."

"Looks like it," said the other bitterly. "Here I haven't seen her for a week—I came two hundred miles on purpose yesterday, and now she won't even look at me. I don't know what's the matter—haven't the least idea—and I can't *get* her to tell me. I have to be off to-morrow at seven o'clock, too—I call it pretty hard lines."

"Let me see," said Mr. Belmore judicially, knitting his brows as if burrowing into the past as he smoked. "Perhaps I can help you out. What have you been writing to her? Telling her all about what you've been doing, and just sending your love at the end? They don't like that, you know."

Mr. Wilson shook his head. "No; upon my soul, I've done nothing but tell her how I—how I was looking forward to—oh, hang it, Belmore, the letters have been all *right,* I know that."

"H'm," said Mr. Belmore, "there's got to be *something* back of it, you know. Seen any girls since you've been gone?"

Mr. Wilson hastened to shake his head more em-

phatically than before. "Not one," he asseverated with
the relief of complete innocence. "Didn't even meet a
soul I knew, except Brower—you remember Dick
Brower? I went into a jeweler's to get my glasses
mended and found him buying a souvenir spoon for
his fiancée."

"O—o—h!" said Mr. Belmore intelligently, "and
did you buy a present for Edith?"

"No, I didn't. She made me promise not to buy
anything more for her; she thinks I'm spending too
much money, and that I ought to economize."

"And did you tell her about Brower?"

"Why, of course I did—as we were coming out this
morning."

Mr. Wilson stared blankly at his friend.

"Chump!" said Mr. Belmore. He bit off the end of
a new cigar and threw it away. "Wilson, my poor
fellow, you're so besotted in ignorance that I don't
know how to let the light in on you. A man is a fool
by the side of his fiancée, anyhow."

"I don't know what you mean," said the bewildered
Wilson stiffly. "*I* don't know what I'm to do."

"No, of course you don't—but Edith does—you can
just trust her for that. A girl *always* knows what a
man ought to do—she can give him cards and spades
and beat him every time."

"Then why doesn't she *tell* me what she wants? I
asked her to, particularly."

"Oh, no! She'll tell you everything the opposite—
that is, half the time. She'll put every obstacle possible in your way, to see if you're man enough to walk

over 'em; that's what she wants to find out; if you're man enough to have your own way in spite of her; and, of course, if you aren't, you're an awful disappointment."

"Are you sure?" said Mr. Wilson deeply, after an awestruck pause. "Half the time, you say. But how am I to find out when she means—I give you my word, Belmore, that I thought—I suppose I could have brought her a small present, anyway, in spite of what she said; a souvenir spoon—but she hates souvenir spoons."

"You'll have to cipher it out for yourself, old man," said Mr. Belmore. "*I* don't set out to interpret any woman's moods. I only give you cold, bare facts. But if I were you," he added impartially, "I'd go down after a while and try and get her alone, you know, and say something. You can, if you try." A swish of skirts outside of the open door made Mr. Wilson jump forward as Mrs. Belmore came in sight with her friend. The latter had her arm around the older woman, and her form drooped toward her as they passed the two men. The eyes of the girl were red, and her lips had a patient quiver. Mr. Wilson gave an exclamation and sprang forward as she disappeared in the further room.

It was some hours later that the husband and wife met unexpectedly upon the stairs with a glad surprise.

"You don't mean to say it's you—alone!" he whispered.

"Wait—is she coming up?" They clutched each

other spasmodically as they listened to the sound of a deflecting footstep. There was a breathless moment, and then the chords of a funeral march boomed forth upon the air. The loud pedal was doing its best to supplement those long and strenuous fingers.

The listeners breathed a sigh of relief.

"He's gone to the station for a time table," whispered the husband with a delighted grin; "though I can stand *him* all right. We had a nice walk with the little girls, after he got tired of playing hide and seek. I wished you were with us. You must be about used up. How are you getting along with her?"

"Oh, pretty well." She let herself be drawn down on the hall window seat at the top of the landing. "You see, Edith really feels dreadfully, poor girl."

"What about?"

"Herbert, she isn't really sure that she loves him."

"Isn't sure! After they've been engaged for a year!"

"That's just it. She says if they had been married out of hand, in the first flush of the novelty, she wouldn't have had time, perhaps, to have any doubts. But it's the seeing him all the time that's made her think."

"Made her think *what?*"

"Whether she loves him or not; whether they are really suited. I remember that I used to feel that way about you, dear. Oh, you know, Herbert, it's a very serious thing for a girl. She says she knows her whole life is at stake; she thinks about it all the time."

G

"How about his?"

"Well, that's what I said," admitted Mrs. Belmore. "She says that she feels that *he* is so rational and self-poised that she makes little difference in his life either way—it has come to her all at once. She says his looking at everything in a matter-of-fact way just chills her; she longs for a whole-souled enthusiasm that can sweep everything before it. She feels that if they are married she will have to keep up the ideal for both of them, and she doesn't know whether she can."

"No, she can't," said Mr. Belmore.

"She says she could if she loved him enough," pursued Mrs. Belmore. "It's the *if* that kills her. She says that when she wakes up in the morning she feels as if she'd die if she didn't see him before night, and when she *does* see him it's all a dreadful disappointment to her; she can't talk to him at all, she feels perfectly hard and stony; then, the moment he's gone, she's crazy to have him back again. She cries herself thin over it."

"She's pretty bony, anyway," said Mr. Belmore impartially.

"Even his appearance changes to her. She says sometimes he looks like a Greek god, so that she could go down on her knees to him, and at other times— Once she happened to catch a glimpse of him in a horrid red sweater, polishing his shoes, and she said she didn't get over it for weeks; he looked positively *ordinary*—like some of the men you see in the trolley cars."

"Oh, good gracious!" protested Mr. Belmore feebly. "Oh, good *gracious,* petty! This is *too* much."

"Hush—don't laugh so loud—be quiet," said his wife anxiously.

"If Wilson *ever* looks like a Greek god to her, she's all right, she loves him—you can tell her so for me. *Wilson!* Here are we sitting up here like a pair of lovers, and they— Hello!"

The hall door opened and shut, the piano lid closed simultaneously with a bang, and there was a swirl of skirts again toward the staircase that scattered the guilty pair on the landing. The hostess heaved a patient sigh.

"They *shall* speak," said Mrs. Belmore when another hour had gone with the situation still unchanged. Her gentle voice had a note of determination. "I can't understand why he doesn't *make* her. She is literally crying her eyes out, because the whole day has been lost. Why didn't you send him into the parlor for a book, as I told you to, when I came up to take care of Dorothy?"

"He wouldn't go—he said he wasn't doing the kindergarten act any more. Hang it, I don't blame him. A man objects to being made a fool of before people, and he's tired of it. Here he goes off again to-morrow for two weeks, and she with no more heart than—"

"Where is he now?" asked Mrs. Belmore.

"Upstairs in my room, smoking."

"*Smoking!* I thought he'd promised her solemnly not to smoke."

"Yes, he did; but he says he doesn't care a—red apple; he's going to have some comfort out of the day. I've left him with a box of cigars; good ones, too. He's having the time of his life."

"O—o—h!" said Mrs. Belmore, with the rapt expression of one who sees beyond the veil. When she spoke it was with impressive slowness. "When you hear me come downstairs with Edith and go in the parlor, you wait a moment and then bring him down —*with his cigar*—into the library. Do you understand?"

"No," said Mr. Belmore.

"Oh, Herbert! If she sees him *smoking*—! There's no time to lose, for I have to get tea to-night. When I call you, leave him and come at once, do you hear? Don't stop a minute—just come, before they get a chance to follow."

"You bet I'll come," said Mr. Belmore, "like a bird to its—I will, really, petty."

That he nearly knocked her down by his wildly tragic rush when she called from the back hall, "Herbert, please come at once! I can't turn off the water," was a mere detail—they clung to each other in silent laughter, behind the enshrouding portières, not daring to move. The footfall of the deserted Edith was heard advancing from the front room to the library, and her clear and solemn voice, as of one actuated only by the lofty dictates of duty, penetrated distinctly to the listeners.

"Alan Wilson, is it possible that you are *smoking?* Have you broken your promised word?"

"Well, they're at it at last," said Mr. Belmore, relapsing into a chair in the kitchen with a sigh of relief, and drawing a folded newspaper from his pocket. "I wouldn't be in his shoes for a farm."

"Oh, it will be all right now," said Mrs. Belmore serenely. She added with some irrelevancy, "I've left the children to undress each other; they've been *so* good. It's been such a different day, though, from what we had planned."

"It's too bad that you have to get the tea."

"Oh, I don't mind that a bit."

She had tucked up the silken skirt of her gown and was deftly measuring out coffee—after the swift, preliminary shaking of the fire with which every woman takes possession of a kitchen—pouring the water into the coffee-pot from the steaming kettle, and then vibrating between the kitchen closet and the butler's pantry with the quick, capable movements of one who knows her ground thoroughly. "Really, it isn't any trouble. Margaret leaves half of the things ready, you know. If you'll just lift down that dish of salad for me—and the cold chicken is beside it. I hate to ask you to get up, but— Thank you. How good the coffee smells! I know you always like the coffee I make."

"You bet I do," said Mr. Belmore with fervor. "Say, petty, you don't think you could come out now and take a look at the garden? I'm almost sure the peas are beginning to show."

"No; I'm afraid there isn't time. We'll have

to give it up for this Sunday." She paused for a great effort. "If you'd like to go by yourself, dear—"

"Wouldn't you mind?"

She paused again, looking at him with her clear-eyed seriousness.

"I don't think I mind now, but I might—afterward."

If he had hesitated, it was for a hardly appreciable second. "And I don't want to go," he protested stoutly, "it wouldn't be the same thing at all without you."

.   .   .   .

"Everything is ready now," said his wife. "Though I do hate to disturb Edith and Alan. I'll just run up and hear the children say their prayers before I put those things on the table. If you would just take a look at the furnace"—it was the sentence Mr. Belmore had been dreading—"and then you can come up and kiss the children good-night."

Mr. Belmore, on his way up from stoking, caught a glimpse projected from the parlor mirror through an aperture in the doorway which the portières had left uncovered. The reflection was of a girl, with tear-stained face and closed eyes, her head upon a young man's shoulder, while his lips were touchingly pressed to her hair. The picture might have been called "After the Storm," the wreckage was so plainly apparent. As Mr. Belmore turned after ascending the flight of stairs he came full in sight of another picture, spread out to view in the room at the end of the hall. He stood unseen in the shadow regarding it.

His wife sat in a low chair near one of the two white beds; little Dorothy's crib was in their room beyond. The three children were perched on the foot of the nearest bed, white-gowned, with rosy faces and neatly brushed hair. While he looked, the youngest child gave a birdlike flutter and jump, and lighted on the floor, falling on her knees, with her bowed head in the mother's lap, her hands upraised. As she finished the murmured prayer, helped by the tender mother voice, she rose and stood to one side, in infantine seriousness, while the next one spread her white plumes for the same flight, waiting afterward in reverent line with the first as the third hovered down.

It was plain to see from the mother's face that she had striven to put all earthly thoughts aside in the performance of this sacred office of ministering to innocence; her eyes must be holy when her children's looked up at her on their way to God.

This was the little inner chapel, the Sanctuary of Home, where she was priestess by Divine right. It would have been an indifferent man, indeed, who had not fallen upon his knees in spirit, in company with this little household of faith, in mute recognition of the love and peace and order that crowned his days.

He kissed the laughing children as they clung to him, before she turned down the light. When she came out of the room he was waiting for her. He put his arm around her as he said, with the darling tenderness that made her life:

"Come along, old sweetness. We've got to go down and stir up those lunatics again. Call *that* 'the happiest time of your life!' *We* know better than that, don't we, petty? I'll tell you what it is: I'll go to church with you next Sunday, if you say so!"

SUCH AS WALK IN DARKNESS

BY SAMUEL HOPKINS ADAMS

Mr. Adams (born at Dunkirk, N. Y., in 1871) has achieved an enviable reputation in the magazine world as a writer of special articles. Among his notable contributions of this order may be mentioned "The Training of Great Cats," which introduced him to "McClure's Magazine," with whose editorial staff he is now connected; "The Department Store" in "Scribner's" series, "The Conduct of Great Businesses," and "The Great American Fraud" (Patent Medicines) in COLLIER'S WEEKLY. The success of these articles is due to the fact that they are not only "stories" in the technical sense of that term as used by newspaper men, but in the literary sense as well. Naturally Mr. Adams also writes good stories in the field of fiction. Two of these have attracted special attention: "The Flying Death," and the present selection, both of which appeared in "McClure's Magazine."

SUCH AS WALK IN DARKNESS

BY SAMUEL HOPKINS ADAMS

IN all the trade of the city you might not find such another quaint business firm as Solomon John and Billy Wigg. The senior partner was a gentle old giant; the junior a brisk and shaggy little dog. It was Solomon John's business to stand on a roaring corner and sell papers; it was Billy Wigg's business to take care of him while he did it, for he was blind. It was our business—Dr. Harvey's and mine—to pay for our papers and pass on, but we seldom strictly minded it. Instead, we would stop to talk to Solomon John, to the detriment of trade, and to be patronized by Billy Wigg, who was much puffed up with self-importance, conceiving himself to be principal owner of the earth and sole proprietor of Solomon John. In the half of which he was correct.

I was very fond of Billy Wigg, despite his airs of superiority. Harvey preferred old Solomon; but this was a semi-professional interest, for my medical friend had contracted the pamphlet habit, which he indulged before scientific bodies made up of gentlemen with weak eyes who knew more about ophthalmology than can be found in many fat tomes. Solomon John was a remarkable case of something quite unpronounceable, and Harvey used to gaze into his

Reprinted by permission from "McClure's Magazine" for August, 1902.

eyes with rapt intensity, while Billy Wigg fidgeted and struggled against the temptation to gnaw such portions of him as were within reach; for Billy Wigg didn't understand, and what he didn't understand he disapproved of on principle. In the light of subsequent events I believe Billy's uneasiness to have been an instance of animal prevision.

To see Billy Wigg conduct his master across that mill-race of traffic that swirled between curb and curb, as he did every morning in time for business, was an artistic pleasure. Something more than a mere pilot was the dog; rather the rudder to whose accurate direction old Solomon responded with precise and prompt fidelity. A tug of the trouser leg from behind would bring the ancient newsboy to a halt. A gentle jerk forward would start him again, and in obedience to a steady pull to one side or the other he would trustingly suffer himself to be conducted around a checked wagon or a halted cable car. All the time Billy Wigg would keep up a running conversation made up of admonition, warning, and encouragement.

"Come on, now"—in a series of sharp yaps as they started from the curb. "Push right ahead. Hold hard. That's all right; it's by. Hurry now. Hurry, I said. *Will* you do as I tell you?" Then, to a too pressing cabby, in an angry bark, "What's the matter with you, anyway? Trying to run folks down? Hey? Well"—apologetically, in response to a jerk on his string—"these fool drivers do stir me up. Wait a bit. Now for it. And here we are."

How many thousand times dog and man had made the trip in safety before the dire day of the accident not even Solomon John can reckon. Harvey and I had started downtown early, while our pair of paper-vending friends chanced to be a little late. As we reached the corner they were already half-way across the street, and Billy Wigg, with all the strength of terror, was striving to haul Solomon John backward.

"What's the matter with Billy?" said Harvey, for from the sidewalk we could not then see the cause of his excitement.

A second later the question was answered, as there plunged into view from behind a car the galloping horse of a derelict delivery wagon.

"Good heavens! Look at the old man," I cried, and in the same breath, "Look at the dog," gasped Harvey.

With one mighty jerk Billy Wigg had torn the leash from his master's hand. Bereft of his sole guidance in the thunder and rush of traffic, the blind man stretched out piteous hands, warding the death he could not see.

"Billy," he quavered, "where are you, Billy? Come back to me, Billy-dog."

For once Billy Wigg was deaf to his master's voice. He was obeying a more imperious call, that unfathomed nobility of dog-nature that responds so swiftly to the summons. He was casting his own life in the balance to save another's. Straight at the horse's throat he launched himself, a forlorn hope. It was a very big horse, and Billy was a very little dog. The up-stroke of the knee caught him full; he was flung, whirling, fell almost under the wheels of a cab, rolled into the gutter, and lay there quiet. The horse had swerved a little, not quite enough. There was a scream, and the blind man went down from the glancing impact of the shoulder. Harvey and I were beside him almost as soon as the crosswalk policeman. The three of us carried him to the sidewalk.

"No need to call an ambulance, officer," said Harvey. "I'm a physician and the man is a friend of mine."

"Bedad, thin, the dawg is a frind of mine," said the big fellow. "Couldn't ye take him along too, sir?"

"Well—rather," said Harvey heartily. "Where is he?" He turned to look for the dog.

Billy Wigg came crawling toward us. Never tell me that dogs have no souls. The eyes in Billy's shaggy little face yearned with a more than human passion of anxiety and love, as, gasping with pain— for he had been cruelly shaken—he dragged himself to his partner's face. At the touch of the warm, eager tongue, Solomon John's eyes opened. He stretched cut his hand and buried it in the heavy fur.

"Hello, Billy," he said weakly. "I was afraid you were hurt. Are you all right, old boy?" And Billy, burrowing a wet nose in Solomon John's neck, wept for joy with loud whines.

Some rapid and expert wire-pulling on the part of Harvey landed our pair of friends in a private hospital, where Solomon John proved a most grateful and gentle patient, and Billy Wigg a most tumul-

tuous one until arrangement was made for the firm
to occupy one and the same cot.   Then he became
tractable, even enduring the indignity of a flannel
jacket and splints with a sort of humorous tolerance.
Every day Harvey came and gazed soulfully into Solomon John's glazed eyes—which is a curious form of
treatment for broken collar-bone, not sanctioned by
any of the authorities who have written on the subject.   It soon became evident that Harvey didn't care
anything about the rib; he had other designs.   On a
day he came to the point.

"Solomon John, would you like to have your sight
back?"

The blind man sat up in his cot and pressed his
hands to his head.

"Do you mean it, sir?" he gasped.   "You—you
wouldn't go to fool an old man about such a thing?"

"Will you let me operate on you to-morrow?"

"Anything you think best, sir.   I don't quite seem
to take it all in yet, sir—not the whole sense of it.
But if it does come out right," added Solomon John
in the simplicity of his soul, "won't Billy Wigg be
surprised and tickled!"

Billy Wigg raged mightily and rent the garments
of his best friends, because he was shut out during the
operation.   When he was admitted after it was over
he howled tumultuously, because Solomon John was
racked with ether sickness, which he mistook for the
throes of approaching dissolution.   Followed then
weeks during which Solomon John wore a white
bandage, in place of the old green eye-shade, and at

frequent intervals sang a solemn but joyous chant
which Billy Wigg accompanied with impatient yelps,
because he couldn't make out what it meant.

> "We're going to have our sight again,
>   Billy Wigg, Billy Wigg:
> We're going to see the world again,
>   Billy, my dog."

It was a long, nerve-trying wait, but the day finally
came when the white bandages were removed. After
the first gasp of rapture, Solomon John looked about
him eagerly.

"Let me see my dog," he said. "Billy, is this you?"
as the junior partner looked with anxious and puzzled eyes into his face. "Well, you're certainly a
mighty handsome doggy, old boy." (Billy Wigg was
homelier than a stack of hay in January, but the eyes
that looked on him were as those of a mother when
she first sees her babe.)

Unhappiness was the portion of Billy in the days
that followed. A partner who wandered about un-
chaperoned and eluded obstacles without relying on
his sense of touch was quite beyond his comprehen-
sion. So he sulked consistently until the time came
for leaving the hospital. Then he chirked up a bit,
thinking, presumably, that Solomon John would resume his old habit of blind reliance upon him when
once the doors had closed behind them. Poor Billy!

It was three weeks after the operation that they left,
Solomon John being discharged as cured. Harvey
exulted. He said it was a great operation and proved
things. I thought, myself, it was a mean trick on

Billy Wigg. My unprofessional diagnosis was that he was on the road to becoming a chronic melancholiac.

The partners called on Harvey soon after the departure from the hospital. They were a study in psychological antithesis; Solomon John bubbling over with boyish happiness, Billy Wigg aged with the weight of woe he was carrying. The old man was touchingly grateful, but his ally surreptitiously essayed to bite a piece out of Harvey's leg when his back was turned. He nursed an unavenged wrong.

Months passed before we saw the pair again. We returned from our European vacation confident of finding them on the same old corner, and sure enough, there they were. But as we approached Harvey seized me by the arm.

"Good heavens! Bob! Look at the old man!"

"What's wrong with him?" said I. "He looks just the same as he used to."

"Just the same as he used to," echoed Harvey bitterly. "Eye-shade and all. All my work gone for nothing. Poor old boy!"

"Billy Wigg's all right, anyway," said I, as that superior animal greeted us with every indication of excitement.

"Think so?" said Harvey. "It strikes me that it isn't exactly welcome that he's trying to express." Then, in a louder voice to Solomon John, "How did it happen, old Sol?"

At the sound of his voice Solomon John whirled about and started to thrust up his shade, as if involuntarily.   Then he held out tremulous hands, crying:

"What! Is that you, Dr. Harvey? God bless you, sir! And is Mr. Roberts with you? Well, well, but this does me good. You're a sight for sore eyes!"

"Not for yours, Solomon John."

"And why not, then? Whist! I forgot," he broke off scaredly, jerking his head toward Billy Wigg, who held us all under jealous scrutiny. "Wait a breath."

Thrusting his hand into his pocket, he whipped it out suddenly. A flight of coins scattered and twinkled and rolled diversely on the sidewalk. "Dear, dear!" cried the old man cunningly. "The old fool that I am! I'll never be rich this way. Pick them up, Billy-boy."

Billy hated it, for picking small coins from a smooth pavement with lip and tooth is no easy job; hated worse leaving his partner to two such unscrupulous characters as he well knew us to be. But he knew his business, and set about it with all his energies.

"Whisper now," said the senior partner as Billy swore under his breath at a slithery and elusive dime. "I've as fine a pair of eyes as you'd want for star-gazing at noonday."

"Then what on earth—"

"Sh-h-h! Soft and easy! The beast's cocking his little ear this way. Sure 'twas all on his account, sirs."

"On Billy's account?" we both exclaimed in a breath.

"You didn't think I'd be faking it?" he asked reproachfully.

We didn't; and we said so. But we required further enlightenment.

"All on account of Billy Wigg there, sirs. The eyesight was a million blessings to me, but 'twas death to poor Billy. Not a pleasure in life would he take after we left the hospital. When I'd walk free and easy along the streets that looked so pretty to my old eyes, the dog'd be crazy with fear that some harm would come to me through him not leading me. At the last he just laid down and set out to die. He'd not sleep, he'd not eat; and the eyes of him when he'd look at me were fit to make a man weep. I sent for a dog doctor—you being away, sir," put in Solomon John in polite parenthesis to my friend. "He says, 'The dog's dying of a broken heart. I've seen it before,' he says. 'What'll I do?' says I. 'He'll not be content till you are as you were before,' says the dog doctor. It was a minute before I sensed what he meant. Then my heart got thick and sick inside me. 'Blind?' I says. 'Is that what you mean?' 'You old fool,' says the dog doctor, 'can't you do a bit of play-acting? You've had enough practice in the part,' he says.

"Over I went and got my stick and put on the old shade that I hadn't ever thought to use again, thanks to you, sir, and tap-tapped across the floor to Billy Wigg. 'Come on, Billy,' says I; 'I want you to take me out for a walk.' Billy jumped up with a kind of choky bark, and I hugged Billy and Billy hugged me,

and—we've been doing business on the corner ever
since."

There was a long pause. Harvey's expression was
queer.   I felt a little queer myself.   It was a queer
story, you know.   Finally I asked the old man if business was good.   Not that I particularly yearned to
know, but it seemed to be time to say something.

"Nicely, sir, thank you," said Solomon John; "but
I want to ask you, Is it a dishonesty, think you, for
me to be wearing my shade like a blind man, and me
able to see a flea on the end of Billy Wigg's tail the
length of the block away?   The Lord's been mighty
good to me, sir—you and the Lord—giving me back
my sight," said Solomon John simply, turning to
Harvey, "and I wouldn't want to do anything that
wasn't just square."

"I wouldn't let it weigh on my mind," said Harvey.

"I'd been thinking of a bit of a sign," proceeded
Solomon John.   "A friend of mine printed it out for
me, but the idea's my own."

After some fumbling under his coat he produced a
placard artfully designed in large and flourishy letters.
This was the order of it:

> I Am NOT Blind
> but
> The Dog
> Thinks I Am.

Billy Wigg seemed pleased because Harvey kicked
me.   No doubt he would have been equally pleased if

I had kicked Harvey. But it happened to be I who laughed. Harvey covered it up by soberly telling Solomon John that the sign was sure to be a grand success.

It was a grand success; quite stupendous, in fact. Old Sol did a business on the strength of it that would have made his eyes pop out if he hadn't kept them tight shut out of respect to Billy's prejudices. Reporters found his simplicity and naïve honesty a mine of "good stuff," and the picture of the firm was in all the papers. Billy Wigg began to suffer from swelled head; became haughty, not to say snobbish. But the fierce light of publicity wore upon the simple soul of Solomon John. He discarded the extraordinary placard, and was glad when he faded away from fame. Billy wasn't. He liked notoriety as well as authority.

Billy continued to exercise his authority. Perhaps tyranny would be nearer the mark. But even so meek a soul as that of Solomon John has limits of endurance beyond which it is not well to press. Only the other day it was that the old man said to Harvey, while Billy Wigg was otherwise engaged:

"It's as bad as being a henpecked husband, sir. Last night, as I was quietly stepping out the window to take a mug of ale with some friends, Billy wakes up, and the fuss he makes rouses the neighborhood. Sure, he wouldn't hark to my going at all. You can see his teeth marks on my shin this minute, sir. Could you give me something harmless to put in his food that'd make him sleep the sounder?"

Harvey said he'd think about it.   He wasn't obliged to.   Less than a week later he got a note in the mail:

"DEAR SIR—I could not stand it any longer. I have Absconded to Buffalo to Take a Rest. Please be Good to Billy Wigg. I inclose his Board and Lodging any place you Put him. He is a good Dog, but too Bossy. I am Going to See Things till my Eyes get Tired. I will come Back in Future.

"Yrs respectfully,

"SOLOMON J. BOLES.

"P.S.—I know you will Treat Billy Good."

The inclosure was a twenty-dollar bill.   It was the price of freedom, and cheap at the price.

THE LOTUS EATERS

BY VIRGINIA TRACY

Virginia Tracy (born July 25, 1874, in New York City) has written in "The Lotus Eaters" what in the opinion of competent critics is the best story of theatrical life that has thus far appeared in American literature. Mr. Richard Harding Davis wrote of it, at the time it appeared in COLLIER'S WEEKLY: "Good as many people will find it, even they will not know how good it is. The people in it are all very real, and the little inside things they said and did are admirably observed." Miss Tracy comes of a theatrical family, and was herself upon the stage until ill health compelled her to abandon the profession. Since then, as a looker-on in Bohemia, she has written dramatic criticism as well as short stories of theatrical life, not great in quantity, but very valuable in their psychological insight.

THE LOTUS EATERS

BY VIRGINIA TRACY

"AND leaves me to starve," said Estella, cutting off a leg of the chicken and throwing it to the nearest dog. "Leaves me to starve in the gutter, and leaves Regina, his own flesh and blood—look at that child, Kate, look at her! What sort of a brute could desert a child like that? Was her mother's comfort, yes, she was!—leaves Regina without a rag to her back." She absent-mindedly put a piece of chicken into her mouth, and leaned her elbows on the table.

"I really don't know what we shall do about the rent," said Mrs. Donnelly. "When he came for it this morning he told Barbara he'd be back this afternoon, and it's a hot day for anybody to be out, let alone a fat fellow like him. You can't put off the landlord himself like you can an agent, anyway. I could pay ten dollars on account next Saturday night. If he won't take that, or your alimony doesn't come, I don't know what'll become of us."

"I'm sure I don't know either," said Estella. "It seems such a nuisance to move. Speak for it, then?"— "Woof! Woof!" said Dooley, the fatter of the Scotch terriers.—"I thought we were going to be so happy here, too, when we first came. He seemed such a nice, unassuming sort of man."

H

Tony, who was washing the household linen in the kitchen, put his head through the doorway. It was a lordly little black head, and belonged to a young fellow of a slender middle height, motions extraordinarily light and free, and blue, humorous, inquisitive, confidential eyes. Said he: "I beg your pardon, Estella, but the big dishpan—has it gone to heaven?"

"It's out on the fire-escape," replied Estella, "with gasoline in it. I put all the old gloves I could find into gasoline this morning, so that if any of us should happen to get an engagement, they'd have clean gloves, anyway."

Tony withdrew. He had not looked at Estella, but at Barbara, the Beauty, who sat in the window-sill, and who continued to look neither at him nor at Estella, nor at the riot of the dogs and the chicken-bones and Regina upon the uncarpeted floor, but across the shining roof-tops to the Palisades.

The mistress of this Harlem flat was Mrs. Estella Baker. Mr. Baker was divorced. He was a prosperous person, and paid a considerable alimony, with which he was not always sufficiently prompt. With Mrs. Baker lived her infant daughter, Regina Rosalys, and her younger sister, Barbara Floyd. Also she had as summer boarders Mr. Anthony Regnault, a young actor who seldom happened to be out of work, Mr. Fred Donnelly, not much older, who seldom happened to be in it, and Mrs. Kate Donnelly, an elderly typewriter, who had married a brother Donnelly, deceased. All the boarders paid far more than their board, when they had it, and nothing at all when they had not. At the present moment, they had been some time through lunch without having as yet cleared away its remains, and Estella and Mrs. Donnelly, whose employer was away on his own vacation, had been regaling the company with accounts of the Russian coronation, which they read from the newspapers that strewed the room. Fred Donnelly, who was busy pinning the edge of his tie over a spot he had just discovered on his shirt-front, gloomily commented upon Estella's last remark: "I guess it'll be a long enough day before any of us get an engagement!"

"You forget Tony!" said his sister-in-law.

"I ain't ever let to," Fred responded with some savagery. "I—can't you stop gorging on those papers a minute? They're two months old!"

"That makes 'em all the lovelier," replied Estella. "Tony threw them off the kitchen shelf this morning, and I felt so good to read it all over again. You feel sure, then, that it's all true."

"Tony's generous with his old newspapers. That's because he's signed for a job. But he don't begin till November. November—Lord! you can't believe there's ever going to be such a month."

"Oh, we may all be working by then," cried Estella, in her voice of tragic fire. "You can't tell. You don't suppose we're going to go on like this, do you?"

"Not if we don't pay the rent, we ain't," said Fred. "We'll have fifteen dollars the week after next, Barbara and me, if we pose for those kinetoscope things. But we owe all that now, in little bills."

"That reminds me, Tony," Estella called, "I wish you could get both the tablecloths ironed by to-night," 'cause you can't do it to-morrow. No; they're going to shut the gas off to-night; we had a notice from 'em yesterday."

"Well, this fellow was just right," declared Mrs. Donnelly, glaring up from her newspaper; "this one that refused to kiss the Czarina's hand. It's a nasty, silly thing to do. They'll never catch me doing it."

"Nor me, I'm afraid," said Tony, reappearing with a bucket that brimmed wet tablecloths. He paused for a moment in the doorway, and leaned there, exceedingly comfortable and cool. Indeed, on this midsummer afternoon, when the unshaded dining-room appeared altogether huddled and tousled and hot, there was in the look of this very competent amateur laundryman something so tranquil, so airy and sylvan, that it might have suggested a beneficent gentleman-dryad but for the absurd great pipe which was hanging out of his mouth. "I'll take these up to the roof now, Estella; I've just hung out the smaller pieces. We can't tell but that later Barbara'll help me take them down. But I do hope, Estella, that the next flat we appropriate will have a coal range. If we are to have no fire to iron with to-morrow, how shall we cook?"

"I suppose we'll have to go out to our meals. I've got my wedding-ring yet. He can force me to part with that, Tommy Baker can, but he can't force me to let our child starve."

"That must be very disenchanting for Tommy,"

Tony answered. "But I think I'll leap out with a chair or two before it comes to our eating up your wedding-ring, Estella."

Regina Rosalys, who was at that moment recuperating from her wrestling matches with the dogs, said suddenly: "Anny Bobs gah go ring."

"No, no, darling. Poor Auntie Barbara hasn't got any ring at all. You lost Auntie Barbara's little blue ring down the stationary washstand, don't you remember?"

"No, no, Anny Bobs gah go ring, big go ring"; Regina's fat little hands formed an oblong about the size of a cucumber. "Big," she persisted, nodding.

"She means that Indian bracelet," said Estella. Tony looked anxiously and a little fearfully at Barbara, and forgot to joke. At that moment the doorbell rang. Tony leaned back into the kitchen and pressed the little electric button which opened the street door.

"Oh!" cried Estella, "that's the expressman with my money now." She rose and ran into the hall.

There was a waiting silence. Tony continued to lean in the doorway and look at the girl in the window-seat. She had gray eyes of a miraculous, deep clearness, but she kept these turned away in a far-off quiet, profound enough to strike cold upon a suitor's heart. Tony had to content himself with the faint bright color in the oval of her cheek; the pale rose of her faded and shrunken cotton blouse stopped in a little drawn circle at her throat; the throat itself was very white and regal-looking under the piled fairness of Barbara's brown hair. One hand dropped, motionless, against her old gray skirt, and Tony smiled to it wistfully. It was a modest smile, under a trick of audacity. Tony was three-and-twenty, and all women had done their best to spoil him, except Barbara, who had remained silent the summer through before his love. By the community before which so much of it had, perforce, to be carried on, the love-making was encouragingly ignored, but the community was beginning to get restless, because from the lady it received no confidence. The summer was sunning itself away, and still Barbara rested, whether or not to be wooed, passive, idle, enigmatic, lovely; and still prayerfully, and with deft derision, Tony continued publicly to woo her. Now, though he could not catch her glance, his eyes spoke declarations twenty times a minute, and formally proposed to her. They besought, commanded, laughed at her, adored her. Suddenly, when there seemed least hope, she turned round and looked at him. It was a very steadfast, searching look, and Tony tingled and rejoiced to meet it. He lifted his head happily, with a singular pride, and at the little motion the girl put her hand sharply to her throat and turned away.

"He's a long time coming upstairs," said Fred.

At that moment Estella ran back into the hall of the flat and closed the door with the effect of a subdued cyclone.

"It's not the expressman!" she called, in a shrieking whisper. "The top of his head looks like the milkman, and his bill's due." Tony laughed aloud.

"Tell him to come again," suggested Kate Donnelly, still fortified by immersion in the coronation glories.

"Told him that last time," said Fred.

"Oh, well, maybe he wasn't coming here," said Estella, listening a moment, and continued, "maybe it was only the janitor, after all. Once before the alimony didn't come, and then it turned out the expressman had brought it two or three times, only the downstairs bell didn't ring, so to-day I asked the janitor to ring the bell every time he went past, so I'd feel quite easy."

The upstairs bell unkindly rang.

"Ssh!" hissed Estella; "pretend we're out."

"Is he to suppose the downstairs door was opened by a spook?" Tony whispered.

"Well, you needn't talk. You did it." She came back into the dining-room, and sat down with infinite non-rustling precautions. "I'm sure I'd like to pay him as well as anybody. Indeed, nobody has the horror of debt I've got. I tremble with it when I wake in the night. It's born in me. I don't know why, but I can't pay what I haven't got, not if I was to coin my blood for it." The bell rang again. "Well, he can just tire himself out at that," Estella added. "I should think he'd know we'd have opened it before if we'd wanted him."

Tony's eyes overran with laughter. Regina threw herself into Barbara's lap, and Barbara put her face into the black mop of Regina's curls, and began to whisper a story to her.

"I wish I was out of the whole business," muttered

Fred: "out of the profession, I mean. I wish I knew another durned thing to do. I had a chance to be a dentist once, but I was too good for it then. When that old aunt of mine in Ireland dies, I bet I take my share of what she leaves and buy an interest in a business. And when you're all down on your luck, you can come to me, people, and I'll help you out."

"My share in that pneumatic tire'll be worth thousands of dollars by then," said Mrs. Donnelly, refolding her newspaper. "They've got a backer for it now who's going to put it right on the market. Will Knowles says there's a fortune in it, and he's an inventor."

"I was thinking the other day it would be nice to invent something," replied Estella; "but I never get mine finished, somehow."

The enemy without gave a final knock and ring, and departed. He was pursued downstairs by the barks of the terriers and the shrieks of Regina, who at that moment rushed, all three, into each other's arms.

"Look here," said Fred; "are you sure it wasn't Mr. Bates come for the rent? He told Barbara he'd be here at three o'clock."

"Mercy! Look out of the window, Barbara, and see who it was." Barbara leaned out and down, watching.

"Well, I vow!" said Mrs. Donnelly. "Do you know what those Gostioffs, or whatever their name is, have been doing? The Czar said everybody could make their crowns out of silver-gilt, because some of 'em are as poor as church mice, and those Gostioffs have been over to Paris and had theirs made out of solid gold!"

"Who told you?"

"It's in the paper. And he's just come of age, a while ago, and paid all his debts."

"Seems rather an excessive person," Tony commented.

Mrs. Donnelly made a little clucking noise to her newspaper: "Tsu! Tsu!—well, poor boy, he does all he can."

"Who?" demanded Fred.

"The Emperor of all the Russias," answered Tony, laughing from under his eyelashes at Kate. "Kate's very partial to him. I sometimes feel quite piqued."

"Well, I don't care. He's a very good man; he wants—"

"They say," remarked Estella dreamily, "that she's got a gold typewriter set with diamonds."

"It was the milkman," announced Barbara, drawing in her head.

Estella had picked up an illustrated weekly, and she now passed it with a tender smile to Mrs. Donnelly. "Wouldn't Barbara look sweet fixed just the way the Czarina is? Those pearl ropes—I'll bet they're yards long—they're just the sort of thing that suits Barbara."

Mrs. Donnelly gravely regarded the Czarina's likeness. "She looks very handsome," she said. "I hope she'll be happy. She's got a kind of a sad look. I knew a girl once, a nice, pretty girl as could be; she looked something like our Barbara, too, only Barbara's the handsomest of the lot—had something that same look at her wedding, and before the very first year was out he had run off to Canada with a pot of money—he was a partner in a wholesale bicycle business—and another woman, and she, poor thing, had to take in boarders."

Estella sat up, clutched her floating yellow dressing-sack about her neck, and with the other hand shoved back the toppling mass of her black hair. "Well!" she cried, "I'd like to know what you mean by that, Kate Donnelly! I didn't think I should ever be insulted at my own lunch-table by people talking as if it were a disgrace to take boarders! You ought to honor me for it, or any other honest way of making my living. I've got my fatherless child to support, and I'm proud of it, and as God is my witness, I think a woman can be a lady, no matter how little money she has. And if you mean to insinuate anything against Tom Baker, I can tell you that whatever my troubles with my husband may have been—and I think you might have had more consideration for Regina than to mention a woman—there never was a breath against his honesty, and he never quarreled with but one of his employers in his life that would bring men he knew home drunk to sleep in the office, and that diamond bracelet I gave him to get the doctor's bill on once when he was out of work, he went and got out and gave it back to me as soon as I got my divorce!" There was a glass pitcher full of lemonade on the table. Estella helped herself to a long drink, and added: "And even so, I shouldn't call you exactly boarders, anyway."

Mrs. Donnelly arose in trembling majesty and took her hat off the mantelpiece. "I'll send you my address, Estella Baker," she said, "as soon as I get one. And you can send your bill in when you like. I wouldn't speak to a dog as you've spoken to me, and I wouldn't take it from you if you were the Queen of England. And as for calling us boarders, I should think you wouldn't, with Tony working like a black slave, and Fred putting off the butcher, and me paying regular every Saturday. I wouldn't have stayed here to have my ears deafened the way you screech, Estella Baker, for anybody but Tony, that was the sweetest child I ever saw when I used to go on as extra in the Amazon marches at his father's theatre, before that sneaking hound of a Gillespie got it away from him—though I've worked hard here to help you, and glad to do it, as you well know. I hope, when I'm gone—"

"Before you go, Kate, dear," said Tony, putting his pipe on the mantelpiece, "we'd better clear the table, or I fear Barbara will be forced to work."

Barbara rose hurriedly, but like a creature moving in a sleep, and Mrs. Donnelly snatched up a plate with one hand, and with the other pushed the young girl back into the window-seat. "Stay where you are," said she, and strode majestically into the kitchen. Her brother-in-law, who had not bestowed so much as a glance upon the previous debate, now lifted a newspaper in his turn. "There's a cut of the Felix house," he said. "Down below, you know, on Riverside Drive, the white stone place. Good print, isn't it? I wish I'd gone in for photography when I had that chance three years ago."

"I never thought I'd much care about having that house," said Estella. "The windows come so low down, I'd always be afraid Regina would fall out. Still, of course, you could put wires across them."

"Forgot the tablecloths," cried Tony, running in and snatching up the bucket. "None of you thought of them, of course—loafers! If I have a sunstroke on the roof, say I died true." Tony peered into the pitcher of lemonade as he passed it. "Oof! Little drops of lemon. Nothing more spirited for the laborer, the poor laborer, Mrs. Tommy?" At the hall door—"I will return to you, Barbara," he said to the back of that young lady's head, and vanished.

"Tony gone pok?" asked Regina.

"I wonder," said Estella, "if Tony's written those words for Barbara to sing Sunday night?"

"Anny Bobs ta Rina pok?" Regina persisted.

"No, no," said Estella, "Auntie Barbara can't take Regina to the park now; it's too hot."

"Too hot?"

"Yes; too hot. Make Auntie sick. Poor Auntie."

"Poo Anny; Anny Bobs ta Rina pok?"

"No; now, Regina, you're naughty."

Regina puffed out an under-lip and nodded: "Rina awn do finey aws," said she plaintively.

"Oh, Regina, why don't you learn to talk plainer?

Oo bid dirl, ess oo is, oo bid dirl! You mostly know what she says, Fred."

"She said, 'Regina wants to go on the flying-horses.'"

"Oh, darling, mamma hasn't any money for that.— No, indeed, Barbara, carfare and everything!—You can go on the flying horses when mamma gets an engagement. Here—here's a nickel. You can play with that."

Regina turned the nickel over and over in the creases of her little warm hand, and Fred returned to his former statement—"I guess it'll be a long day before any of us gets an engagement."

"I'll bet you anything you like," cried Estella, "that I'll be starring in my own play before the year's out. That play's bound to succeed, because it speaks right to people's hearts. I wrote every word of it out of my own soul. There isn't a word in it without a throb, and yet the comedy interest's good, too. I think Barbara'll be quite sweet in that. She's a little tall for comedy, but then—. You know Sam Tannehill? He says it's the greatest play that's been written in America since 'The Banker's Daughter.'"

Mrs. Donnelly, who had been going to and from the kitchen with the dishes, now swept away the table-cloth, and Estella, still clutching the lemonade, and waving the butter-knife, leaned back to give her free play. She concluded, "He asked me why I didn't let Olga Nethersole have it."

"Well, dearie," said Mrs. Donnelly, "why don't you? I'm sure you deserve a little luck."

"Well," said Estella, "I guess not. Nobody'll ever play that part but me. There's plenty of managers would be glad to take the play, and put their own old stars into it; night and day I'm afraid some one will steal my ideas. If I could only get a good part in New York and show people just once what I could do, there'd be plenty of managers ready to back me in my play afterward!"

Fred yawned. "Estella," said he, "when you do get an engagement you quarrel with the stage-manager and come home."

Estella planted her elbows on the table. "That's because they've got such old fuss-budgets of stage-managers. I guess after I've sat up all night wearing myself to pieces studying my art, I'm not going to be dictated to by those ignorant things. It was mean of that old Dawkins, though, to fight with me, when I'd had my pink crêpe dress made for their old piece, and I hadn't even got it paid for yet. Wasn't that a sweet dress, Kate? I wore my real coral and gold belt with it that Tommy gave me while we were married. He always said he did like me to look nice, Tommy did. I've got plenty of clothes to take an engagement if I could only get one. I wish the dogs hadn't broken Whopper, and I'd ask her when we any of us were going to get anything."

"We always ask her that, and she always lies. We'd better ask her when the alimony's coming."

Estella looked at the pieces of the broken planchette which were scattered over the floor. "They looked so cunning breaking it up, and Tony would name her that," she added, with apparent irrelevance. "Hand me the cards, Fred, and let me see if I can see anything."

As she shuffled the pack her mind went back to the pink crêpe.

"If she likes to fix it over I'll let Barbara wear that dress to Mrs. Wade's Sunday night, and I can take her blue waist; you know, Kate, that one you made out of the old pair of sleeves."

She looked cordially at Barbara, but the girl did not answer, nor turn her head.

"She's dreaming," said Fred. "Love's young dream, Barbara? Estella, do you see a dark man?"

"Let her be," pleaded Mrs. Donnelly; "maybe she is really thinking about Tony."

"You make me tired, Kate," said the fraternal Fred; "you bet Tony can do his own love-making. You bet he can look after himself. I wonder," he added in a half-voice, "if she says things to him, though, when they're alone. He keeps on so.

"You never can tell," Estella sighed.

"She might be very glad to have the chance of him!" Mrs. Donnelly almost cried aloud.

"I guess my sister doesn't need to be glad of anybody, Kate Donnelly, and he's very unsettled and extravagant; I've always heard so."

"Oh, rot!" said Fred, getting in ahead of his sister-in-law. "What of it? He's only a boy, and most of the year he's more money than he knows what to do with. I don't know why it should be worse for him to throw gold dollars around than for anybody else to do it."

"Slander loves a shining mark," said Mrs. Donnelly, sententiously.

Fred laughed. "Well there's nothing so very shining about Tony, except a first-class job in the future. But, of course, he's lucky to have that, at his age; and I daresay it is his luck and his good looks and those kid ways of his starts those notions. He's really a corking fellow, Tony is, and straight, as far as I know. But if he buys a girl a pair of gloves—and I don't say he doesn't like a pretty girl—there's as much cackle as if another man had bought her Fifth Avenue. And he's too easy-tempered; he lets stories get around about him, things that matter. Look at that old gander last week at Reilly's—said it was Mrs. Rexal who got him that part with Rexal, and—you know what people say."

"Oh!" said Barbara, "it's all cowardly. It's a lie." ("Why, she's awake after all," laughed Fred.) She turned in upon them from the window, and her live voice broke into the room with its curious little throaty richness. "I—I don't deceive myself about Tony. I daresay he's wild, I daresay he's unreliable, but we must all know that he was never—base." Her face flushed and paled, her hands clinched in her lap. "We're unsteady and extravagant ourselves, Estella, and what should we have done this summer: who would have given us any pleasure, who would have helped us, who would have worked for us, what should we have done here without Tony? I remember all the time, even if we're only a caprice of his, even if he doesn't mean a word he says, we are his debtors a thousand, thousand times."

The hall door opened, and they heard Tony banging the bucket and whistling "My girl's a high-born lady," as he went into his own room.

"My dear! my dear!" Estella warned her.

"That's right, Barbara," said Fred. "I tell you the truth, I didn't think you had so much sense. There's nothing the matter with Tony except a first-class appetite for being happy. Look at him all this summer—till his next season's manager puts a stop to it—goes and makes a darned jockey of himself, for ten dollars a week, riding their plug steeplechasers in a backwoods melodrama. Does anybody say a word for him about that? Why, no! You'd think they all did it! But he went to dinner at the Waldorf last night with a fellow I know that had made some money at Brighton, and a couple of girls, and I'll bet you everybody on Broadway's talking about it."

"At the Waldorf? Is that where he was?" cried Barbara. "Last night!" She leaned forward and stared at Fred intently. Something in her accent recalled to the assemblage their own last night's dinner; the little hot untidy dining-room, and the scramble in getting the dishes washed up, and the fact that the ice had given out. Only Estella remembered for the first time that Barbara had dressed her hair elaborately yesterday afternoon, and had tried to press out her white lace waist, and had scorched it. She remembered in the same flash that the morning before Tony had praised the stately habit of dressing for dinner. She pushed away the cards, and in her turn looked at Barbara, as Barbara was looking at Fred.

"Was *that* where he was?" said the girl again.

"I'm sure he had every right to be!" cried Kate.

"I'm sure we should be the last to question that right," Barbara said.

" 'Feathered like a peacock, just as gay,' " sang Tony's whistle, clipped suddenly by the sound of splashing water.

"That boy's got his head under the faucet again!" exclaimed Mrs. Donnelly. "He'll give himself neuralgia."

"Why, Barbara!" Estella cried; "yesterday was—"

"Oh, yes," she moved her hands helplessly in her lap; "I was twenty yesterday."

"Oh, dearie! I'm so sorry! I never thought of it."

"Tony never knew of it," said Kate.

"Why, no," Barbara replied; "why should he?"

"Here he comes now," said Fred.

He came in as radiant with idleness as he had lately been with work, and very fresh from his encounter with the faucet, whose drops were still shining, bright and cold, in his black hair. There was what Estella called a diván at one side of the room; Tony composed himself upon its cushions with a fan and a glass of lemonade, and lounged there, staring at the ceiling like a contented child. He found a considerable diversion in teaching himself to drink without changing his attitude, and while he was acquiring this art, the talk tried to jerk itself past his interruption. Everybody had been a little startled by Barbara's outbreak, everybody felt that Fred would better have kept his knowledge to himself, and a little uneasy bewilderment, as at a treachery to Tony, shadowed more lively interests and quieted the long talk. They looked rather gravely at the profile view which was once more accorded them of Barbara's head.

"What's the matter, Estella?" asked Tony, glancing at the newspapers. "Aren't there any murders?" At the continued silence he lifted his head. "Hello! What's the scandal?"

"You are!" said Estella. "The idea of you being around here, anyhow, and me with a sister that's just twenty!"

"There has to be somebody to watch Fred," said Tony.

"It's Fred's been giving you away. Oh, he didn't mean to! But he says you throw your money around."

"He wants to show you what a beautiful nature I have," said the accused. He looked lovingly at Fred, because he had black murder in his heart. He looked with anxious stealth at Barbara, but Barbara seemed not to notice.

"He says people say things about you," Estella continued.

"Slander loves a shining mark," repeated Mrs. Donnelly, with solemn emphasis.

"Nice Kate!" said Tony. He went and sat down on the floor by her chair, and stroked her hand. "Good Kate! Pretty Kate!"

"I'm sure," continued Mrs. Donnelly, pretending to push him off, "nobody could be a better boy around the house than he is. Could they, now, could they? I bet you'd all want him back fast enough if he went away! I've known him since he was no bigger than that," measuring about the height of a footstool, "and never saw a cross word come out of his mouth, and I can tell you, if this never having a cent is hard on us, he's had more money to throw away when he was a child on a rocking-horse than would pay this miserable old rent time and again, and not a complaint out of him."

"Good Tony!" said that gentleman. He added in a tone of profound conviction, "Noble Tony!"

Estella studied him with her chin in her hand. "Yes," she said, "you're a very sweet boy. But—you're Irish."

"I once had a father, Mrs. Baker, and he was French."

"Well, goodness, that only makes it worse!"

"Oh, dear!" said Tony drowsily, "where French and Irish meet and make a mixture that is not discreet. That's for you, Barbara, who love the poets!" He opened his eyes and stared sadly at his hostess. "It's inelegant to display such a prejudice against the foreign, dear Estella."

"I hope you've written those new verses to Gus Fenwicke's song, since you're so smart; Barbara won't have time to learn them for Sunday night, Tony Regnault, if you've put them off again, and she won't sing the old ones. Mr. Fenwicke's going to be there to hear her Sunday, and he's going to sing himself."

"Dear me, how unnecessary of him," said Tony. He went back to the couch where his banjo lay, and began to touch an air upon it as he spoke the lines. Certainly, he looked at Barbara.

"The sleeping princess quiet lay
And dreamed the empty years away,
    Her love delayed;
And princes came and princes went,
And mighty kings magnificent
As they above her beauty bent
    Were all afraid, afraid.

"And no man knew what word would wake,
Nor for what fortune's golden sake,
    Or deed of love,
That shining princess would arise,
Unveil the kindness of her eyes
And stretch the hand that he would prize
    All worlds above, above.

"A beggar at the palace gate
Had a light heart to tempt his fate
    And entered in;
He wished no other joy but this,
And this for death he would not miss:
He touched her sweet mouth with a kiss—
    She waked for him, for him!"

"Oh!" cried Mrs. Donnelly, "isn't that lovely!"

"That last line doesn't rhyme, Tony," said Estella, with severity.

"Will you sing it, Barbara?" Tony asked.

"Thank you," she said. "It is very charming. You were very kind to write it. But I don't think I shall sing it. I don't think I shall sing at all."

Said Tony: "That pink thing you have on is very becoming to you, my own."

"You mustn't call Barbara that, Tony!" cried Estella. "It doesn't sound well. I can't have it."

"Not even when it isn't true?" Tony pleaded. "Not even to please Barbara? If you'll move over a little, Barbara, I'll sit by you a minute." He secured to himself a part of the window seat, and remained there, swinging his heels and playing "Daisy" on the banjo. Barbara's slim young stateliness, aided by her trailing skirts, made her look almost as tall as he, and far more resolute. She seemed to him, as he studied her out of the corner of an eye, to be very pale and very tragically sweet.

"I'm glad, Estella," he said, "that you are beginning to awaken to a sense of your responsibilities about us. We shall be almost grown up in a minute. 'These pretty babes went hand in hand'—you remember what happened to *their* wicked guardian, Mrs. Baker, after the robin-redbreasts had covered them with leaves? I am afraid Barbara would be rather long for robin-redbreasts; she would keep them busy."

Estella smiled disdainfully. "You look like a yard of pump-water, the both of you," said she.

"The each of us, Estella. And it's still incorrect to be cross with my physique—Napoleon was once slender. Barbara's, to be sure," lifting Barbara's lovely wrist between his thumb and finger, and critically regarding it—"Barbara's, to be sure, is no great shakes."

She did not smile, she did not even withdraw her hand. Tony laid it carefully in her lap. "Cheer up, Anny Bobs!" he whispered.

At this moment the entire apartment was filled with the roar of Regina's rage. "Mahmu a my nicky. Mahmu a my nicky."

"What?" said every one; "what is it?"

"Mahmu a my nicky! A my nicky! Bah Mahmu!"

Fred was stooping over Regina. "Mohammed ate my nickel," he translated. Mohammed was the older terrier.

"A my nicky," assented Regina.

"Ate her nickel? Heavens, swallowed it! It'll kill him!" Estella fell on her knees and glared down the throat of Mohammed, who wagged his tail feebly.

"Bah Mahmu!" cried Regina, beating the air and howling lustily. "A my nicky! Mahmu a my nicky!"

"Do you think it'll kill him?" persisted Estella; "was Stella's old boy? Did want doctor?"

"Wa my nicky!" entreated Regina.

"It seems to me extremely forehanded of him," said Tony to Regina. "You know you nearly ate it yourself."

Regina stopped crying and stared at him. She began slowly to smile and dimple, and presently extended a hand. "Nicky," said she.

Tony laid a copper on her palm. "Penny," he said; "not nicky. 'Nough."

Regina went over to Estella and pulled her arm. "Mah-ma, nicky."

Estella closed Mohammed's mouth with her fingers and kissed his nose. "Him eat nickels?" she inquired.

"No, I haven't got another nickel for you, Regina,

I haven't got— Oh, don't cry. Here, you can have my pearl heart. And here," reaching for a clean napkin and a blue pencil from a crowded trunk-lid at her back, "we'll make a rag dolly, shall we?"

Tony leaped upon her, and wrenched the napkin from her grasp. "I would never wish to interfere with any of your little diversions, Estella," said he, returning in triumph to his seat, "but it is I who wash the linen."

"Oh, Lord, oh, Lord, oh, Lord!" yawned Fred. "What a deadly drag it is! I wonder shall I ever work again?"

"I wonder," said Estella, "why it's always us who can't get parts? We can all act."

"Well," said Fred, "we could if we were let. But the question now is—Mr. Bates told Barbara he'd be here after that blamed rent at three o'clock, and it's about that now; what are we going to tell him?"

"If I could only get a backer for my play," began Estella. "Oh, I wish you'd stop fooling with that banjo, Tony, you put me out so!"

"Say, look here, Tony!" cried Fred, "since you've got a job coming to you—I know it isn't the proper thing, but—couldn't you get something in advance from your management?"

"Oh!" cried Mrs. Donnelly, "and start out in debt, and be all the season getting even!"

Tony looked hopefully at Barbara, but Barbara positively frowned.

"Unh-unh!" said Tony, shaking his head at Fred; "nev-er bor-row from the man-age-ment. If you do,

you'll nev-er save a cent;"—he struck a discreet tinkle
from the banjo, and added: "In the mean-time, who
will pay the rent?"

"Without turning her head round to the company,
Barbara said: "I daresay we shan't have to pay the
rent at all, if I marry Mr. Bates."

They were too surprised to speak, but as they gradually recovered their breath, they turned and stared
at her; all but Tony, who went on touching the banjo
and looking at it carefully. Estella leaned forward
and knocked on the table with the handle of the butter-
knife. "What do you mean by that?" she said.

Barbara put up one hand and smoothed her back
hair with deliberate fingers. "When I went into the
hall this morning to see if I couldn't inveigle him to
go away"—Tony lifted his head quickly and angrily,
and frowned from Barbara to Estella—"as I was
asked to do," Barbara continued, "he asked me if I
would marry him. Or, rather, he asked me to think
about it. He is coming back at three to—to help us
think about it. He wants to speak to you, Estella."

"Well, I'm not going to have anything to do with
it!" Estella cried. "And you needn't frown at me,
Tony Regnault, for I was taking the curling irons out
of the gas-range that very minute, or I would have
gone out to him myself. Nobody shall ever say I
forced her into it. I wouldn't wreck the life of my
own sister, not if he was to pay me for it in diamonds!
But God knows, Tony, what's to become of her, the
way things are; for even if ever she can make up her
mind, and marry you, you're all alike, you actors; I

wouldn't trust a girl's heart to the best of you, though
it's true Jim Folso did take care of his mother till the
day she died—I know that myself—sent her ten dollars a week year out and in; he's had to borrow it
from Tommy many a time. No, sir, she'll have to
decide it for her own self, Barbara will."

And at this moment, as though by special arrangement with a dramatic deity, there was a ring at the
front door.

"It needn't be he, you know," said Estella, confronting a circle of stricken faces.

But it was he. Fred went to the door and ushered
in a large, plump, blond gentleman in the elder middle
years. He had his coat on his arm and his hat in his
hand, and he was mopping his face and forehead with
a huge clean handkerchief.

"Good-day, all," said he. "No, don't trouble yourself for me, ma'am," to Estella, who had risen, mute
and regal, and was schooling herself to the manner of
a dowager empress. He accepted a chair, however,
and looked around with simple confidence upon the
company. "It is hot! When you come to my time of
life, you feel the stairs."

"You'll have a glass of lemonade, Mr. Bates," said
Tony. He brought a glassful and his own fan to the
landlord, and the two men looked at each other as the
glass changed hands.

"Thank you," said Mr. Bates, "I don't object."

An embarrassed silence followed these civilities.
Tony had cuddled on to the couch again with his
inevitable banjo, and the terriers had come forward,

and were sniffing at Mr. Bates's legs. Dooley drew back suddenly and showed his teeth; Mohammed instantly broke into a volley of shrill yelps.

"Knows I'm the landlord," tactfully remarked Mr. Bates, setting down his glass, and smiling jovially around. He snapped his fingers at Dooley, "Nice boy, good fellow." The dogs thrust their bodies back and their heads forward, and continued to grumble and to growl. "Well, I guess from what Miss Barbara told me this morning, you didn't want to see me to-day."

"I'll be frank with you, Mr. Bates," said Estella. "My allowance hasn't come yet. God is my witness, I expected it the day before yesterday. Though why I should expect it from a man that forsakes his own child, and that I never would have married if I hadn't been infatuated with him—a girl's infatuation, Mr. Bates, you know what that is—I don't know. But I was so sure it would come to-day, while that lace sale was on at Siegel & Cooper's. I thought of dressing to be ready right after lunch—didn't I, Barbara? But it hasn't come. I'm sure you're the last man, Mr. Bates, that would want me to take the bread out of my child's mouth."

"Must be a pretty mean man," said Mr. Bates; "won't spend money to keep his own little girl. But you know, Mrs. Baker, I know people talk, especially the Irish, but owners have to make their property pay, someways."

"Oh, well," said Estella, "after all, this isn't a flat you could really expect much rent for. If I'd had my

money this month, there's a lot of things I'd have
spoken to you about. We haven't any awnings, for one
thing, and it makes the place like a bake-oven, and it
makes it look like a tenement; though, for that matter, there isn't a tenement but what has awnings.
And that woman in the flat over us, you'll have to
speak to her. She says insulting things about my
dogs, down the airshaft. Yes, she does; she means
to insult me, because I told her she ought to be
ashamed to let her parrot use such language. I
couldn't let Regina listen to it, Mr. Bates, indeed I
couldn't. And the storeroom leaks, or a pipe's burst
in it, or something, and I shan't pay my rent at all if
my Saratoga trunk is damaged, for there's a lot of
wardrobe in it and things no money could replace.
My white satin—I only wore it two weeks—is in
there, and my husband's miniature's in that trunk. I
shouldn't like to see that damaged."

"Well, well," said Mr. Bates, heartlessly putting
the miniature of Mr. Baker to one side: "I guess you
know it isn't altogether about the rent I came. I guess
maybe Miss Barbara's told you about what I said to
her this morning. No, ma'am; no, gent'men, don't
go. I know it's not the usual thing, but you've always
seemed sort of like a family here, and I know you'll
all talk about it when I'm gone, so might's well have
it now. And I'm counting that maybe you'll kind of
help me out. I'm not supposing"—he turned a pair of
patient eyes on Barbara, and the tame, kindly loving-
ness in them seemed at once to shield and to caress
her—"I'm not supposing Miss Barbara's what's called

in love with me. 'Twouldn't be natural, but I think she might like me if she came to know me and gave me a fair show. Especially when she knows more o' the way people get along than she does now; she'd see how different I'd treat her from the way a lot of men do that have got wives and don't know how to use 'em. I always thought this was a kind of rough world for women, and I'd like to do what's really right by one of them."

Nobody answered, but Tony lifted a long grave look to his.

"And so I thought," continued Mr. Bates, "that some of you who haven't such fancy ideas as it's natural enough she's got, would speak to her, and tell her that if—if you don't see something as pretty as you'd like, it's best to take something that's all wool."

He was greatly pleased at this flower of speech, and looked up quickly and brightly at Barbara, and Barbara smiled. She had a slow smile of infinite possibilities, and Mr. Bates looked at it a little before he proceeded: "I've got money; a couple of hundred thousand, one way and another, and more making—and I've got health and good habits, and the store I set by her, you wouldn't believe it. Well, I guess she's kind of notiony and high-spirited, and I don't seem much to her, but I'm relying you'll tell her those are things make life comfortable and worth having just the same; and I should think you, Mrs. Baker, that's had your own troubles in your time, would feel kind o' scared to have anything so pretty and so kind of high-headed and proud around like this."

"God is my witness, Mr. Bates—" began Estella, leaning forward.

"Not," hurriedly continued the suitor, "not as I've got anything to say against your profession. Those that like it—why let 'em, I say. But it ain't the life for a woman, is it? Now, is it? Nor, I shouldn't think myself, for a man either. I don't mean any disrespect, but it does seem to me a lady like Miss Barbara's got something more coming to her than this, and what's more," he added, meditatively, "it seems like it don't pay."

Tony, who was leaning on his knees, with his chin in his hands, lifted his guileless eyes, and said sweetly: "It's only fair to the profession, Mr. Bates, to tell you that we are not its most victorious exponents."

"Likely, likely," admitted Mr. Bates, a little mystified. "But we can keep a woman out of it, Mr. Reeno, and take her clean away from all this stage business."

"You don't think," inquired Tony—this was the only base advantage Tony took—"you don't think she ought to have anything to say about it herself—the being taken clean away from all this stage business?"

"Not when she's got a man to look after her," said Mr. Bates, "and to give her a comfortable home."

"Oh!" admitted Tony, and confided a twinkle to the flooring.

"Well, my dear," said Estella, "it's a very great responsibility for me, and I don't want to urge you. But if I'd married Mr. Fettercamp when he wanted me to, we'd all be rolling in our own carriages this minute.   There was his sister married an Italian prince, and she wasn't a circumstance to Barbara.   She's dead now, poor girl, but she married him.   But, no, I would have Tommy Baker because I loved him—indeed, I did, Barbara Floyd, I loved him madly—but there's no use marrying for love when you can't even be sure he'll send you your alimony right.   And because I wrecked my life, Barbara, I'd like to see you marry somebody worthy.   I'd say the same if it was Regina.   Regina—Regina Baker, don't you put that penny in your mouth.   Come here—come here to mama."

Regina advanced slowly, and Estella gathered the curls out of her warm little neck and face, and hastily polished off her face with a handkerchief.   "Don't you know Mr. Bates, darling?   What do nice little girls say to gentlemen?"

Regina ducked her head, made an unintelligible sound and extended her hand.

"How-de-do, miss," said Mr. Bates, shaking the hand.   "I'm sorry I didn't think to bring you some candy.   Better luck next time, eh?   Why, why, you mustn't begin to cry, little girl.   Don't you want to be friends with me?"   Regina nodded.   "Don't you want to grow up and have a pony to ride and learn the piano?"

"Awn go finey aws," said Regina.

"She wants to go on the flying horses," translated the patient Fred.   "Merry-go-round, you know."

"And so she shall!" assented Mr. Bates.

Regina glowed with joy.   "An Anny Bobs?"

"And Auntie Barbara?" Mr. Bates repeated after Fred; "why, yes, indeed."

Regina, in a kind of vacuous triumph, smiled around the room and had an inspiration. "An Tony?"

"Why," responded Mr. Bates hesitatingly, "maybe he wouldn't want to."

A perfect torrent of joyous sounds intended to be affirmative burst from Regina's lips. In the vigor of her confidence she flung herself upon the legs of Mr. Bates and beat his knees. "Oh, yef! As time, as time, aw lone, Rina an Anny Bobs an Tony go finey aws, go roun an roun an roun, an Tony caw go ring!"

There was a suspicion of thickness in the voice of the translator: "Once, last time, nobody else happened to be there. Tony and Barbara rode, too, and Tony caught the gold ring; you know, with those little blunt swords."

"Why, he's a very clever young man," Mr. Bates affably replied.

Regina smote his knees and shrieked with joy. "Oh, yef!" she repeated, "an Anny Bobs gah go ring."

"You said it was Mr. Tony caught the gold ring, little girl."

"That's what she means to say," said Fred.

"No! no!" Regina passionately insisted. "Anny Bobs *gah* go ring! Anny Bobs gah go ring *now!* Rina fine it."

"Well, well, Regina," Estella interrupted, "Mr. Bates can't talk to you all day!"

"I paid it her as a reward of merit. I assure you,

I gave the man a dime for it," said Tony, softly, with
a little blush.

Mr. Bates passed over the insignificance of Tony's
shabby boyhood with the good temper of a potentate.
"Well," said he, giving his face a final wipe, "I guess
I've said what I laid out to.   I didn't come here to
talk soft.   That part of it's just my business, and
hers—if she'll have it."   He got up and took his hat
and went over to Barbara.   "Miss Barbara," he said,
"if you can make out to like me—like me well enough
to have me—you'll never regret it."   He held out his
hand, and Barbara gave him hers with her long boyish clasp.   Kate followed him to the door, and let him
out.

An unpleasant silence settled upon the company.
Its members were suddenly set face to face with decision and responsibility; they were crowded and jostled and made to feel strange and ill at ease, here in
the dilapidated cheer of their own home, by the en-
croaching wisdom of other worlds.   Barbara continued
to sit idly in the blinding sunshine like a person passive
before the issue of events, and indifferent to it.   The
fierce light seemed to set her apart from counsel and
from tenderness, and to blare aloud her beauty.

Estella, after two or three clearings of her throat,
inquired with a kind of trembling pomp: "And what
do you think about it yourself, my dear?"

Barbara rose and came slowly to the table.   She
stood stroking the edge of it with her hand, and finally
she said: "I'll tell you what I think.   I think that if
I were married to Mr. Bates, I shouldn't have to run

out into the hall to ogle landlords to cheat them out
of their rent.   I think I shouldn't have to pretend to
be out when the milkman comes, nor wheedle the
butcher, nor have the gas turned off.   I shouldn't have
to walk out of a filthy mess like this"—Estella gasped
—"dressed as if I were going to a beauty show, because I wanted work, and into offices where I should
be looked over as if I were a horse.   I think I shouldn't
owe every stitch I wear and everything I put into my
mouth to my sister's divorced husband.   That's what
I think.   I think I should be looked out for and taken
care of and kept away from hurt, as other women
are!"

Estella began: "Well, of all the—"

"And I think," continued Barbara, her voice rising
to a hysteric pitch, "that my husband would be respected everywhere, and would work for me and be
true and good, and not depend for his pleasures upon a
friend's getting some money, and taking him out to
dinner with girls—"

"Oh! oh! Barbara!" cried Fred.

"It was such a good dinner, Barbara!" said Tony.
Unquestionably, his smile was coming back.

The dogs at the same moment began to quarrel over
a bone, and their voices rose in ear-splitting dispute.
Estella cuffed one of them, and the other carried the
bone into the sitting-room, from whence issued ecstatic
lickings and crunchings.

In the comparative pause Mrs. Donnelly's tearful
indignation burst upon Barbara:

"We all know what you mean by that last, Barbara

Floyd," she cried. "And I guess there are other people besides you in this house that are sick and tired of being poor, and the fuss there is about meals, and that have spent all their money on you, and whose fathers were rich and famous, and thought nothing of living at Delmonico's before ever you were born. If the butcher is swindled out of his meat, I don't see but you eat your share of it. If you think it's messy here, why don't you get up and clean it? Tony's scrubbed the kitchen while you've been lolling there, and you wouldn't know how to cook anything but a boiled egg and a pickle to this day if it wasn't for Tony. You're a bad, ungrateful girl, Barbara Floyd, and Tony—"

Estella pitched her voice above the voices of Mrs. Donnelly and the dogs: "Don't you try to bully my sister, Kate Donnelly, she—"

Tony struck the table sharply with his hand. "Come, Barbara," he said. "We must get the washing down now." He held the door open for her, and without looking round she went past him into the hall.

At the head of the top flight of stairs there was a door with a heavy sliding weight, and Tony, who had run upstairs in advance, pushed it open, and with a wave of the hand, like a lavish host, welcomed Barbara to the great, shining roof. It was very wide and hot, and silent, and little airs that the sidewalk never knew drifted over its cornices. Said Tony: "To where, beyond the voices, there is peace."

Barbara stepped out fearlessly between the glare of the red roofs and the glare of the blue and golden sky. With a happy breath, she turned her unshielded face up to the light. This stretch of gleaming tin had long been their private garden, and they had known it in many kinds of weather. "Oh, Tony!" she said, in a little soft, fluttered, laughing voice, "we needn't bother about the washing yet, need we?"

"Come," said Tony. "I've found a place where we can see the river. I found it for us this morning. Mustn't tell!"

"No," she said, and put her hand out to him, like a child. "Show me."

Behind its newer and broader substitute an old chimney rose out of the roof's western bulwark, from which it parted company a few feet above the ground in an angle of crumbling brick and mortar. Tony jumped into the niche of this angle and held down a hand to Barbara. "Step up and I'll lift you," he directed. She was beside him in an instant, and found herself breast-high above the parapet, which served as an elbow rest. It was too broad to let them see straight down into the common, cluttered street, and beyond the shops and the low buildings over the way stumbled the vine-smothered huts of squatters; past a bit of leafy, broken ground the wide green of market gardens was dotted with the gold of sunflowers and the scarlet of geraniums, a single close-shorn lawn was banked with the white and the mystic blue of hydrangeas. Further yet, between the shimmer of poplars and the frown of purple hills, the river flashed and drifted.

"It's good here," said Tony.

Barbara stretched her arm across the parapet as

though she stretched it into the coolness of fresh water. "There's a yacht—a white one, watch! Going down the river! Let's pretend it's going straight to sea, Tony—what fun! Across the sea."

"We're going with it, you know. Just ourselves, of course, and a telescope, maybe, and plenty of honey wrapped up in a five-pound note. All the little fishes will come and beg us for the honey, and you'll give it to them out of your hands till I shall be jealous. It isn't nice to be jealous. I wouldn't let even a little fish suffer it, if I were you, Barbara. Why, Barbara! what foolishness you talk! And you don't even hear me!"

"I wish I could see all this from my own window," she said.

"Ah, but you can't. I had to show it to you, Barbara. It was quite easy to find, but you know you never found it." The little rosy ruffle of Barbara's sleeve lay on the rough edge of the parapet, and Tony bent his head and kissed it. "I was sure you'd like it here. Be good," he said.

The voices of some children singing ring games on a near fire-escape rose with an accent of their own natures to the two truants on the housetop. Otherwise they seemed the only living souls in a universe made up of two expanses: below them, the wide, sparkling, burning roofs, with one distant fringe of leaves and waters, and above, the radiant, hot blue, luminous and quivering, and scarcely tinged by the white clouds which slowly sailed across it and banked themselves on the horizon into palaces and temples. Toward the

west, where the sun blazed in a splendor that even the
eyes of lovers dared not meet, the heavens were almost white—not in pallor, but effulgence, like light in-
carnate.   Small, lazy breezes floated through the sunshine, and brushed, fresh and sweet, against their faces.

"Barbara," said Tony, leaning forward and catching her by both wrists, "where did Regina find my
ring?"

She was startled both by the suddenness of his attack and by the strength of his hold, and straining
back upon his grasp she remained alert and silent, like
a deer.   He waited a moment, but she continued passionately quiet, passionately studious of his face.   In
the pause, the voices of the children arose with a new
clearness:

> "And on his breast he wore a Star,
>   Pointing to the East and West."

"Barbara!"

"Hush!" she insisted.   Her breath was fluttering on
her lips, and her eyes shining into his:

> "Go choose your East, go choose your West,
>   Go choose the one that you love best."

"You kept that ring!" he said.   "You kept it—because of me!"   Almost as he spoke she had leaped
down and away from him, and was running across
the roof.

He caught up with her on the low platform of
wooden slats amid the flutter of the wet linens.
"Help me take these in," she called to him.   "Estella will be angry."   She was struggling with the

clothespins, and their fingers met over a row of pillow-slips.

"They're not dry yet. Listen, I—"

"There's a breeze come up. It will dry them in a minute." She was moving further and further away.

"Why, see, my sweet, you don't know what you're saying! I want to tell you—"

"Oh," she cried, pausing oppressedly, "what does everybody tell me? That you are idle, that you are extravagant, that you—that you—that girls—"

"Barbara," he said, "though they follow me in their thousands and their ten thousands, though their dead bodies strew my pathway, I will be blind to them. I love you, Barbara."

She retreated again, making as though to reach the door, and he stood still in a sudden bitterness, with a little wound in the dignity of his love. The next instant he was startled to see her, who was so light and true of step, stumble and lose her footing on a broken slat and sink down in a heap with her hands over her face.

He ran up and bent over her without touching her. "Oh, my dear!" he asked; "what is it? Are you hurt? Or were you angry? Would you like me to go away? What is it?"

She lifted her face to his and put her arms around his neck.

"I was thinking of you," she said.

.   .   .   .

Half an hour later, as they still sat on the platform, the roof rang with their names, and from under their damp canopy of tablecloths and towels they perceived Estella in the doorway.

"Come on!" she called. "Why, whatever's kept you? Come on! The alimony's come, and we're all going to Coney Island for dinner!"

"Don't be so noisy, Estella," said Tony. "We're engaged."

"Really? Really, Barbara? Well, I'm glad of it. Yes, Regina," she called over her shoulder, "come up. Mama's here. Well, I'm very glad. And I'll have my white satin cleaned for her as soon as I can. How jolly we're going out to dinner! Like a party for you, Barbara."

"Splendid!" said Tony. "The alimony-baked meats did coldly furnish forth the marriage tables."

He sprang up and handed Barbara to her feet. There fell to the ground something Barbara had been showing Tony—a slender ribbon, as long as a watch-chain, and, dangling from its end, a great, clumsy, ridiculous gilt ring. Regina, who came staggering through the doorway, fell upon this latter object with a shriek of joyous recognition. "Anny Bobs gah go ring!" she cried. "Rina awn go finey aws, go finey aws, go roun an roun an roun!"

FOR THE LOVE OF A MAN

BY JACK LONDON

Jack London (born in San Francisco, January 12, 1876) belongs in authorship as in life wholly to the new century of the nation. His is the literature of present action, preferably that produced under the impulse of the undying primitive emotions, whether of man or other animals. While he has written several short stories, none seems quite so typical of his genius as a chapter from his novel "The Call of the Wild," containing an episode that in itself forms a complete "animal story." Accordingly, this has been selected for reproduction in the present series, and is here published under its original chapter title, "For the Love of a Man."

FOR THE LOVE OF A MAN

BY JACK LONDON

WHEN John Thornton froze his feet in the previous December, his partners had made him comfortable and left him to get well, going on themselves up the river to get out a raft of saw-logs for Dawson. He was still limping slightly at the time he rescued Buck, but with the continued warm weather even the slight limp left him. And here, lying by the river bank through the long spring days, watching the running water, listening lazily to the songs of birds and the hum of nature, Buck slowly won back his strength.

A rest comes very good after one has traveled three thousand miles, and it must be confessed that Buck waxed lazy as his wounds healed, his muscles swelled out, and the flesh came back to cover his bones. For that matter, they were all loafing—Buck, John Thornton, and Skeet and Nig—waiting for the raft to come that was to carry them down to Dawson. Skeet was a little Irish setter who early made friends with Buck, who, in a dying condition, was unable to resent her first advances. She had the doctor trait which some dogs possess; and as a mother cat washes her kittens, so she washed and cleansed Buck's wounds. Regularly, each morning after he had finished his breakfast, she

From "The Call of the Wild." Copyright, 1903, by Jack London.

performed her self-appointed task, till he came to look
for her ministrations as much as he did for Thornton's.
Nig, equally friendly, though less demonstrative, was
a huge black dog, half bloodhound and half deer-
hound, with eyes that laughed and a boundless good
nature.

To Buck's surprise these dogs manifested no jeal-
ousy toward him. They seemed to share the kindli-
ness and largeness of John Thornton. As Buck grew
stronger they enticed him into all sorts of ridiculous
games, in which Thornton himself could not forbear
to join; and in this fashion Buck romped through his
convalescence and into a new existence. Love, genu-
ine passionate love, was his for the first time. This he
had never experienced at Judge Miller's down in the
sun-kissed Santa Clara Valley. With the Judge's sons,
hunting and tramping, it had been a working partner-
ship; with the Judge's grandsons, a sort of pompous
guardianship; and with the Judge himself, a stately
and dignified friendship. But love that was feverish
and burning, that was adoration, that was madness, it
had taken John Thornton to arouse.

This man had saved his life, which was something;
but, further, he was the ideal master. Other men saw
to the welfare of their dogs from a sense of duty and
business expediency; he saw to the welfare of his as
if they were his own children, because he could not
help it. And he saw further. He never forgot a
kindly greeting or a cheering word, and to sit down
for a long talk with them ("gas" he called it) was as
much his delight as theirs. He had a way of taking

Buck's head roughly between his hands, and resting
his own head upon Buck's, of shaking him back and
forth, the while calling him ill names that to Buck
were love names. Buck knew no greater joy than that
rough embrace and the sound of murmured oaths,
and at each jerk back and forth it seemed that his
heart would be shaken out of his body, so great was its
ecstasy. And when, released, he sprang to his feet,
his mouth laughing, his eyes eloquent, his throat vibrant with unuttered sound, and in that fashion remained without movement, John Thornton would rev-
erently exclaim, "God! you can all but speak!"

Buck had a trick of love expression that was akin to
hurt. He would often seize Thornton's hand in his
mouth and close so fiercely that the flesh bore the
impress of his teeth for some time afterward. And as
Buck understood the oaths to be love words, so the
man understood this feigned bite for a caress.

For the most part, however, Buck's love was expressed in adoration. While he went wild with happiness when Thornton touched him or spoke to him, he
did not seek these tokens. Unlike Skeet, who was
wont to shove her nose under Thornton's hand and
nudge and nudge till petted, or Nig, who would stalk
up and rest his great head on Thornton's knee, Buck
was content to adore at a distance. He would lie by
the hour, eager, alert, at Thornton's feet, looking up
into his face, dwelling upon it, studying it, following
with keenest interest each fleeting expression, every
movement or change of feature. Or, as chance might
have it, he would lie further away, to the side or rear,

watching the outlines of the man and the occasional movements of his body. And often, such was the communion in which they lived, the strength of Buck's gaze would draw John Thornton's head around, and he would return the gaze, without speech, his heart shining out of his eyes as Buck's heart shone out.

For a long time after his rescue, Buck did not like Thornton to get out of his sight. From the moment he left the tent to when he entered it again, Buck would follow at his heels. His transient masters since he had come into the Northland had bred in him a fear that no master could be permanent. He was afraid that Thornton would pass out of his life as Perrault and François and the Scotch half-breed had passed out. Even in the night, in his dreams, he was haunted by this fear. At such times he would shake off sleep and creep through the chill to the flap of the tent, where he would stand and listen to the sound of his master's breathing.

But in spite of this great love he bore John Thornton, which seemed to bespeak the soft civilizing influence, the strain of the primitive, which the Northland had aroused in him, remained alive and active. Faithfulness and devotion, things born of fire and roof, were his; yet he retained his wildness and wiliness. He was a thing of the wild, come in from the wild to sit by John Thornton's fire, rather than a dog of the soft Southland stamped with the marks of generations of civilization. Because of his very great love, he could not steal from this man, but from any other man, in any other camp, he did not hesitate an instant; while the cunning with which he stole enabled him to escape detection.

His face and body were scored by the teeth of many dogs, and he fought as fiercely as ever and more shrewdly. Skeet and Nig were too good-natured for quarreling—besides, they belonged to John Thornton; but the strange dog, no matter what the breed or valor, swiftly acknowledged Buck's supremacy or found himself struggling for life with a terrible antagonist. And Buck was merciless. He had learned well the law of club and fang, and he never forewent an advantage or drew back from a foe he had started on the way to Death. He had lessoned from Spitz, and from the chief fighting dogs of the police and mail, and knew there was no middle course. He must master or be mastered; while to show mercy was a weakness. Mercy did not exist in the primordial life. It was misunderstood for fear, and such misunderstandings made for death. Kill or be killed, eat or be eaten, was the law; and this mandate, down out of the depths of Time, he obeyed.

He was older than the days he had seen and the breaths he had drawn. He linked the past with the present, and the eternity behind him throbbed through him in a mighty rhythm to which he swayed as the tides and seasons swayed. He sat by John Thornton's fire, a broad-breasted dog, white-fanged and long-furred; but behind him were the shades of all manner of dogs, half-wolves and wild wolves, urgent and prompting, tasting the savor of the meat he ate, thirsting for the water he drank, scenting the wind with him, listening with him and telling him the sounds made by the wild life in the forest, dictating his moods, directing his actions, lying down to sleep with him when he lay down, and dreaming with him and beyond him and becoming themselves the stuff of his dreams.

So peremptorily did these shades beckon him that each day mankind and the claims of mankind slipped further from him. Deep in the forest a call was sounding, and as often as he heard this call, mysteriously thrilling and luring, he felt compelled to turn his back upon the fire and the beaten earth around it, and to plunge into the forest, and on and on, he knew not where or why; nor did he wonder where or why, the call sounding imperiously, deep in the forest. But as often as he gained the soft unbroken earth and the green shade, the love for John Thornton drew him back to the fire again.

Thornton alone held him. The rest of mankind was as nothing. Chance travelers might praise or pet him; but he was cold under it all, and from a too demonstrative man he would get up and walk away. When Thornton's partners, Hans and Pete, arrived on the long-expected raft, Buck refused to notice them till he learned they were close to Thornton; after that he tolerated them in a passive sort of way, accepting favors from them as though he favored them by accepting. They were of the same large type as Thornton, living close to the earth, thinking simply and seeing clearly; and ere they swung the raft into the big eddy by the saw-mill at Dawson, they understood Buck and

his ways, and did not insist upon an intimacy such as obtained with Skeet and Nig.

For Thornton, however, his love seemed to grow and grow. He, alone among men, could put a pack upon Buck's back in the summer traveling. Nothing was too great for Buck to do when Thornton commanded. One day (they had grub-staked themselves from the proceeds of the raft and left Dawson for the head waters of the Tanana) the men and dogs were sitting on the crest of a cliff which fell away, straight down, to naked bed-rock three hundred feet below. John Thornton was sitting near the edge, Buck at his shoulder. A thoughtless whim seized Thornton, and he drew the attention of Hans and Pete to the experiment he had in mind. "Jump, Buck!" he commanded, sweeping his arm out and over the chasm. The next instant he was grappling with Buck on the extreme edge, while Hans and Pete were dragging them back into safety.

"It's uncanny," Pete said, after it was over and they had caught their speech.

Thornton shook his head. "No, it is splendid, and it is terrible, too. Do you know, it sometimes makes me afraid."

"I'm not hankering to be the man that lays hands on you while he's around," Pete announced conclusively, nodding his head toward Buck.

"Py Jingo!" was Hans's contribution. "Not mine-self either."

It was at Circle City, ere the year was out, that Pete's apprehensions were realized. "Black" Burton, a man evil-tempered and malicious, had been picking a quarrel with a tenderfoot at the bar, when Thornton stepped good-naturedly between. Buck, as was his custom, was lying in a corner, head on paws, watching his master's every action. Burton struck out, without warning, straight from the shoulder. Thornton was sent spinning, and saved himself from falling only by clutching the rail of the bar.

Those who were looking on heard what was neither bark nor yelp, but a something which is best described as a roar, and they saw Buck's body rise up in the air as he left the floor for Burton's throat. The man saved his life by instinctively throwing out his arm, but was hurled backward to the floor with Buck on top of him. Buck loosed his teeth from the flesh of the arm and drove in again for the throat. This time the man succeeded only in partly blocking, and his throat was torn open. Then the crowd was upon Buck, and he was driven off; but while a surgeon checked the bleeding, he prowled up and down, growling furiously, attempting to rush in, and being forced back by an array of hostile clubs. A "miners' meeting," called on the spot, decided that the dog had sufficient provocation, and Buck was discharged. But his reputation was made, and from that day his name spread through every camp in Alaska.

Later on, in the fall of the year, he saved John Thornton's life in quite another fashion. The three partners were lining a long and narrow poling-boat down a bad stretch of rapids on the Forty-Mile Creek. Hans and Pete moved along the bank, snubbing with

a thin manila rope from tree to tree, while Thornton
remained in the boat, helping its descent by means of
a pole, and shouting directions to the shore.   Buck, on
the bank, worried and anxious, kept abreast of the
boat, his eyes never off his master.

At a particularly bad spot, where a ledge of barely
submerged rocks jutted out into the river, Hans cast
off the rope, and, while Thornton poled the boat out
into the stream, ran down the bank with the end in his
hand to snub the boat when it had cleared the ledge.
This it did, and was flying down-stream in a current
as swift as a mill-race, when Hans checked it with the
rope and checked too suddenly.   The boat flirted over
and snubbed in to the bank bottom up, while Thornton, flung sheer out of it, was carried down-stream
toward the worst part of the rapids, a stretch of wild
water in which no swimmer could live.

Buck had sprung in on the instant; and at the end
of three hundred yards, amid a mad swirl of water,
he overhauled Thornton.   When he felt him grasp his
tail, Buck headed for the bank, swimming with all his
splendid strength.   But the progress shoreward was
slow; the progress down-stream amazingly rapid.
From below came the fatal roaring where the wild
current went wilder and was rent in shreds and spray
by the rocks which thrust through like the teeth of an
enormous comb.   The suck of the water as it took the
beginning of the last steep pitch was frightful, and
Thornton knew that the shore was impossible.   He
scraped furiously over a rock, bruised across a second,
and struck a third with crushing force.   He clutched

its slippery top with both hands, releasing Buck, and above the roar of the churning water shouted: "Go, Buck! Go!"

Buck could not hold his own, and swept on downstream, struggling desperately, but unable to win back. When he heard Thornton's command repeated, he partly reared out of the water, throwing his head high, as though for a last look, then turned obediently toward the bank. He swam powerfully and was dragged ashore by Pete and Hans at the very point where swimming ceased to be possible and destruction began.

They knew that the time a man could cling to a slippery rock in the face of that driving current was a matter of minutes, and they ran as fast as they could up the bank to a point far above where Thornton was hanging on. They attached the line with which they had been snubbing the boat to Buck's neck and shoulders, being careful that it should neither strangle him nor impede his swimming, and launched him into the stream. He struck out boldly, but not straight enough into the stream. He discovered the mistake too late, when Thornton was abreast of him and a bare half-dozen strokes away while he was being carried helplessly past.

Hans promptly snubbed with the rope, as though Buck were a boat. The rope thus tightening on him in the sweep of the current, he was jerked under the surface, and under the surface he remained till his body struck against the bank and he was hauled out. He was half drowned, and Hans and Pete threw themselves upon him, pounding the breath into him and the

water out of him. He staggered to his feet and fell
down. The faint sound of Thornton's voice came to
them, and though they could not make out the words
of it, they knew that he was in his extremity. His
master's voice acted on Buck like an electric shock.
He sprang to his feet and ran up the bank ahead of the
men to the point of his previous departure.

Again the rope was attached and he was launched,
and again he struck out, but this time straight into
the stream. He had miscalculated once, but he would
not be guilty of it a second time. Hans paid out the
rope, permitting no slack, while Pete kept it clear of
coils. Buck held on till he was on a line straight above
Thornton; then he turned, and with the speed of an
express train headed down upon him. Thornton saw
him coming, and, as Buck struck him like a battering
ram, with the whole force of the current behind him,
he reached up and closed with both arms around the
shaggy neck. Hans snubbed the rope around the tree,
and Buck and Thornton were jerked under the water.
Strangling, suffocating, sometimes one uppermost and
sometimes the other, dragging over the jagged bottom, smashing against rocks and snags, they veered
in to the bank.

Thornton came to, belly downward and being violently propelled back and forth across a drift log by
Hans and Pete. His first glance was for Buck, over
whose limp and apparently lifeless body Nig was setting up a howl, while Skeet was licking the wet face
and closed eyes. Thornton was himself bruised and
battered, and he went carefully over Buck's body, when

he had been brought around, finding three broken ribs.

"That settles it," he announced. "We camp right here." And camp they did, till Buck's ribs knitted and he was able to travel.

That winter, at Dawson, Buck performed another exploit, not so heroic, perhaps, but one that put his name many notches higher on the totem-pole of Alaskan fame. This exploit was particularly gratifying to the three men; for they stood in need of the outfit which it furnished, and were enabled to make a long-desired trip into the virgin East, where miners had not yet appeared. It was brought about by a conversation in the Eldorado Saloon, in which men waxed boastful of their favorite dogs. Buck, because of his record, was the target for these men, and Thornton was driven stoutly to defend him. At the end of half an hour one man stated that his dog could start a sled with five hundred pounds and walk off with it; a second bragged six hundred for his dog; and a third, seven hundred.

"Pooh! pooh!" said John Thornton; "Buck can start a thousand pounds."

"And break it out? and walk off with it for a hundred yards?" demanded Matthewson, a Bonanza King, he of the seven hundred vaunt.

"And break it out, and walk off with it for a hundred yards," John Thornton said coolly.

"Well," Matthewson said, slowly and deliberately, so that all could hear, "I've got a thousand dollars that says he can't. And there it is." So saying, he slammed a sack of gold dust of the size of a bologna sausage down upon the bar.

Nobody spoke. Thornton's bluff, if bluff it was, had been called. He could feel a flush of warm blood creeping up his face. His tongue had tricked him. He did not know whether Buck could start a thousand pounds. Half a ton! The enormousness of it appalled him. He had great faith in Buck's strength and had often thought him capable of starting such a load; but never, as now, had he faced the possibility of it, the eyes of a dozen men fixed upon him, silent and waiting. Further, he had no thousand dollars; nor had Hans or Pete.

"I've got a sled standing outside now, with twenty fifty-pound sacks of flour on it," Matthewson went on with brutal directness; "so don't let that hinder you."

Thornton did not reply. He did not know what to say. He glanced from face to face in the absent way of a man who has lost the power of thought and is seeking somewhere to find the thing that will start it going again. The face of Jim O'Brien, a Mastodon king and old-time comrade, caught his eyes. It was as a cue to him, seeming to rouse him to do what he would never have dreamed of doing.

"Can you lend me a thousand?" he asked, almost in a whisper.

"Sure," answered O'Brien, thumping down a plethoric sack by the side of Matthewson's. "Though it's little faith I'm having, John, that the beast can do the trick."

The Eldorado emptied its occupants into the street

to see the test. The tables were deserted, and the dealers and gamekeepers came forth to see the outcome of the wager and to lay odds. Several hundred men, furred and mittened, banked around the sled within easy distance. Matthewson's sled, loaded with a thousand pounds of flour, had been standing for a couple of hours, and in the intense cold (it was sixty below zero) the runners had frozen fast to the hard-packed snow. Men offered odds of two to one that Buck could not budge the sled. A quibble arose concerning the phrase "break out." O'Brien contended it was Thornton's privilege to knock the runners loose, leaving Buck to "break it out" from a dead standstill. Matthewson insisted that the phrase included breaking the runners from the frozen grip of the snow. A majority of the men who had witnessed the making of the bet decided in his favor, whereat the odds went up to three to one against Buck.

There were no takers. Not a man believed him capable of the feat. Thornton had been hurried into the wager, heavy with doubt; and now that he looked at the sled itself, the concrete fact, with the regular team of ten dogs curled up in the snow before it, the more impossible the task appeared. Matthewson waxed jubilant.

"Three to one!" he proclaimed. "I'll lay you another thousand at that figure, Thornton. What d'ye say?"

Thornton's doubt was strong in his face, but his fighting spirit was aroused—the fighting spirit that soars above odds, fails to recognize the impossible, and is deaf to all save the clamor for battle. He called Hans and Pete to him. Their sacks were slim, and with his own the three partners could rake together only two hundred dollars. In the ebb of their fortunes, this sum was their total capital; yet they laid it unhesitatingly against Matthewson's six hundred.

The team of ten dogs was unhitched, and Buck, with his own harness, was put into the sled. He had caught the contagion of the excitement, and he felt that in some way he must do a great thing for John Thornton. Murmurs of admiration at his splendid appearance went up. He was in perfect condition, without an ounce of superfluous flesh, and the one hundred and fifty pounds that he weighed were so many pounds of grit and virility. His furry coat shone with the sheen of silk. Down the neck and across the shoulders, his mane, in repose as it was, half bristled and seemed to lift with every movement, as though excess of vigor made each particular hair alive and active. The great breast and heavy fore legs were no more than in proportion with the rest of the body, where the muscles showed in tight rolls underneath the skin. Men felt these muscles and proclaimed them hard as iron, and the odds went down to two to one.

"Gad, sir! Gad, sir!" stuttered a member of the latest dynasty, a king of the Skookum Benches. "I offer you eight hundred for him, sir, before the test, sir; eight hundred just as he stands."

Thornton shook his head and stepped to Buck's side.

"You must stand off from him," Matthewson protested. "Free play and plenty of room."

The crowd fell silent; only could be heard the voices of the gamblers vainly offering two to one. Everybody acknowledged Buck a magnificent animal, but twenty fifty-pound sacks of flour bulked too large in their eyes for them to loosen their pouchstrings.

Thornton knelt down by Buck's side. He took his head in his two hands and rested cheek on cheek. He did not playfully shake him, as was his wont, or murmur soft love curses; but he whispered in his ear. "As you love me, Buck. As you love me," was what he whispered. Buck whined with suppressed eagerness.

The crowd was watching curiously. The affair was growing mysterious. It seemed like a conjuration. As Thornton got to his feet, Buck seized his mittened hand between his jaws, pressing in with his teeth and releasing slowly, half reluctantly. It was the answer, in terms, not of speech, but of love. Thornton stepped well back.

"Now, Buck," he said.

Buck tightened the traces, then slacked them for a matter of several inches. It was the way he had learned.

"Gee!" Thornton's voice rang out, sharp in the tense silence.

Buck swung to the right, ending the movement in a plunge that took up the slack and with a sudden jerk arrested his one hundred and fifty pounds. The load quivered, and from under the runners arose a crisp crackling.

"Haw!" Thornton commanded.

Buck duplicated the manœuvre, this time to the left. The crackling turned into a snapping, the sled pivoting and the runners slipping and grating several inches to the side. The sled was broken out. Men were holding their breaths, intensely unconscious of the fact.

"Now, *mush!*"

Thornton's command cracked out like a pistol-shot. Buck threw himself forward, tightening the traces with a jarring lunge. His whole body was gathered compactly together in the tremendous effort, the muscles writhing and knotting like live things under the silky fur. His great chest was low to the ground, his head forward and down, while his feet were flying like mad, the claws scarring the hard-packed snow in parallel grooves. The sled swayed and trembled, half-started forward. One of his feet slipped, and one man groaned aloud. Then the sled lurched ahead in what appeared a rapid succession of jerks, though it never really came to a dead stop again . . . half an inch . . . an inch . . . two inches. . . . The jerks perceptibly diminished; as the sled gained momentum, he caught them up, till it was moving steadily along.

Men gasped and began to breathe again, unaware that for a moment they had ceased to breathe. Thornton was running behind, encouraging Buck with short, cheery words. The distance had been measured off, and as he neared the pile of firewood which marked the end of the hundred yards, a cheer began to grow and grow, which burst into a roar as he passed the firewood and halted at command. Every man was tearing himself loose, even Matthewson. Hats and mittens were flying in the air. Men were shaking hands, it did not matter with whom, and bubbling over in a general incoherent babel.

But Thornton fell on his knees beside Buck. Head was against head, and he was shaking him back and forth. Those who hurried up heard him cursing Buck, and he cursed him long and fervently, and softly and lovingly.

"Gad, sir! Gad, sir!" spluttered the Skookum Bench king. "I'll give you a thousand for him, sir, a thousand, sir—twelve hundred, sir."

Thornton rose to his feet. His eyes were wet. The tears were streaming frankly down his cheeks. "Sir," he said to the Skookum Bench king, "no, sir. You can go to hell, sir. It's the best I can do for you, sir."

Buck seized Thornton's hand in his teeth. Thornton shook him back and forth. As though animated by a common impulse, the onlookers drew back to a respectful distance; nor were they again indiscreet enough to interrupt.

THE HALL BEDROOM

BY MARY E. WILKINS FREEMAN

Mrs. Freeman (born in 1862, at Randolph, Mass.) achieved under her maiden name of Mary Eleanor Wilkins a reputation as the foremost realist among our American short story writers, and now threatens to link in the public mind her married name with the highest order of imaginative fiction. In the present selection, a tale of the fourth dimension, by clever story-telling art, she causes that most contracted of habitable cells, a city hall bedroom, to expand into infinite vistas, not only of space, but of sight, sound, sense, and their other unnamed brothers of the family of sense-perceptions.

THE HALL BEDROOM

BY MARY E. WILKINS FREEMAN

name is Mrs. Elizabeth Jennings. I am
ighly respectable woman. I may style
a gentlewoman, for in my youth
es. I was well brought up, and
ng ladies' seminary. I also
and was that most genteel
ecary. His shop was on
street in Rockton, the town
where I lived until the death
y parents had died when I had
rt time, so I was left quite alone in
as not competent to carry on the
ss by myself, for I had no knowl-
ad had a mortal terror of giving
ad of medicines. Therefore I was
sell at a considerable sacrifice, and the
ds, some five thousand dollars, were all I had
world. The income was not enough to support
in any kind of comfort, and I saw that I must in
ome way earn money. I thought at first of teaching,
but I was no longer young, and methods had
changed since my school days. What I was able to
teach, nobody wished to know. I could think of
only one thing to do: take boarders. But the same

objection to that business as to teaching held good in
Rockton. Nobody wished to board. My husband
had rented a house with a number of bedrooms, an
I advertised, but nobody applied. Finally my c
was running very low, and I became despera
packed up my furniture, rented a large house
town and moved here. It was a ventur
with many risks. In the first place
exorbitant, in the next I was e
However, I am a person of cons
and have inventive power, and
the occasion presses. I adve
manner, although that act
that is, the last penny of
was forced to draw on my pr
first supplies, a thing which I
on any account to do. But the g
a reward, for I had several appli
days after my advertisement appear
Within two weeks my boarding-hous
lished, I became very successful, and
would have been uninterrupted had it not
the mysterious and bewildering occurrences
I am about to relate. I am now forced to leav
house and rent another. Some of my old board
accompany me, some, with the most unreasonable
nervousness, refuse to be longer associated in any
way, however indirectly, with the terrible and uncanny happenings which I have to relate. It remains
to be seen whether my ill luck in this house will
follow me into another, and whether my whole pros-

THE HALL BEDROOM

BY MARY E. WILKINS FREEMAN

MY name is Mrs. Elizabeth Jennings. I am
a highly respectable woman. I may style
myself a gentlewoman, for in my youth
I enjoyed advantages. I was well brought up, and
I graduated at a young ladies' seminary. I also
married well. My husband was that most genteel
of all merchants, an apothecary. His shop was on
the corner of the main street in Rockton, the town
where I was born, and where I lived until the death
of my husband. My parents had died when I had
been married a short time, so I was left quite alone in
the world. I was not competent to carry on the
apothecary business by myself, for I had no knowledge of drugs, and had a mortal terror of giving
poisons instead of medicines. Therefore I was
obliged to sell at a considerable sacrifice, and the
proceeds, some five thousand dollars, were all I had
in the world. The income was not enough to support
me in any kind of comfort, and I saw that I must in
some way earn money. I thought at first of teaching,
but I was no longer young, and methods had
changed since my school days. What I was able to
teach, nobody wished to know. I could think of
only one thing to do: take boarders. But the same

objection to that business as to teaching held good in
Rockton. Nobody wished to board. My husband
had rented a house with a number of bedrooms, and
I advertised, but nobody applied. Finally my cash
was running very low, and I became desperate. I
packed up my furniture, rented a large house in this
town and moved here. It was a venture attended
with many risks. In the first place the rent was
exorbitant, in the next I was entirely unknown.
However, I am a person of considerable ingenuity,
and have inventive power, and much enterprise when
the occasion presses. I advertised in a very original
manner, although that actually took my last penny,
that is, the last penny of my ready money, and I
was forced to draw on my principal to purchase my
first supplies, a thing which I had resolved never
on any account to do. But the great risk met with
a reward, for I had several applicants within two
days after my advertisement appeared in the paper.
Within two weeks my boarding-house was well established, I became very successful, and my success
would have been uninterrupted had it not been for
the mysterious and bewildering occurrences which
I am about to relate. I am now forced to leave the
house and rent another. Some of my old boarders
accompany me, some, with the most unreasonable
nervousness, refuse to be longer associated in any
way, however indirectly, with the terrible and uncanny happenings which I have to relate. It remains
to be seen whether my ill luck in this house will
follow me into another, and whether my whole pros-

perity in life will be forever shadowed by the Mystery of the Hall Bedroom. Instead of telling the strange story myself in my own words, I shall present the Journal of Mr. George H. Wheatcroft. I shall show you the portions beginning on January 18 of the present year, the date when he took up his residence with me. Here it is:

"January 18, 1883. Here I am established in my new boarding-house. I have, as befits my humble means, the hall bedroom, even the hall bedroom on the third floor. I have heard all my life of hall bedrooms, I have seen hall bedrooms, I have been in them, but never until now, when I am actually established in one, did I comprehend what, at once, an ignominious and sternly uncompromising thing a hall bedroom is. It proves the ignominy of the dweller therein. No man at thirty-six (my age) would be domiciled in a hall bedroom, unless he were himself ignominious, at least comparatively speaking. I am proved by this means incontrovertibly to have been left far behind in the race. I see no reason why I should not live in this hall bedroom for the rest of my life, that is, if I have money enough to pay the landlady, and that seems probable, since my small funds are invested as safely as if I were an orphan-ward in charge of a pillar of a sanctuary. After the valuables have been stolen, I have most carefully locked the stable door. I have experienced the revulsion which comes sooner or later to the adventurous soul who experiences nothing but defeat and so-called ill luck. I have swung to the opposite extreme. I have lost in everything—I have lost in love, I have lost in money, I have lost in the struggle for preferment, I have lost in health and strength. I am now settled down in a hall bedroom to live upon my small income, and regain my health by mild potations of the mineral waters here, if possible; if not, to live here without my health—for mine is not a necessarily fatal malady—until Providence shall take me out of my hall bedroom. There is no one place more than another where I care to live. There is not sufficient motive to take me away, even if the mineral waters do not benefit me. So I am here and to stay in the hall bedroom. The landlady is civil, and even kind, as kind as a woman who has to keep her poor womanly eye upon the main chance can be. The struggle for money always injures the fine grain of a woman; she is too fine a thing to do it; she does not by nature belong with the gold grubbers, and it therefore lowers her; she steps from heights to claw and scrape and dig. But she can not help it oftentimes, poor thing, and her deterioration thereby is to be condoned. The landlady is all she can be, taking her strain of adverse circumstances into consideration, and the table is good, even conscientiously so. It looks to me as if she were foolish enough to strive to give the boarders their money's worth, with the due regard for the main chance which is inevitable. However, that is of minor importance to me, since my diet is restricted.

"It is curious what an annoyance a restriction in

diet can be even to a man who has considered himself somewhat indifferent to gastronomic delights. There was to-day a pudding for dinner, which I could not taste without penalty, but which I longed for. It was only because it looked unlike any other pudding that I had ever seen, and assumed a mental and spiritual significance. It seemed to me, whimsically no doubt, as if tasting it might give me a new sensation, and consequently a new outlook. Trivial things may lead to large results: why should I not get a new outlook by means of a pudding? Life here stretches before me most monotonously, and I feel like clutching at alleviations, though paradoxically, since I have settled down with the utmost acquiescence. Still one can not immediately overcome and change radically all one's nature. Now I look at myself critically and search for the keynote to my whole self, and my actions, I have always been conscious of a reaching out, an overweening desire for the new, the untried, for the broadness of further horizons, the seas beyond seas, the thought beyond thought. This characteristic has been the primary cause of all my misfortunes. I have the soul of an explorer, and in nine out of ten cases this leads to destruction. If I had possessed capital and sufficient push, I should have been one of the searchers after the North Pole. I have been an eager student of astronomy. I have studied botany with avidity, and have dreamed of new flora in unexplored parts of the world, and the same with animal life and geology. I longed for riches in order to discover the power and sense of possession of the rich. I longed for love in order to discover the possibilities of the emotions. I longed for all that the mind of man could conceive as desirable for man, not so much for purely selfish ends, as from an insatiable thirst for knowledge of a universal trend. But I have limitations, I do not quite understand of what nature—for what mortal ever did quite understand his own limitations, since a knowledge of them would preclude their existence?—but they have prevented my progress to any extent. Therefore behold me in my hall bedroom, settled at last into a groove of fate so deep that I have lost the sight of even my horizons. Just at present, as I write here, my horizon on the left, that is my physical horizon, is a wall covered with cheap paper. The paper is an indeterminate pattern in white and gilt. There are a few photographs of my own hung about, and on the large wall space beside the bed there is a large oil painting which belongs to my landlady. It has a massive tarnished gold frame, and, curiously enough, the painting itself is rather good. I have no idea who the artist could have been. It is of the conventional landscape type in vogue some fifty years since, the type so fondly reproduced in chromos—the winding river with the little boat occupied by a pair of lovers, the cottage nestled among trees on the right shore, the gentle slope of the hills and the church spire in the background—but still it is well done. It gives me the impression of an artist without the slightest originality of design, but much of technique. But for some inexplicable reason the picture frets me. I find myself gazing at it when I do not wish to do so. It seems to compel my attention like some intent face in the room. I shall ask Mrs. Jennings to have it removed. I will hang in its place some photographs which I have in a trunk.

"January 26. I do not write regularly in my journal. I never did. I see no reason why I should. I see no reason why any one should have the slightest sense of duty in such a matter. Some days I have nothing which interests me sufficiently to write out, some days I feel either too ill or too indolent. For four days I have not written, from a mixture of all three reasons. Now, to-day I both feel like it and I have something to write. Also I am distinctly better than I have been. Perhaps the waters are benefiting me, or the change of air. Or possibly it is something else more subtle. Possibly my mind has seized upon something new, a discovery which causes it to react upon my failing body and serves as a stimulant. All I know is, I feel distinctly better, and am conscious of an acute interest in doing so, which is of late strange to me. I have been rather indifferent, and sometimes have wondered if that were not the cause rather than the result of my state of health. I have been so continually balked that I have settled into a state of inertia. I lean rather comfortably against my obstacles. After all, the worst of the pain always lies in the struggle. Give up and it is rather pleasant than otherwise. If one did not kick, the pricks would not in the least matter. However, for some reason, for the last few days, I seem to have awakened from my state of quiescence. It means future trouble for me, no doubt, but in the meantime I am not sorry. It began with the picture—the large oil painting. I went to Mrs. Jennings about it yesterday, and she, to my surprise —for I thought it a matter that could be easily arranged—objected to having it removed. Her reasons were two; both simple, both sufficient, especially since I, after all, had no very strong desire either way. It seems that the picture does not belong to her. It hung here when she rented the house. She says if it is removed, a very large and unsightly discoloration of the wall-paper will be exposed, and she does not like to ask for new paper. The owner, an old man, is traveling abroad, the agent is curt, and she has only been in the house a very short time. Then it would mean a sad upheaval of my room, which would disturb me. She also says that there is no place in the house where she can store the picture, and there is not a vacant space in another room for one so large. So I let the picture remain. It really, when I came to think of it, was very immaterial after all. But I got my photographs out of my trunk, and I hung them around the large picture. The wall is almost completely covered. I hung them yesterday afternoon, and last night I repeated a strange experience which I have had in some degree every night since I have been here, but was not sure whether it deserved the name of experience, but was not rather one of those dreams in which one dreams one is awake. But last night it came again, and now I know. There is something very singular about this room. I am very much interested. I will write down for future reference the events of last night. Concerning those of the preceding nights since I have slept in this room, I will simply say that they have been of a similar nature, but, as it were, only the preliminary stages, the prologue to what happened last night.

"I am not depending upon the mineral waters here as the one remedy for my malady, which is sometimes of an acute nature, and indeed constantly threatens me with considerable suffering unless by medicine I can keep it in check. I will say that the medicine which I employ is not of the class commonly known as drugs. It is impossible that it can be held responsible for what I am about to transcribe. My mind last night and every night since I have slept in this room was in an absolutely normal state. I take this medicine, prescribed by the specialist in whose charge I was before coming here, regularly every four hours while awake. As I am never a good sleeper, it follows that I am enabled with no inconvenience to take any medicine during the night with the same regularity as during the day. It is my habit, therefore, to place my bottle and spoon where I can put my hand upon them easily without lighting the gas. Since I have been in this room, I have placed the bottle of medicine upon my dresser at the side of the room opposite the bed. I have done this rather than place it nearer, as once I jostled the bottle and spilled most of the contents, and it is not easy for me to replace it, as it is expensive. Therefore I placed it in security on the dresser, and, indeed, that is but three or four steps from my bed, the room being so small. Last night I wakened as usual, and I knew, since I had fallen asleep about eleven, that it must be in the neighborhood of three. I wake with almost clock-like regularity and it is never necessary for me to consult my watch.

"I had slept unusually well and without dreams, and I awoke fully at once, with a feeling of refreshment to which I am not accustomed. I immediately got out of bed and began stepping across the room in the direction of my dresser, on which I had set my medicine-bottle and spoon.

"To my utter amazement, the steps which had hitherto sufficed to take me across my room did not suffice to do so. I advanced several paces, and my outstretched hands touched nothing. I stopped and went on again. I was sure that I was moving in a straight direction, and even if I had not been I knew it was impossible to advance in any direction in my tiny apartment without coming into collision either with a wall or a piece of furniture. I continued to walk falteringly, as I have seen people on the stage: a step, then a long falter, then a sliding step. I kept my hands extended; they touched nothing. I stopped again. I had not the least sentiment of fear or consternation. It was rather the very stupefaction of surprise. 'How is this?' seemed thundering in my ears. 'What is this?'

"The room was perfectly dark. There was nowhere any glimmer, as is usually the case, even in a so-called dark room, from the walls, picture-frames, looking-glass or white objects. It was absolute gloom. The house stood in a quiet part of the town. There were many trees about; the electric street lights were extinguished at midnight; there was no moon and the sky was cloudy. I could not distinguish my one window, which I thought strange, even on such a dark night. Finally I changed my plan of motion and turned, as nearly as I could estimate, at right angles. Now, I thought, I must reach soon, if I kept on, my writing-table underneath the window; or, if I am going in the opposite direction, the hall door. I reached neither. I am telling the unvarnished truth when I say that I began to count my steps and carefully measure my paces after that, and I traversed a space clear of furniture at least twenty feet by thirty—a very large apartment. And as I walked I was conscious that my naked feet were pressing something which gave rise to sensations the like of which I had never experienced before. As nearly as I can express it, it was as if my feet pressed something as elastic as air or water, which was in this case unyielding to my weight. It gave me a curious sensation of buoyancy and stimulation. At the same time this surface, if surface be the right name, which I trod, felt cool to my feet with the coolness of vapor or fluidity, seeming to overlap the soles. Finally I stood still; my surprise was at last merging into a measure of consternation. 'Where am I?' I thought. 'What am I going to do?' Stories that I had heard of travelers being taken from their

beds and conveyed into strange and dangerous places,
Middle Age stories of the Inquisition flashed through
my brain. I knew all the time that for a man who
had gone to bed in a commonplace hall bedroom in a
very commonplace little town such surmises were
highly ridiculous, but it is hard for the human mind
to grasp anything but a human explanation of phe-
nomena. Almost anything seemed then, and seems
now, more rational than an explanation bordering upon
the supernatural, as we understand the supernatural. At last I called, though rather softly, 'What does
this mean?' I said quite aloud, 'Where am I? Who is
here? Who is doing this? I tell you I will have no
such nonsense. Speak, if there is anybody here.' But
all was dead silence. Then suddenly a light flashed
through the open transom of my door. Somebody
had heard me—a man who rooms next door, a decent
kind of man, also here for his health. He turned on
the gas in the hall and called to me. 'What's the
matter?' he asked, in an agitated, trembling voice.
He is a nervous fellow.

"Directly, when the light flashed through my transom, I saw that I was in my familiar hall bedroom.
I could see everything quite distinctly—my tumbled
bed, my writing-table, my dresser, my chair, my little
wash-stand, my clothes hanging on a row of pegs, the
old picture on the wall. The picture gleamed out
with singular distinctness in the light from the transom. The river seemed actually to run and ripple,
and the boat to be gliding with the current. I gazed
fascinated at it, as I replied to the anxious voice:

" 'Nothing is the matter with me,' said I. 'Why?'

" 'I thought I heard you speak,' said the man outside. 'I thought maybe you were sick.'

" 'No,' I called back. 'I am all right. I am trying to find my medicine in the dark, that's all. I can see now you have lighted the gas.'

" 'Nothing is the matter?'

" 'No; sorry I disturbed you. Good-night.'

" 'Good-night.' Then I heard the man's door shut after a minute's pause. He was evidently not quite satisfied. I took a pull at my medicine-bottle, and got into bed. He had left the hall-gas burning. I did not go to sleep again for some time. Just before I did so, some one, probably Mrs. Jennings, came out in the hall and extinguished the gas. This morning when I awoke everything was as usual in my room. I wonder if I shall have any such experience to-night.

"January 27. I shall write in my journal every day until this draws to some definite issue. Last night my strange experience deepened, as something tells me it will continue to do. I retired quite early, at half-past ten. I took the precaution, on retiring, to place beside my bed, on a chair, a box of safety matches, that I might not be in the dilemma of the night before. I took my medicine on retiring; that made me due to wake at half-past two. I had not fallen asleep directly, but had had certainly three hours of sound, dreamless slumber when I awoke. I lay a few minutes hesitating whether or not to strike a safety match and light my way to the dresser, whereon stood my medicine-bottle. I hesitated, not because I had the least sensation of fear, but because of the same shrinking from a nerve shock that leads one at times to dread the plunge into an icy bath. It seemed much easier to me to strike that match and cross my hall bedroom to my dresser, take my dose, then return quietly to my bed, than to risk the chance of floundering about in some unknown limbo either of fancy or reality.

"At last, however, the spirit of adventure, which has always been such a ruling one for me, conquered. I rose. I took the box of safety matches in my hand, and started on, as I conceived, the straight course for my dresser, about five feet across from my bed. As before, I traveled and traveled and did not reach it. I advanced with groping hands extended, setting one foot cautiously before the other, but I touched nothing except the indefinite, unnameable surface which my feet pressed. All of a sudden, though, I became aware of something. One of my senses was saluted, nay, more than that, hailed, with imperiousness, and that was, strangely enough, my sense of smell, but in a hitherto unknown fashion. It seemed as if the odor reached my mentality first. I reversed the usual process, which is, as I understand it, like this: the odor when encountered strikes first the olfactory nerve, which transmits the intelligence to the brain. It is as if, to put it rudely, my nose met a rose, and then the nerve belonging to the sense said to my brain, 'Here is a rose.' This time my brain said, 'Here is a rose,' and my sense then recognized it. I say rose, but it was not a rose, that is, not the fragrance of any rose which I had ever known. It was undoubtedly a flower-odor, and rose came perhaps the nearest to it. My mind realized it first with what seemed a leap of rapture. 'What is this delight?' I asked myself. And then the ravishing fragrance smote my sense. I breathed it in and it seemed to feed my thoughts, satisfying some hitherto unknown hunger. Then I took a step further and another fragrance appeared, which I liken to lilies for lack of something better, and then came violets, then mignonette. I can not describe the experience, but it was a sheer delight, a rapture of sublimated sense. I groped further and further, and always into new waves of fragrance. I seemed to be wading breast-high through flower-beds of Paradise, but all the time I touched nothing with my groping hands. At last a sudden giddiness as of surfeit overcame me. I realized that I might be in some unknown peril. I was distinctly afraid. I struck one of my safety matches, and I was in my hall bedroom, midway between my bed and my dresser. I took my dose of medicine and went to bed, and after a while fell asleep and did not wake till morning.

"January 28. Last night I did not take my usual dose of medicine. In these days of new remedies and mysterious results upon certain organizations, it occurred to me to wonder if possibly the drug might have, after all, something to do with my strange experience.

"I did not take my medicine. I put the bottle as

usual on my dresser, since I feared if I interrupted
further the customary sequence of affairs I might fail
to wake. I placed my box of matches on the chair beside the bed. I fell asleep about quarter past eleven
o'clock, and I waked when the clock was striking two
—a little earlier than my wont. I did not hesitate
this time. I rose at once, took my box of matches
and proceeded as formerly. I walked what seemed a
great space without coming into collision with anything. I kept sniffing for the wonderful fragrances of
the night before, but they did not recur. Instead, I
was suddenly aware that I was tasting something, some
morsel of sweetness hitherto unknown, and, as in the
case of the odor, the usual order seemed reversed, and
it was as if I tasted it first in my mental consciousness.
Then the sweetness rolled under my tongue. I thought
involuntarily of 'Sweeter than honey or the honey-
comb' of the Scripture. I thought of the Old Testa-
ment manna. An ineffable content as of satisfied
hunger seized me. I stepped further, and a new savor
was upon my palate. And so on. It was never cloying,
though of such sharp sweetness that it fairly stung.
It was the merging of a material sense into a spiritual
one. I said to myself, 'I have lived my life and always
have I gone hungry until now.' I could feel my brain
act swiftly under the influence of this heavenly food
as under a stimulant. Then suddenly I repeated the
experience of the night before. I grew dizzy, and an
indefinite fear and shrinking were upon me. I struck
my safety match and was back in my hall bedroom.
I returned to bed, and soon fell asleep. I did not take

my medicine. I am resolved not to do so longer. I am feeling much better.

"January 29. Last night to bed as usual, matches in place; fell asleep about eleven and waked at half-past one. I heard the half-hour strike; I am waking earlier and earlier every night. I had not taken my medicine, though it was on the dresser as usual. I again took my match-box in hand and started to cross the room, and, as always, traversed strange spaces, but this night, as seems fated to be the case every night, my experience was different. Last night I neither smelled nor tasted, but I heard—my Lord, I heard! The first sound of which I was conscious was one like the constantly gathering and receding murmur of a river, and it seemed to come from the wall behind my bed where the old picture hangs. Nothing in nature except a river gives that impression of at once advance and retreat. I could not mistake it. On, ever on, came the swelling murmur of the waves, past and ever past they died in the distance. Then I heard above the murmur of the river a song in an unknown tongue which I recognized as being unknown, yet which I understood; but the understanding was in my brain, with no words of interpretation. The song had to do with me, but with me in unknown futures for which I had no images of comparison in the past; yet a sort of ecstasy as of a prophecy of bliss filled my whole consciousness. The song never ceased, but as I moved on I came into new sound-waves. There was the pealing of bells which might have been made of crystal, and might have summoned to the gates of heaven.

There was music of strange instruments, great harmonies pierced now and then by small whispers as of love, and it all filled me with a certainty of a future of bliss.

"At last I seemed the centre of a mighty orchestra which constantly deepened and increased until I seemed to feel myself being lifted gently but mightily upon the waves of sound as upon the waves of a sea. Then again the terror and the impulse to flee to my own familiar scenes was upon me. I struck my match and was back in my hall bedroom. I do not see how I sleep at all after such wonders, but sleep I do. I slept dreamlessly until daylight this morning.

"January 30. I heard yesterday something with regard to my hall bedroom which affected me strangely. I can not for the life of me say whether it intimidated me, filled me with the horror of the abnormal, or rather roused to a greater degree my spirit of adventure and discovery. I was down at the Cure, and was sitting on the veranda sipping idly my mineral water, when somebody spoke my name. 'Mr. Wheatcroft?' said the voice politely, interrogatively, somewhat apologetically, as if to provide for a possible mistake in my identity. I turned and saw a gentleman whom I recognized at once. I seldom forget names or faces. He was a Mr. Addison whom I had seen considerable of three years ago at a little summer hotel in the mountains. It was one of those passing acquaintances which signify little one way or the other. If never renewed, you have no regret; if renewed, you accept the renewal with no hesitation. It is in every way negative. But just now, in my feeble, friendless state, the sight of a face which beams with pleased remembrance is rather grateful. I felt distinctly glad to see the man. He sat down beside me. He also had a glass of the water. His health, while not as bad as mine, leaves much to be desired.

"Addison had often been in this town before. He had in fact lived here at one time. He had remained at the Cure three years, taking the waters daily. He therefore knows about all there is to be known about the town, which is not very large. He asked me where I was staying, and when I told him the street, rather excitedly inquired the number. When I told him the number, which is 240, he gave a manifest start, and after one sharp glance at me sipped his water in silence for a moment. He had so evidently betrayed some ulterior knowledge with regard to my residence that I questioned him.

" 'What do you know about 240 Pleasant Street?' said I.

" 'Oh, nothing,' he replied, evasively, sipping his water.

"After a little while, however, he inquired, in what he evidently tried to render a casual tone, what room I occupied. 'I once lived a few weeks at 240 Pleasant Street myself,' he said. 'That house always was a boarding-house, I guess.'

" 'It had stood vacant for a term of years before the present occupant rented it, I believe,' I remarked. Then I answered his question. 'I have the hall bedroom on the third floor,' said I. 'The quarters are pretty straitened, but comfortable enough as hall bed-rooms go.'

"But Mr. Addison had showed such unmistakable consternation at my reply that then I persisted in my questioning as to the cause, and at last he yielded and told me what he knew.   He had hesitated both because he shrank from displaying what I might consider an unmanly superstition, and because he did not wish to influence me beyond what the facts of the case warranted.   'Well, I will tell you, Wheatcroft,' he said.   'Briefly all I know is this: When last I heard of 240 Pleasant Street it was not rented because of foul play which was supposed to have taken place there, though nothing was ever proved.   There were two disappearances, and—in each case—of an occupant of the hall bedroom which you now have.   The first disappearance was of a very beautiful girl who had come here for her health and was said to be the victim of a profound melancholy, induced by a love disappointment.   She obtained board at 240 and occupied the hall bedroom about two weeks; then one morning she was gone, having seemingly vanished into thin air.   Her relatives were communicated with; she had not many, nor friends either, poor girl, and a thorough search was made, but the last I knew she had never come to light.   There were two or three arrests, but nothing ever came of them.   Well, that was before my day here, but the second disappearance took place when I was in the house—a fine young fellow who had overworked in college.   He had to pay his own way.   He had taken cold, had the grip, and that and the overwork about

finished him, and he came on here for a month's rest
and recuperation. He had been in that room about
two weeks, a little less, when one morning he wasn't
there. Then there was a great hullabaloo. It seems
that he had let fall some hints to the effect that there
was something queer about the room, but, of course,
the police did not think much of that. They made arrests right and left, but they never found him, and the
arrested were discharged, though some of them are
probably under a cloud of suspicion to this day. Then
the boarding-house was shut up. Six years ago
nobody would have boarded there, much less occupied that hall bedroom, but now I suppose new
people have come in and the story has died out.
I dare say your landlady will not thank me for reviving it.'

"I assured him that it would make no possible difference to me. He looked at me sharply, and asked
bluntly if I had seen anything wrong or unusual about
the room. I replied, guarding myself from falsehood
with a quibble, that I had seen nothing in the least unusual about the room, as indeed I had not, and have
not now, but that may come. I feel that that will
come in due time. Last night I neither saw, nor heard,
nor smelled, nor tasted, but I—felt. Last night, having
started again on my exploration of, God knows what,
I had not advanced a step before I touched something.
My first sensation was one of disappointment. 'It is
the dresser, and I am at the end of it now,' I thought.
But I soon discovered that it was not the old painted
dresser which I touched, but something carved, as

nearly as I could discover with my unskilled finger-tips, with winged things.   There were certainly long keen curves of wings which seemed to overlay an arabesque of fine leaf and flower work.   I do not know what the object was that I touched.   It may have been a chest. I may seem to be exaggerating when I say that it somehow failed or exceeded in some mysterious respect of being the shape of anything I had ever touched. I do not know what the material was.   It was as smooth as ivory, but it did not feel like ivory; there was a singular warmth about it, as if it had stood long in hot sunlight.   I continued, and I encountered other objects I am inclined to think were pieces of furniture of fashions and possibly of uses unknown to me, and about them all was the strange mystery as to shape.   At last I came to what was evidently an open window of large area.   I distinctly felt a soft, warm wind, yet with a crystal freshness, blow on my face. It was not the window of my hall bedroom, that I know.   Looking out, I could see nothing.   I only felt the wind blowing on my face.

"Then suddenly, without any warning, my groping hands to the right and left touched living beings, beings in the likeness of men and women, palpable creatures in palpable attire.   I could feel the soft silken texture of their garments which swept around me, seeming to half infold me in clinging meshes like cobwebs.   I was in a crowd of these people, whatever they were, and whoever they were, but, curiously enough, without seeing one of them I had a strong sense of recognition as I passed among them.

Now and then a hand that I knew closed softly over mine; once an arm passed around me. Then I began to feel myself gently swept on and impelled by this softly moving throng; their floating garments seemed to fairly wind me about, and again a swift terror overcame me. I struck my match, and was back in my hall bedroom. I wonder if I had not better keep my gas burning to-night? I wonder if it be possible that this is going too far? I wonder what became of those other people, the man and the woman who occupied this room? I wonder if I had better not stop where I am?

"January 31. Last night I saw—I saw more than I can describe, more than is lawful to describe. Something which nature has rightly hidden has been revealed to me, but it is not for me to disclose too much of her secret. This much I will say, that doors and windows open into an out-of-doors to which the outdoors which we know is but a vestibule. And there is a river; there is something strange with respect to that picture. There is a river upon which one could sail away. It was flowing silently, for to-night I could only see. I saw that I was right in thinking I recognized some of the people whom I encountered the night before, though some were strange to me. It is true that the girl who disappeared from the hall bedroom was very beautiful. Everything which I saw last night was very beautiful to my one sense that could grasp it. I wonder what it would all be if all my senses together were to grasp it? I wonder if I had better not keep my gas burning to-night? I wonder—"

This finishes the journal which Mr. Wheatcroft left in his hall bedroom. The morning after the last entry he was gone. His friend, Mr. Addison, came here, and a search was made. They even tore down the wall behind the picture, and they did find something rather queer for a house that had been used for boarders, where you would think no room would have been let run to waste. They found another room, a long narrow one, the length of the hall bedroom, but narrower, hardly more than a closet. There was no window, nor door, and all there was in it was a sheet of paper covered with figures, as if somebody had been doing sums. They made a lot of talk about those figures, and they tried to make out that the fifth dimension, whatever that is, was proved, but they said afterward they didn't prove anything. They tried to make out then that somebody had murdered poor Mr. Wheatcroft and hid the body, and they arrested poor Mr. Addison, but they couldn't make out anything against him. They proved he was in the Cure all that night and couldn't have done it. They don't know what became of Mr. Wheatcroft, and now they say two more disappeared from that same room before I rented the house.

The agent came and promised to put the new room they discovered into the hall bedroom and have everything new—papered and painted. He took away the picture; folks hinted there was something queer about that, I don't know what. It looked innocent enough, and I guess he burned it up. He said if I would stay he would arrange it with the owner, who everybody says is a very queer man, so I should not have to pay much if any rent. But I told him I couldn't stay if he was to give me the rent. That I wasn't afraid of anything myself, though I must say I wouldn't want to put anybody in that hall bedroom without telling him all about it; but my boarders would leave, and I knew I couldn't get any more. I told him I would rather have had a regular ghost than what seemed to be a way of going out of the house to nowhere and never coming back again. I moved, and, as I said before, it remains to be seen whether my ill luck follows me to this house or not. Anyway, it has no hall bedroom.

THE DAMNED THING

BY AMBROSE BIERCE

Ambrose Bierce (born in Ohio in 1842) served as a line officer during the Civil War, and, as a newspaper man, has been managing lines and columns ever since. He is the pink of paragraphic drill-masters; however ill-assorted may be the conceits that present themselves, he marshals the awkward squad into very effective uniformity. The column may be motley in array, but it presents a line of satiric points admirable for even brilliancy. Mr. Bierce's fiction is as fantastic as his satire, and similarly consistent in its quality of effectiveness. From its unconventional title to its pseudo-scientific conclusion the present selection holds the reader, sceptic as he remains, hypnotized by its clever art.

THE DAMNED THING

BY AMBROSE BIERCE

I

BY the light of a tallow candle, which had been placed on one end of a rough table, a man was reading something written in a book. It was an old account book, greatly worn; and the writing was not, apparently, very legible, for the man sometimes held the page close to the flame of the candle to get a stronger light upon it. The shadow of the book would then throw into obscurity a half of the room, darkening a number of faces and figures; for besides the reader, eight other men were present. Seven of them sat against the rough log walls, silent and motionless, and, the room being small, not very far from the table. By extending an arm any one of them could have touched the eighth man, who lay on the table, face upward, partly covered by a sheet, his arms at his sides. He was dead.

The man with the book was not reading aloud, and no one spoke; all seemed to be waiting for something to occur; the dead man only was without expectation. From the blank darkness outside came in, through the aperture that served for a window, all the ever unfamiliar noises of night in the wilderness—the long, nameless note of a distant coyote; the stilly pulsing thrill of tireless insects in trees; strange cries of night birds, so different from those of the birds of day; the drone of great blundering beetles, and all that mysterious chorus of small sounds that seem always to have been but half heard when they have suddenly ceased, as if conscious of an indiscretion. But nothing of all this was noted in that company; its members were not overmuch addicted to idle interest in matters of no practical importance; that was obvious in every line of their rugged faces—obvious even in the dim light of the single candle. They were evidently men of the vicinity—farmers and woodmen.

The person reading was a trifle different; one would have said of him that he was of the world, worldly, albeit there was that in his attire which attested a certain fellowship with the organisms of his environment. His coat would hardly have passed muster in San Francisco: his footgear was not of urban origin, and the hat that lay by him on the floor (he was the only one uncovered) was such that if one had considered it · as an article of mere personal adornment he would have missed its meaning. In countenance the man was rather prepossessing, with just a hint of sternness; though that he may have assumed or cultivated, as appropriate to one in authority. For he was a coroner. It was by virtue of his office that he had possession of the book in which he was reading; it had been found among the dead man's effects—in his cabin, where the inquest was now taking place.

When the coroner had finished reading he put the book into his breast pocket. At that moment the door was pushed open and a young man entered. He, clearly, was not of mountain birth and breeding: he was clad as those who dwell in cities. His clothing was dusty, however, as from travel. He had, in fact, been riding hard to attend the inquest.

The coroner nodded; no one else greeted him.

"We have waited for you," said the coroner. "It is necessary to have done with this business to-night."

The young man smiled. "I am sorry to have kept you," he said. "I went away, not to evade your summons, but to post to my newspaper an account of what I suppose I am called back to relate."

The coroner smiled.

"The account that you posted to your newspaper," he said, "differs probably from that which you will give here under oath."

"That," replied the other, rather hotly and with a visible flush, "is as you choose. I used manifold paper and have a copy of what I sent. It was not written as news, for it is incredible, but as fiction. It may go as a part of my testimony under oath."

"But you say it is incredible."

"That is nothing to you, sir, if I also swear that it is true."

The coroner was apparently not greatly affected by the young man's manifest resentment. He was silent for some moments, his eyes upon the floor. The men about the sides of the cabin talked in whispers, but seldom withdrew their gaze from the face of the corpse. Presently the coroner lifted his eyes and said: "We will resume the inquest."

The men removed their hats. The witness was sworn.

"What is your name?" the coroner asked.

"William Harker."

"Age?"

"Twenty-seven."

"You knew the deceased, Hugh Morgan?"

"Yes."

"You were with him when he died?"

"Near him."

"How did that happen—your presence, I mean?"

"I was visiting him at this place to shoot and fish. A part of my purpose, however, was to study him, and his odd, solitary way of life. He seemed a good model for a character in fiction. I sometimes write stories."

"I sometimes read them."

"Thank you."

"Stories in general—not yours."

Some of the jurors laughed. Against a sombre background humor shows high lights. Soldiers in the intervals of battle laugh easily, and a jest in the death chamber conquers by surprise.

"Relate the circumstances of this man's death," said the coroner. "You may use any notes or memoranda that you please."

The witness understood. Pulling a manuscript from his breast pocket he held it near the candle, and turning the leaves until he found the passage that he wanted, began to read.

II

" . . . The sun had hardly risen when we left the house. We were looking for quail, each with a shotgun, but we had only one dog. Morgan said that our best ground was beyond a certain ridge that he pointed out, and we crossed it by a trail through the *chaparral*. On the other side was comparatively level ground, thickly covered with wild oats. As we emerged from the *chaparral*, Morgan was but a few yards in advance. Suddenly, we heard, at a little distance to our right, and partly in front, a noise as of some animal thrashing about in the bushes, which we could see were violently agitated.

" 'We've started a deer,' I said. 'I wish we had brought a rifle.'

"Morgan, who had stopped and was intently watching the agitated *chaparral*, said nothing, but had cocked both barrels of his gun, and was holding it in readiness to aim. I thought him a trifle excited, which surprised me, for he had a reputation for exceptional coolness, even in moments of sudden and imminent peril.

" 'O, come!' I said. 'You are not going to fill up a deer with quail-shot, are you?'

"Still he did not reply; but, catching a sight of his face as he turned it slightly toward me, I was struck by the pallor of it. Then I understood that we had serious business on hand, and my first conjecture was that we had 'jumped' a grizzly. I advanced to Morgan's side, cocking my piece as I moved.

"The bushes were now quiet, and the sounds had ceased, but Morgan was as attentive to the place as before.

" 'What is it? What the devil is it?' I asked.

" 'That Damned Thing!' he replied, without turning his head. His voice was husky and unnatural. He trembled visibly.

"I was about to speak further, when I observed the wild oats near the place of the disturbance moving in the most inexplicable way. I can hardly describe it. It seemed as if stirred by a streak of wind, which not only bent it, but pressed it down—crushed it so that it did not rise, and this movement was slowly prolonging itself directly toward us.

"Nothing that I had ever seen had affected me so strangely as this unfamiliar and unaccountable phenomenon, yet I am unable to recall any sense of fear. I remember—and tell it here because, singularly enough, I recollected it then—that once, in looking carelessly out of an open window, I momentarily mistook a small tree close at hand for one of a group of larger trees at a little distance away. It looked the same size as the others, but, being more distinctly and sharply defined in mass and detail, seemed out of harmony with them. It was a mere falsification of the law of aerial perspective, but it startled, almost terrified me. We so rely upon the orderly operation of familiar natural laws that any seeming suspension of them is noted as a menace to our safety, a warning of unthinkable calamity. So now the apparently causeless movement of the herbage, and the slow, undeviating approach of the line of disturbance were distinctly disquieting. My companion appeared actually frightened, and I could hardly credit my senses when I saw him suddenly throw his gun to his shoulders and fire both barrels at the agitated grass! Before the smoke of the discharge had cleared away I heard a loud savage cry—a scream like that of a wild animal—and, flinging his gun upon the ground, Morgan sprang away and ran swiftly from the spot. At the same instant I was thrown violently to the ground by the impact of something unseen in the smoke—some soft, heavy substance that seemed thrown against me with great force.

"Before I could get upon my feet and recover my gun, which seemed to have been struck from my hands, I heard Morgan crying out as if in mortal agony, and mingling with his cries were such hoarse, savage sounds as one hears from fighting dogs. Inexpressibly terrified, I struggled to my feet and looked in the direction of Morgan's retreat; and may heaven in mercy spare me from another sight like that! At a distance of less than thirty yards was my friend, down upon one knee, his head thrown back at a frightful angle, hatless, his long hair in disorder and his whole body in violent movement from side to side, backward and forward. His right arm was lifted and seemed to lack the hand—at least, I could see none. The other arm was invisible. At times, as my memory now reports this extraordinary scene, I could discern but a part of his body; it was as if he had been partly blotted out—I can not otherwise express it—then a shifting of his position would bring it all into view again.

"All this must have occurred within a few seconds, yet in that time Morgan assumed all the postures of a determined wrestler vanquished by superior weight and strength. I saw nothing but him, and him not always distinctly. During the entire incident his shouts and curses were heard, as if through an enveloping uproar of such sounds of rage and fury as I had never heard from the throat of man or brute!

"For a moment only I stood irresolute, then, throwing down my gun, I ran forward to my friend's assistance. I had a vague belief that he was suffering from a fit or some form of convulsion. Before I could reach his side he was down and quiet. All sounds had ceased, but, with a feeling of such terror as even these awful events had not inspired, I now saw the same mysterious movement of the wild oats prolonging itself from the trampled area about the prostrate man toward the edge of a wood. It was only when it had reached the wood that I was able to withdraw my eyes and look at my companion. He was dead."

III

The coroner rose from his seat and stood beside the dead man. Lifting an edge of the sheet he pulled it away, exposing the entire body, altogether naked and showing in the candle light a clay-like yellow. It had, however, broad maculations of bluish-black, obviously caused by extravasated blood from contusions. The chest and sides looked as if they had been beaten with a bludgeon. There were dreadful lacerations; the skin was torn in strips and shreds.

The coroner moved round to the end of the table and undid a silk handkerchief, which had been passed under the chin and knotted on the top of the head. When the handkerchief was drawn away it exposed what had been the throat. Some of the jurors who had risen to get a better view repented their curiosity, and turned away their faces. Witness Harker went to the open window and leaned out across the sill, faint and sick. Dropping the handkerchief upon the dead man's neck, the coroner stepped to an angle of the room, and from a pile of clothing produced one garment after another, each of which he held up a moment for inspection. All were torn, and stiff with blood. The jurors did not make a closer inspection. They seemed rather uninterested. They had, in truth, seen all this before; the only thing that was new to them being Harker's testimony.

"Gentlemen," the coroner said, "we have no more evidence, I think. Your duty has been already explained to you; if there is nothing you wish to ask you may go outside and consider your verdict."

The foreman rose—a tall, bearded man of sixty, coarsely clad.

"I should like to ask one question, Mr. Coroner," he said. "What asylum did this yer last witness escape from?"

"Mr. Harker," said the coroner, gravely and tranquilly, "from what asylum did you last escape?"

Harker flushed crimson again, but said nothing, and the seven jurors rose and solemnly filed out of the cabin.

"If you have done insulting me, sir," said Harker, as soon as he and the officer were left alone with the dead man, "I suppose I am at liberty to go?"

"Yes."

Harker started to leave, but paused, with his hand on the door latch. The habit of his profession was strong in him—stronger than his sense of personal dignity. He turned about and said:

"The book that you have there—I recognize it as Morgan's diary. You seemed greatly interested in it; you read in it while I was testifying. May I see it? The public would like—"

"The book will cut no figure in this matter," replied the official, slipping it into his coat pocket; "all the entries in it were made before the writer's death."

As Harker passed out of the house the jury re-entered and stood about the table, on which the now covered corpse showed under the sheet with sharp definition. The foreman seated himself near the candle, produced from his breast pocket a pencil and scrap of paper, and wrote rather laboriously the following verdict, which with various degrees of effort all signed:

"We, the jury, do find that the remains come to their death at the hands of a mountain lion, but some of us thinks, all the same, they had fits."

IV

In the diary of the late Hugh Morgan are certain interesting entries having, possibly, a scientific value as suggestions. At the inquest upon his body the book was not put in evidence; possibly the coroner thought it not worth while to confuse the jury. The date of the first of the entries mentioned can not be ascertained; the upper part of the leaf is torn away; the part of the entry remaining is as follows:

" . . . would run in a half circle, keeping his head turned always toward the centre and again he would stand still, barking furiously. At last he ran away into the brush as fast as he could go. I thought at first that he had gone mad, but on returning to the house found no other alteration in his manner than what was obviously due to fear of punishment.

"Can a dog see with his nose? Do odors impress some olfactory centre with images of the thing emitting them? . . .

"Sept. 2.—Looking at the stars last night as they rose above the crest of the ridge east of the house, I observed them successively disappear—from left to right. Each was eclipsed but an instant, and only a few at the same time, but along the entire length of the ridge all that were within a degree or two of the crest were blotted out. It was as if something had passed along between me and them; but I could not see it, and the stars were not thick enough to define its outline. Ugh! I don't like this. . . ."

Several weeks' entries are missing, three leaves being torn from the book.

"Sept. 27.—It has been about here again—I find evidences of its presence every day. I watched again all of last night in the same cover, gun in hand, double-charged with buckshot. In the morning the fresh foot-prints were there, as before. Yet I would have sworn that I did not sleep—indeed, I hardly sleep at all. It is terrible, insupportable! If these amazing experiences are real I shall go mad; if they are fanciful I am mad already.

"Oct. 3.—I shall not go—it shall not drive me away. No, this is *my* house, *my* land. God hates a coward. . . .

"Oct. 5.—I can stand it no longer; I have invited Harker to pass a few weeks with me—he has a level head. I can judge from his manner if he thinks me mad.

"Oct. 7.—I have the solution of the problem; it came to me last night—suddenly, as by revelation. How simple—how terribly simple!

"There are sounds that we can not hear. At either end of the scale are notes that stir no chord of that imperfect instrument, the human ear. They are too high or too grave. I have observed a flock of blackbirds occupying an entire treetop—the tops of several trees —and all in full song. Suddenly—in a moment—at absolutely the same instant—all spring into the air and fly away. How? They could not all see one another —whole treetops intervened. At no point could a leader have been visible to all. There must have been a signal of warning or command, high and shrill above the din, but by me unheard. I have observed, too, the same simultaneous flight when all were silent, among not only blackbirds, but other birds—quail, for example, widely separated by bushes—even on opposite sides of a hill.

"It is known to seamen that a school of whales

basking or sporting on the surface of the ocean, miles apart, with the convexity of the earth between them, will sometimes dive at the same instant—all gone out of sight in a moment. The signal has been sounded— too grave for the ear of the sailor at the masthead and his comrades on the deck—who nevertheless feel its vibrations in the ship as the stones of a cathedral are stirred by the bass of the organ.

"As with sounds, so with colors. At each end of the solar spectrum the chemist can detect the presence of what are known as 'actinic' rays. They represent colors—integral colors in the composition of light— which we are unable to discern. The human eye is an imperfect instrument; its range is but a few octaves of the real 'chromatic scale.' I am not mad; there are colors that we can not see.

"And, God help me! the Damned Thing is of such a color!"

THE NEXT CORNER

BY GUY WETMORE CARRYL

Guy Wetmore Carryl (born in New York, March 4, 1873; died 1904) during his brief literary career made his name very familiar to readers of light literature by his many clever contributions to the leading magazines. In the last year of his life three books of his appeared of a distinctly higher order than his previous work. These are "The Lieutenant-Governor," "The Transgression of Andrew Vane," and "Zut and Other Parisians," from which last book the present selection has been taken.

THE NEXT CORNER

BY GUY WETMORE CARRYL

ANTHONY CAZEBY was a man whom the disposition, sufficient ready money, and a felicitous combination of an adventurous magnificent constitution had introduced to many and various sensations, but he was conscious that, so far as intensity went, no one of them all had approached for a moment that with which he emerged from the doorway of the Automobile Club, and, winking at the sting of the keen winter air, looked out across the place de la Concorde, with its globes of light, swung, like huge pearls on invisible strings, across the haze of the January midnight. He paused for a moment, as if he would allow his faculties to obtain a full and final grasp of his situation, and motioned aside the trim little club chasseur who stood before him, with one cotton-gloved hand stretched out expectantly for a supposititious carriage-check.

"Va, mon petit, je vais à pied!"

Afoot! Cazeby smiled to himself at the tone of sudden caprice which rang in his voice, and, turning his fur collar high up about his ears, swung off rapidly toward the Cours la Reine. After all, the avenue d'Eylau was only an agreeable stroll's length distant. Why not go home afoot? But then, on the other

hand, why go home at all? As this thought leaped
suddenly at Cazeby's throat out of the void of the
great unpremeditated, he caught his breath, stopped
suddenly in the middle of the driveway, and then went
on more slowly, thinking hard.

It had been that *rarissima avis* of social life, even
in Paris, a perfect dinner. Cazeby had found himself
wondering, at more than one stage of its smooth and
imposing progress, how the Flints could afford to do
it. But on each recurrence of the thought he dis-
missed it with a little frown of vexation. If there
was one thing more than another upon which Cazeby
prided himself, it was originality of thought, word,
and deed, and he was annoyed to find himself, even
momentarily, on a mental level with the gossips of the
American and English colonies, whose time is equally
divided between wondering how the Choses can afford to do what they do, and why the Machins can
not afford to do what they leave undone.

People had said many things of Hartley Flint, and
still more of his wife, but no one had ever had the
ignorance or the perversity to accuse them of ineffi-
ciency in the matter of a dinner. Moreover, on this
particular occasion, they were returning the hospitality of the Baroness Klemftt, who had, at the close
of the Exposition, impressed into her service the chef
of the Roumanian restaurant, and whose dinners
were, in consequence, the wonder and despair of four
foreign colonies. After her latest exploit Hartley
Flint had remarked to his wife that it was "up to them
to make good," which, being interpreted, was to say

that it was at once his duty and his intention to repay the Baroness in her own sterling coin. The fact that the men of the party afterward commended Hartley's choice of wines, and that the women expressed the opinion that "Kate Flint looked *really* pretty!" would seem to be proof positive that the operation of "making good" had been an unqualified success.

Now, Cazeby was wondering whether he had actually enjoyed it all. Under the circumstances it seemed to him incredible, and yet he could not recall a qualm of uneasiness from the moment when the maître d'hôtel had thrown open the doors of the private dining room, until the Baroness had smiled at her hostess out of a cloud of old Valenciennes, and said, "Now there are *two* of us who give impeccable dinners, Madame Flint." Even now, even facing his last ditch, Cazeby was conscious of a little thrill of self-satisfaction. He had said the score of clever things which each of his many hostesses expected of him, and had told with great effect his story of the little German florist, which had grown, that season, under the persuasive encouragement of society's applause, from a brief anecdote into a veritable achievement of Teutonic dialect. Also, he had worn a forty-franc orchid, and had left it in his coffee-cup because it had begun to wilt. In brief, he had been Anthony Cazeby at his extraordinary best, a mixture of brilliancy and eccentricity, without which, as Mrs. Flint was wont to say, no dinner was complete.

But the sublime and the ridiculous are not the only contrasting conditions that lie no further than a step apart, and Cazeby was painfully conscious of having, in the past five minutes, crossed the short interval which divides gay from grave. Reduced to its lowest terms, his situation lay in his words to the little chasseur. With the odor of the rarest orchid to be found in Vaillant-Rozeau's whole establishment yet clinging to his lapel, Anthony Cazeby was going home on foot because the fare from the Concorde to the avenue d'Eylau was one franc fifty, and one franc fifty precisely ninety centimes more than he possessed in the world. For a moment he straightened himself, threw back his head, and looked up at the dull saffron of the low-hanging sky, in an attempt to realize this astounding fact, and then went back to his thinking.

Well, it was not surprising. The life of a popular young diplomat with extravagant tastes is not conducive to economy, and the forty thousand dollars which had come to Cazeby at the beginning of his twenty-eighth year had proved but a bad second-best in the struggle with Parisian gayety. His bibelots, his servants, Auteuil, Longchamp, his baccarat at the Prince de Tréville's, a dancer at the Folies-Marigny, Monte Carlo, Aix, Trouville—they had all had their share, and now the piper was waiting to be paid and the exchequer was empty. It was an old story. Other men of his acquaintance had done the same, but they had had some final resource. The trouble was, as Cazeby had already noted, that, in his case, the final resource was not, as in theirs, pecuniary. Quite on the contrary, it was a tidy little weapon, of Smith and Wesson make, which lay in the upper right-hand

drawer of his marqueterie desk. He had looked long at
it that same afternoon, with all his worldly wealth, in
the shape of forty-two francs sixty, spread out beside
it. That was before he had taken a fiacre to Vaillant-
Rozeau's.

At the very moment when Cazeby was contemplat-
ing these doubtful assets, a grim old gentleman was
seated at another desk, three thousand miles away,
engaged upon a calculation of the monthly profits
derived from a wholesale leather business. But
Cazeby père was one of the hopeless persons who believe in economy. He was of the perverted opinion
that money hardly come by should be thoughtfully
spent, or, preferably, invested in government bonds,
and he had violent prejudices against "industrials,"
games of chance, and young men who preferred the
gayety of a foreign capital to the atmosphere of "the
Swamp." Also he was very rich. But Anthony had
long since ceased to regard his father as anything
more than a chance relation. He could have told
what would be the result of a frank confession of his
extremity as accurately as if the avowal had been
already made. There would have been some brief
reference to the sowing of oats and their reaping, to
the making of a metaphorical bed and the inevitable
occupancy thereof, and to other proverbial illustra-
tions which, in a financial sense, are more ornamental
than useful—and nothing more. The essential spark
of sympathy had been lacking between these two since
the moment when the most eminent physician in New
York had said, "It is a boy, sir—but—we can not

hope to save the mother." The fault may have lain on the one side, or the other, or on both, or on neither; but certain it is that to Anthony's imagination Cazeby senior had never appealed in the light of a final resource.

Somehow, in none of his calculations had the idea of invoking assistance ever played a part. Naturally, as a reasoning being, he had foreseen the present crisis for some months, but at the time when the inevitable catastrophe first became clear to him it was already too late to regain his balance, since the remainder of his inheritance was so pitifully small that any idea of retrieving his fortunes through its instrumentality was simply farcical. The swirl of the rapids, as he had then told himself, had already caught his boat. All that was left to do was to go straight on to the sheer of the fall, with his pennant flying and himself singing at the helm. Then, on the brink, a well-placed bullet—no bungling for Anthony Cazeby!—and the next day people would be talking of the shocking accident which had killed him in the act of cleaning his revolver, and saying the usual things about a young man with a brilliant future before him and everything in life for which to live.

And this plan he had carried out in every detail— save the last, to which he was now come; and his was the satisfying conviction that not one of the brilliant, careless men and women among whom he lived and moved and had his being suspected for a moment that the actual circumstances differed in the least from the outward appearances. He thought it all over care-

fully now, and there was no play in the entire game
that he felt he would have liked to have changed.

Sentiment had no part in the make-up of Anthony
Cazeby. Lacking from early childhood the common
ties of home affection, and by training and profession
a diplomat, he added to a naturally undemonstrative
nature the non-committal suavity of official poise.
But that was not all. He had never been known to
be ill at ease. This was something which gained him
a reputation for studious self-control. As a matter of
fact it was due to nothing of the sort. No one had
ever come fairly at the root of his character except
Cazeby père, who once said, in a fit of passion, "You
don't care a brass cent, sir, whether you live and are
made President of the United States, or die and are
eternally damned!" And that was exactly the point.

Something of all this had passed through Cazeby's
mind, when he was suddenly aroused to an appreciation of his whereabouts by the sound of a voice, to
find that the curious instinct of direction which under-
lies advanced inebriety and profound preoccupation
alike had led him up the avenue du Trocadéro, and
across the place, and that he had already advanced
some little way along the avenue d'Eylau in the direction of his apartment. The street was dimly
lighted, but, just behind him, the windows of a tiny
wine-shop gave out a subdued glow, and from within
came the sound of a violin. Then Cazeby's attention
came around to the owner of the voice. This was
a youngish man of medium stature, in the familiar
street dress of a French laborer, jacket and waist-

coat of dull blue velveteen, peg-top trousers of heavy corduroy, a crimson knot at his throat, and a dark Tam o' Shanter pulled low over one ear. As their eyes met, he apparently saw that Cazeby had not heard his first remark, and so repeated it.

"I have need of a drink!"

There was nothing of the beggar in his tone or manner. Both were threatening, rather; and, as soon as he had spoken, he thrust his lower jaw forward, in the fashion common to the thug of any and every nationality when the next move is like to be a blow. But, for once, these manifestations of hostility failed signally of effect. Cazeby was the last person in the world to select as the object of sudden attack, with the idea that panic would make him easy prey. In his present state of mind he went further than preserving his equanimity: he was even faintly amused. It was not that he did not comprehend the other's purpose, but, to his way of thinking, there was something distinctly humorous in the idea of holding up a man with only sixty centimes to his name, and menacing him with injury, when he himself was on his way to the upper right-hand drawer of the marqueterie desk.

"I have need of a drink," repeated the other, coming a step nearer. "Thou art not deaf, at least?"

"No," said Cazeby, pleasantly, "no, I am not deaf, and I, too, have need of a drink. Shall we take it together?" And, without waiting for a reply, he turned and stepped through the doorway of the little wineshop. The Frenchman hesitated, shrugged his shoulders with an air of complete bewilderment, and, after an instant, also entered the shop and placed himself at the small table where Cazeby was already seated.

"A vitriol for me," he said.

Cazeby had not passed three years in Paris for nothing. He received this remarkable request with the unconcern of one to whom the slang of the exterior boulevards is sufficiently familiar, and, as the proprietor leaned across the nickeled slab of his narrow counter with an air of interrogation, duplicated his companion's order.

"*Deux vitriols!*"

The proprietor, vouchsafing the phrase a grin of appreciation, lumbered heavily around to the table, filled two small glasses from a bottle of cheap cognac, and stood awaiting payment, hands on hips.

"*Di-ze sous,*" he said.

There was no need to search for the exact amount. Cazeby spun his fifty-centime piece upon the marble, added his remaining two sous by way of *pourboire,* and disposed of the brandy at a gulp.

"Have you also need of a cigarette?" he inquired, politely, tendering the other his case.

For some minutes, as they smoked, the diplomat and the vagabond took stock of each other in silence. In many ways they were singularly alike. There was in both the same irony of lip line, the same fair chiseling of chin and nostril and brow, the same weariness of eye. The difference was one of dress and bearing alone, and, in those first moments of mutual analysis, Cazeby realized that there was about this street-lounger a vague air of the gentleman, a subtle suggestion of good birth and breeding, which even his slouching manner and coarse speech were not wholly able to conceal; and his guest was conscious that in Cazeby he had to deal with no mere society puppet, but with one in whom the limitations of position had never wholly subdued the devil-may-care instincts of the vagabond. The one was a finished model of a man of the world, the other a caricature, but the clay was the same.

"I am also hungry," said the latter suddenly.

"In that respect," responded Cazeby, in the same tone of even politeness, "I am, unfortunately, unable to assist you, unless you will accept the hospitality of my apartment. It is but a step, and I am rather an expert on bacon and eggs. Also," he added, falling into the idiom of the faubourgs, "there is a means there of remedying the dryness of the sponge in one's throat. My name is Antoine."

"I am Bibi-la-Raie," said the other shortly. Then he continued, with instinctive suspicion, "It is a strange fashion thou hast of introducing a type to these gentlemen."

"As a matter of fact," said Cazeby, "I do not live over a poste. But whether or not you will come is something for you to decide. It is less trouble to cook eggs for one than for two."

Bibi-la-Raie reflected briefly. Finally he had recourse to his characteristic shrug.

"After all, what difference?" he said. "As well now as another time. I follow thee!"

The strangely assorted companions entered Cazeby's

apartment as the clock was striking one, and pressure of an electric button, flooding the salon with light, revealed a little tea-table furnished with cigarettes and cigars, decanters of Scotch whiskey and liqueurs, and Venetian goblets of oddly tinted glass. Cazeby shot a swift glance at his guest as this array sprang into view, and was curiously content to observe that he manifested no surprise. Bibi-la-Raie had flung himself into a great leather chair with an air of being entirely at ease.

"Not bad, thy little box," he observed. "Is it permitted?"

He indicated the table with a nod.

"Assuredly," said Cazeby. "Do as if you were at home. I shall be but a moment with the supper."

When he returned from the kitchen, bearing a smoking dish of bacon and eggs, butter, rye bread, and Swiss cheese, Bibi-la-Raie was standing in rapt contemplation before an etching of the "Last Judgment."

"What a genius, this animal of a Michel Ange!" he said.

"Rather deft at times," replied Cazeby, arranging the dishes on the larger table.

"*Je te crois!*" said Bibi, enthusiastically. "Without him—what? Evidently, it was not Léon Treize who built Saint Pierre!"

The eggs had been peculiarly obstinate, as it happened, and a growing irritability had taken possession of Anthony. As they ate in silence, the full force of his tragic position returned to him. Even the unwontedness of his chance encounter with Bibi-la-Raie

had not wholly dispelled the cloud that had been gradually settling around him since he emerged from the
Automobile Club, and, as they finished the little repast,
he turned suddenly upon his guest, in a burst of
irritation.

"Who are you?" he said. "And what does all this
mean? Was I mistaken, when you first spoke to me,
in thinking you a mere *voyou?* Surely not! You
meant to rob me. You speak the argot of the forti-
fications. Yet here I find you discoursing on Michel
Angelo as though you were the conservateur of the
Uffizzi! What am I to think?"

Bibi-la-Raie lighted another cigarette, blew forth
the smoke in a thin, gray wisp, and thrust his thumbs
into the armholes of his velveteen waistcoat.

"And *you,*" he said, slowly, abandoning the familiar address he had been using, "who are *you?* No,
you were not mistaken in thinking I meant to rob you.
Such is my profession. But does a gentleman reply,
in ordinary, to the summons of a thief by paying that
thief a drink? Does he invite him to his apartment
and cook a supper for him? What am *I* to think?"

There was a brief pause, and then he faced his host
squarely.

"Are you absolutely resolved to put an end to it all
to-night?" he demanded.

Cazeby made a small sign of bewilderment.

"*Ah, mon vieux,*" continued the other. "That, you
know, is of no use with me. You ask me who I am.
For one thing, I am one who has lived too long in
touch with desperate men not to know the look in the

eyes when the end has come. You think you are going to blow out your brains to-night."

"Your wits are wandering; that's all," said Cazeby, compassionately.

"Oh, far from it!" said Bibi-la-Raie, with a short laugh. "But one does not fondle one's revolver in the daytime without a good reason, nor does one leave it *on top* of letters postmarked this morning unless one has been fondling it—*quoi?*"

Cazeby was at the marqueterie desk in two strides, tugging at the upper right-hand drawer. It was locked. He turned about slowly, and, half seating himself on the edge of the desk, surveyed his guest coolly.

"The revolver is in your pocket," he said.

"No," answered Bibi, with an air of cheerfulness. "I have one of my own. But the key is."

"Why?" said Cazeby.

Bibi helped himself to yellow chartreuse, and appeared to reflect.

"I am not sure that I know why, myself," he said finally. "Perhaps, because you have done me a kindness and I would not like to have you burn your fingers in a moment of absent-mindedness. Perhaps, because we might disagree, and I should not care to take the chance of your shooting first!"

He squinted at the liqueur, swallowed it slowly and with extreme appreciation, smacked his lips, and then, cocking his feet up on Cazeby's brass club fender, began to smoke again, staring into the dwindling fire. His host watched him in silence, until he should be ready to speak, which he presently began to do, with his cigarette drooping from the corner of his mouth and moving in time to his words. He had suddenly and curiously become a man of the world—of the grand monde—and his speech had shaken off all trace of slang, and was tinged instead with the faint club sarcasm which one hears in the glass card-room of the Volney or over coffee on the roof of the Automobile. Moreover, it was beautiful French. Not Mounet himself could have done better.

"The only man to whom one should confide personal secrets," said Bibi-la-Raie, "is he whom one has never seen before and will, as is probable, never see again. I could tell you many things, Monsieur Cazeby, since that is your name—I have seen your morning's mail, you know!—but, for the moment, let it suffice to say that the *voyou* who accosted you this evening is of birth as good as yours—pardon, but probably better! *Wein, weib, und gesang*—you know the saying. Add cards and the race-course, and you have, complete, the short ladder of five rungs down which I have been successful in climbing. I shall presume to the extent of supposing that you have just accomplished the same descent. One learns much thereby, but more after one has reached the ground. In many ways I am afraid experience has made me cynical, but in one it has taught me optimism. I have found, and I think I shall continue to find, that there is always something worth looking into around the next corner of even the darkest street. The rue des Sablons, for instance. It was very dark to-night, very damp, and very cold. Assuredly, as I turned into the avenue d'Eylau I had no reason to foresee a supper, Russian cigarettes, and *chartreuse jaune*. And yet, *me viola!* Now what most of us lack—what you, in particular, seem to lack, Monsieur Cazeby—is the tenacity needful if one is to get to that next turning."

"There are streets darker than the rue des Sablons," put in Anthony, falling in with the other's whimsical humor, "and that have no turning."

"You speak from conjecture, not experience," said Bibi-la-Raie. "You can never have seen one."

He glanced about the room, with the air of one making a mental inventory.

"First," he added, "there come the pawnshop, the exterior boulevards, the somewhat insufficient shelter of the Pont Royal. No, you have not come to the last corner."

"All that," said Cazeby, "is simply a matter of philosophy. Each of us has his own idea of what makes life worth the while. When that is no longer procurable, then that is the last corner."

"For instance—"

"For instance, my own case. You have analyzed my situation sufficiently well—though when you said I was about to blow out my brains—"

"It was a mere guess," interrupted Bibi, "founded on circumstantial evidence. Then I *thought* so. Now I *know* it."

"Let us grant you are right," continued Cazeby, with a smile. "I have my own conception of what I require to make existence tolerable. It includes this apartment, or its equivalent, a horse, two servants, two clubs, and a sufficient income to dress, eat, entertain, and amuse myself in the manner of my class— an extravagant and unreasonable standard, if you will, but such is my conviction. Now, granted that the moment has come when it is no longer possible for me to have these things, and when there is no prospect of my situation being bettered, I can not conceive what advantage there can be in continuing to live."

"I perceive you are a philosopher," said the other. "How about the religious view?"

Cazeby shrugged his shoulders.

"As to that," he said, "my religious views are, so far as I know, stored away in the little church which I was forced to attend three times on every Sunday of my boyhood. They did not come out with me on the last occasion, and I have never met them since."

"Excellent!" said Bibi. "It is the same with me. But I think you are mistaken in your conviction of what makes life worth living. I had my own delusions in the time. But I have had a deal of schooling since then. There are many things as amusing as luxury—even on the exterior boulevards. Of course, actual experience is essential. One never knows what one would do under given conditions."

He turned suddenly, and looked Cazeby in the eye.

"What, for example, would you do if you were in my place?" he asked.

"As you say, one never knows," said his host. "I *think* that, in your place, I should improve the opportunity you find open, and carry out your late and laudable intention of robbing Monsieur Antoine Cazeby. I may be influenced by my knowledge that such a proceeding would not irritate or incommode him in the least, but that is what I think I should do.

"I shall not need these things to-morrow," he added, indicating his surroundings with a gesture. "You were quite right about the pistol. As to your prospective booty, I regret to say that I spent my last sixty centimes on our cognac, but there is a remarkably fine scarfpin on the table in my dressing-room."

"A sapphire, surrounded by black pearls," put in the other. "You were rather long in cooking those eggs."

"A sapphire, surrounded by black pearls," agreed Cazeby. "Yes, upon reflection, I am quite sure that that is what I should do."

Bibi-la-Raie smiled pleasantly.

"I am glad to find we are of one mind," he said. "Of course, mine was made up, but it is more agreeable to know that I am causing you no inconvenience. I suppose it is unnecessary to add that resistance will be quite useless. I have the only available revolver, and, moreover, I propose to tie you into this extremely comfortable chair. It is not," he added, "that I do not trust you, although our acquaintance is, unfortunately, too recent to inspire complete confidence. No, I have my convictions as well as you, Monsieur Cazeby, and one of them, curiously enough, is that, in spite of appearances, I am doing you a kindness in putting it out of your power, for to-night at least, to do yourself an injury. Who knows? Perhaps, in the morn-

ing, you may find that there is something around the
next corner, after all.   If not, there is no harm done.
Your servants come in early?"

"At seven o'clock," said Anthony, briefly.

"Exactly.   And I will leave the key in the drawer."
Bibi was expeditious.   When he had bound Cazeby
firmly, and with an art that showed practice, he disappeared into the dressing-room, returning in less than
a minute with the sapphire scarfpin and several other
articles of jewelry in his hand.

"I should like to add to these," he said, going to
the bookcase, "this little copy of Omar Khayyám.   He
is a favorite of mine.   There is something about his
philosophy which seems to accord with our own.   But
—'the bird of time has but a little way to flutter' "—
He paused at the door.

"Can I do anything for you before I go?" he
inquired politely.

"Be good enough to turn off the light," said the
other.   "The button is on the right of the door."

"Good-night," said Bibi-le-Raie.

"Good-night—brother!" said Cazeby.

Then he heard the door of the apartment close
softly.

Anthony was awakened from a restless sleep by the
sound of its opening.   Through the gap between the
window draperies the gray light of the winter morning was creeping in.   His wrists and ankles were ach-
ing from the pressure of the curtain cords with which
he had been bound, and he was gratified when, after
a brief interval, the salon door was opened in its turn

and the invaluable Jules came in, in shirt-sleeves and long white apron, carrying a handful of letters.

That impassive person was probably never nearer to being visibly surprised. For a breath he stopped, and the pupils of his round eyes dilated like those of a cat in a dim light. But his training stood him in good stead, and when he spoke his voice was as innocent of emotion as if he had been announcing dinner.

"Monsieur desires to be untied?"

Left to himself, Cazeby turned his attention to his letters, and from the top of the pile picked up a cablegram. He was still reflecting upon the singular experience of the night, in an attempt to analyze his present emotions. Was he in any whit changed by his enforced reprieve? He was glad to think not. Above all minor faults he abhorred vacillation of purpose. No, his situation and his purpose remained unaltered. But he was conscious, nevertheless, of an unwonted thrill at the thought that, but for the merest chance, it would have been for others to open the envelope he was even now fingering. Jules would already have found him—he wondered, with the shadow of a smile, whether Jules would still have been unsurprised!—and would have brought up the concierge and the police—

Suddenly the cable message jumped at him through his revery as if, at that moment, the words had been instantaneously printed on what was before blank paper, and he realized that it was from his father's solicitor:

"Mr. Cazeby died eight o'clock this evening after making will your favor whole property. Waiting instructions.
"MILLIKEN."

Anthony straightened himself with a long sigh, and, putting aside the curtain, looked out across the mansards, wet and gleaming under a thin rain. His hand trembled a little on the heavy velvet, and he frowned at it, and, going across to the table, poured himself out a swallow of brandy.

With the glass at his lips he paused, his eyes upon the chair where Bibi-la-Raie had sat and wherein he himself had passed five hours. Then, very ceremoniously, he bowed and dipped his glass toward an imaginary occupant.

"Merci, Monsieur!" he said.

THE PHONOGRAPH AND THE GRAFT

BY O. HENRY

*Sidney Porter (born about 1865 in the
State of Texas) has had a strange and
varied career befitting the picaresque hu-
morist that he is. He has tried his facile
hand at all sorts of incongruous employ-
ments, and poked his investigating nose
into many strange corners of the continent.
He has been cowboy, sheep-herder, merchant,
miner, druggist; and has traveled, note-
book in hand, throughout Latin America,
chiefly the Central American military autoc-
racies miscalled republics. "The Phonograph and the Graft" deals humorously,
but nevertheless significantly, with official
corruption in one of these last-named coun-
tries. Hitherto he has successfully hidden his
identity under the pen-name of "O. Henry,"*

THE PHONOGRAPH AND
THE GRAFT

BY O. HENRY

I LOOKED in at the engine-room of the Bloom-field-Cater Mfg. Co. (Ltd.), for the engineer was Kirksy, and there was a golden half-hour between the time he shut down steam and washed up that I coveted. For Kirksy was an improvisatore, and he told stories from the inside outward, finely leaving his spoken words and his theme to adjust themselves as best they might.

I found Kirksy resting, with his pipe lighted, smut-faced and blue overalled.

" 'Tis a fair afternoon," I said, "but bids to be colder."

"Did I ever tell you," began Kirksy honorably, "about the time Henry Horsecollar and me took a phonograph to South America?" and I felt ashamed of my subterfuge, and dropped into the wooden chair he kicked toward me.

"Henry was a quarter-breed, quarter-back Chero-kee, educated East in the idioms of football and West in contraband whiskey, and a gentleman, same as you or me. He was easy and romping in his ways; a man about six foot, with a kind of rubber-tire move-ment. Yes, he was a little man about five foot five, or five foot eleven. He was what you would call a medium tall man of average smallness. Henry had quit college once, and the Muscogee jail three times —once for introducing, and twice for selling, whiskey in the Territories. Henry Horsecollar never let any cigar stores come up and stand behind him. He didn't belong to that tribe of Indians.

"Henry and me met at Texarkana, and figured out this phonograph scheme. He had $360 which came to him out of a land allotment in the reservation. I had run down from Little Rock on account of a distressful scene I had witnessed on the street there. A man stood on a box and passed around some gold watches, screw case, stem-winders, Elgin movement, very elegant. Twenty bucks they cost you over the counter. At three dollars the crowd fought for the tickers. The man happened to find a valise full of them handy, and he passed them out like putting hot biscuits on a plate. The backs were hard to unscrew, but the crowd put its ear to the case, and they ticked mollifying and agreeable. Three of those watches were genuine tickers; but the rest, they were only kickers. Hey? Why, empty cases with one of them horny black bugs that fly around electric lights in 'em. Them bugs kick off minutes and seconds industrious and beautiful. The man I was speaking of cleaned up $288, and went away, because he knew that when it came time to wind watches in Little Rock an entomologist would be needed, and he wasn't one.

"So, as I say, Henry had $360 and I had $288. The

phonograph idea was Henry's, but I took to it freely, being fond of machinery of all kinds.

" 'The Latin races,' says Henry, explaining easy in his idioms he learned at college, 'are peculiarly adapted to be victims of the phonograph. They possess the artistic temperament. They yearn for music and color and gayety. They give up wampum to the hand-organ man or the four-legged chicken when they're months behind with the grocery and the breadfruit tree.'

" 'Then,' says I, 'we'll export canned music to the Latins; but I'm mindful of Mr. Julius Cæsar's account of 'em where he says, "*Omnia Gallia in tres partes divisa est,*" which is the same as to say, "We will need all of our gall in devising means to tree them parties." ' I hated to make a show of education, but I was disinclined to be overdone in syntax by a mere Indian, to whom we owe nothing except the land on which the United States is situated.

"We bought a fine phonograph in Texarkana—one of the best make—and half a trunkful of records. We packed up, and took the T. and P. for New Orleans. From that celebrated centre of molasses and disfranchised coon songs we took a steamer for—yes, I think it was South America or Mexico—I am full of inability to divulge the location of it—'tis on the rural delivery route, 'tis colored yellow on the map, and branded with the literature of cigar boxes.

"We landed on a smiling coast at a town they denounced by the name, as near as I can recollect, of Sore-toe-kangaroo. 'Twas a palatable enough place to look at. The houses were clean and white, sticking about among the scenery like hard-boiled eggs served with lettuce. There was a block of skyscraper mountains in the suburbs, and they kept pretty quiet, like they were laying one finger on their lips and watching the town. And the sea was remarking 'Sh-sh-sh!' on the beach; and now and then a ripe cocoanut would fall kerblip in the sand, and that was all there was doing. Yes, I judge that town was considerably on the quiet. I judge that after Gabriel quits blowing his horn, and the car starts, with Philadelphia swinging to the last strap, and Pine Gulley, Arkansas, hanging on to the hind rail, Sore-toe-kangaroo will wake up and ask if anybody spoke.

"The captain went ashore with us, and offered to conduct what he seemed to like to call the obsequies. He introduced Henry and me to the United States Consul, and a roan man, the head of the Department of Mercenary and Licentious Dispositions, the way it read upon his sign.

" 'I touch here again a week from to-day,' says the captain.

" 'By that time,' we told him, 'we'll be amassing wealth in the interior towns with our galvanized prima donna and correct imitations of Sousa's band excavating a march from a tin mine.'

" 'Ye'll not,' says the captain. 'Ye'll be hypnotized. Any gentleman in the audience who kindly steps upon the stage and looks this country in the eye will be converted to the hypothesis that he's but a fly in the Elgin creamery. Ye'll be standing knee deep in the surf waiting for me, and your machine for making Hamburger steak out of the hitherto respected art of music will be playing "There's no place like home."

"Henry skinned a twenty off his roll, and received from the Bureau of Mercenary Dispositions a paper bearing a red seal and a dialect story, and no change.

"Then we got the consul full of red wine, and struck him for a horoscope. He was a thin, youngish kind of man, I should say past fifty, sort of French-Irish in his affections, and puffed up with disconsolation. Yes, he was a flattened kind of a man, in whom drink lay stagnant, inclined to corpulence and misery. Yes, I think he was a kind of Dutchman, being very sad and genial in his ways.

" 'The marvelous invention,' he says, 'entitled the phonograph, has never before invaded these shores. The people have never heard it. They would not believe it if they should. Simple-hearted children of nature, progress has never condemned them to accept the work of a can-opener as an overture, and rag-time might incite them to a bloody revolution. But you can try the experiment. The best chance you have is that the populace may not wake up when you play. There's two ways,' says the consul, 'they may take it. They may become inebriated with attention, like an Atlanta colonel listening to "Marching through Georgia," or they will get excited and transpose the key of the music with an axe and yourselves into a dungeon. In the latter case,' says the consul, 'I'll do my duty by cabling to the State Department, and I'll wrap the Stars and Stripes around you when you come to be shot, and threaten them with the vengeance of the greatest gold export and financial reserve nation on earth. The flag is full of bullet holes now,' says the consul, 'made in that way. Twice before,' says the consul, 'I have cabled our Government for a couple of gunboats to protect American citizens. The first time the Department sent me a pair of gum boots. The other time was when a man named Pease was going to be executed here. They referred that appeal to the Secretary of Agriculture. Let us now disturb the señor behind the bar for a subsequence of the red wine.'

"Thus soliloquized the consul of Sore-toe-kangaroo to me and Henry Horsecollar.

"But, notwithstanding, we hired a room that afternoon in the Calle de los Angeles, the main street that runs along the shore, and put our trunks there. 'Twas a good-sized room, dark and cheerful, but small. 'Twas on a various street, diversified by houses and conservatory plants. The peasantry of the city passed to and fro on the fine pasturage between the sidewalks. 'Twas, for the world, like an opera chorus when the Royal Kafoozlum is about to enter.

"We were rubbing the dust off the machine and getting fixed to start business the next day when a big, fine-looking white man in white clothes stopped at the door and looked in. We extended the invitations, and he walked inside and sized us up. He was chewing a long cigar, and wrinkling his eyes, meditative, like a girl trying to decide which dress to wear to the party.

" 'New York?' he says to me finally.

" 'Originally, and from time to time,' I says, 'Hasn't it rubbed off yet?'

" 'It's simple,' says he, 'when you know how. It's the fit of the vest. They don't cut vests right anywhere else. Coats, maybe, but not vests.'

"The white man looks at Henry Horsecollar and hesitates.

" 'Injun,' says Henry; 'tame Injun.'

" 'Mellinger,' says the man—'Homer P. Mellinger. Boys, you're confiscated. You're babes in the wood without a chaperon or referee, and it's my duty to start you going. I'll knock out the props and launch you proper in the pellucid waters of Sore-toe-kangaroo. You'll have to be christened, and if you'll come with me I'll break a bottle of wine across your bows, according to Hoyle.'

"Well, for two days Homer P. Mellinger did the honors. That man cut ice in Sore-toe-kangaroo. He was It. He was the Royal Kafoozlum. If me and Henry was babes in the wood, he was a Robin Redbreast from the topmost bough. Him and me and Henry Horsecollar locked arms and toted that phonograph around and had wassail and diversions. Everywhere we found doors open we went in and set the machine going, and Mellinger called upon the people to observe the artful music and his lifelong friends, the two Señors Americanos. The opera chorus was agitated with esteem, and followed us from house to house. There was *vino tinto* and *vino blanco* to drink with every tune. The aborigines had acquirements of a pleasant thing in the way of drinks that gums itself to the recollection. They chop off the end of a green cocoanut, and pour in on the liquor of it French brandy and gin. We had them and other things.

"Mine and Henry's money was counterfeit. Everything was on Homer P. Mellinger. That man could find rolls of bills in his clothes where Hermann the Wizard couldn't have conjured out an omelette. He could have founded universities and had enough left to buy the colored vote of his country. Henry and me wondered what his graft was. One evening he told us.

" 'Boys,' says he, 'I've deceived you. Instead of a painted butterfly, I'm the hardest worked man in this country. Ten years ago I landed on its shores, and two years ago on the point of its jaw. Yes, I reckon I can get the decision over this ginger-cake commonwealth at the end of any round I choose. I'll confide in you because you are my countrymen and guests, even if you have committed an assault upon my adopted shores with the worst system of noises ever set to music.

" 'My job is private secretary to the President of this Republic, and my duties are running it. I'm not headlined in the bills, but I'm the mustard in the salad dressing. There isn't a law goes before Congress, there isn't a concession granted, there isn't an import duty levied, but what H. P. Mellinger he cooks and seasons it. In the front office I fill the President's ink-stand and search visiting statesmen for dynamite; in the back room I dictate the policy of the government. You'd never guess how I got the pull. It's the only graft of its kind in the world. I'll put you wise. You remember the topliner in the old copy-books—"Honesty is the best policy." That's it. I'm the only honest man in this republic. The government knows it; the people know it; the boodlers know it; the foreign investors know it. I make the government keep its faith. If a man is promised a job he gets it. If outside capital buys a concession they get the goods. I run a monopoly of square dealing here. There's no competition. If Colonel Diogenes were to flash his lantern in this precinct he'd have my address inside of two minutes. There isn't big money in it, but it's a sure thing, and lets a man sleep of nights.'

"Thus Homer P. Mellinger made oration to me and Henry Horsecollar in Sore-toe-kangaroo. And, later, he divested himself of this remark:

" 'Boys, I'm to hold a *soirée* this evening with a gang of leading citizens, and I want your assistance. You bring the musical corn sheller and give the affair the outside appearance of a function. There's important business on hand, but it mustn't show. I can talk to you people. I've been pained for years on account of not having anybody to blow off and brag to. I get homesick sometimes, and I'd swap the entire perquisites of office for just one hour to have a stein and a caviare sandwich somewhere on Thirty-fourth Street, and stand and watch the street cars go by, and smell the peanut roaster at old Giuseppe's fruit stand.'

" 'Yes,' said I, 'there's fine caviare at Billy Renfrow's café, corner of Thirty-fourth and—"

" 'God knows it,' interrupts Mellinger, 'and if you'd

told me you knew Billy Renfrow I'd have invented
tons of ways of making you happy. Billy was my side
kicker in New York. That is a man who never knew
what crooked was. Here I am working Honesty for a
graft, but that man loses money on it. *Carrambos!*
I get sick at times of this country. Everything's rot-
ten. From the Executive down to the coffee pickers,
they're plotting to down each other and skin their
friends. If a mule driver takes off his hat to an official, that man figures it out that he's a popular idol,
and sets his pegs to stir up a revolution and upset the
administration. It's one of my little chores as private
secretary to smell out these revolutions and affix the
kibosh before they break out and scratch the paint off
the government property. That's why I'm down here
now in this mildewed coast town. The Governor of
the district and his crew are plotting to uprise. I've
got every one of their names, and they're invited to
listen to the phonograph to-night, compliments of H.
P. M. That's the way I'll get them in a bunch, and
things are on the programme to happen to them.'

"We three were sitting at table in the cantina of the
Purified Saints. Mellinger poured out wine, and was
looking some worried; I was thinking.

" 'They're a sharp crowd,' he says, kind of fretful.
'They're capitalized by a foreign syndicate after rubber, and they're loaded to the muzzle for bribing. I'm
sick,' goes on Mellinger, 'of comic opera. I want to
smell East River and wear suspenders again. At
times I feel like throwing up my job, but I'm d—n
fool enough to be sort of proud of it. "There's Mel-

linger," they say here, "*Por Dios!* you can't touch him
with a million." I'd like to take that record back and
show it to Billy Renfrow some day; and that tightens
my grip whenever I see a fat thing that I could corral
just by winking one eye—and losing my graft. By
——! they can't monkey with me. They know it.
What money I get I make honest and spend it. Some
day I'll make a pile and go back and eat caviare with
Billy. To-night I'll show you how to handle a bunch
of corruptionists. I'll show them what Mellinger,
private secretary, means when you spell it with the
cotton and tissue paper off.'

"Mellinger appears shaky, and breaks his glass
against the neck of the bottle.

"I says to myself, 'White man, if I'm not mistaken
there's been a bait laid out where the tail of your eye
could see it.'

"That night, according to arrangements, me and
Henry took the phonograph to a room in a 'dobe
house in a dirty side street, where the grass was knee
high. 'Twas a long room, lighted with smoky oil
lamps. There was plenty of chairs and a table at the
back end. We set the phonograph on the table. Mellinger was there, walking up and down, disturbed in
his predicaments. He chewed cigars and spat 'em out,
and he bit the thumb nail of his left hand.

"By and by the invitations to the musicale came
sliding in by pairs and threes and spade flushes. Their
color was of a diversity, running from a three-days'
smoked meerschaum to a patent-leather polish. They
were as polite as wax, being devastated with enjoy-

ments to give Señor Mellinger the good evenings. I
understood their Spanish talk—I ran a pumping engine two years in a Mexican silver mine, and had it
pat—but I never let on.

"Maybe fifty of 'em had come, and was seated,
when in slid the king bee, the Governor of the district. Mellinger met him at the door and escorted
him to the grand stand. When I saw that Latin man
I knew that Mellinger, private secretary, had all the
dances on his card taken. That was a big, squashy
man, the color of a rubber overshoe, and he had an
eye like a head waiter's.

"Mellinger explained, fluent, in the Castilian idioms, that his soul was disconcerted with joy at introducing to his respected friends America's greatest invention, the wonder of the age. Henry got the cue
and run on an elegant brass-band record and the
festivities became initiated. The Governor man had
a bit of English under his hat, and when the music
was choked off he says:

"'Ver-r-ree fine. Gr-r-r-r-racias, the American
gentleemen, the so esplendeed moosic as to playee.'

"The table was a long one, and Henry and me sat
at the end of it next the wall. The Governor sat at
the other end. Homer P. Mellinger stood at the side
of it. I was just wondering how Mellinger was
going to handle his crowd, when the home talent suddenly opened the services.

"That Governor man was suitable for uprisings
and policies. I judge he was a ready kind of man,
who took his own time. Yes, he was full of atten-

tions and immediateness. He leaned his hands on the table and imposed his face toward the secretary man.

" 'Do the American Señors understand Spanish?' he asks in his native accents.

" 'They do not,' says Mellinger.

" 'Then, listen,' goes on the Latin man, prompt. 'The musics are of sufficient prettiness, but not of necessity. Let us speak of business. I well know why we are here, since I observe my compatriots. You had a whisper yesterday, Señor Mellinger, of our proposals. To-night we will speak out. We know that you stand in the President's favor, and we know your influence. The government will be changed. We know the worth of your services. We esteem your friendship and aid so much that'—Mellinger raises his hand, but the Governor man bottles him up. 'Do not speak until I have done.'

"The Governor man then draws a package wrapped in paper from his pocket, and lays it on the table by Mellinger's hand.

" 'In that you will find one hundred thousand dollars in money of your country. You can do nothing against us, but you can be worth that for us. Go back to the capital and obey our instructions. Take that money now. We trust you. You will find with it a paper giving in detail the work you will be expected to do for us. Do not have the unwiseness to refuse.'

"The Governor man paused, with his eyes fixed on Mellinger, full of expressions and observances. I looked at Mellinger, and was glad Billy Renfrow couldn't see him then. The sweat was popping out on his forehead, and he stood dumb, tapping the little package with the ends of his fingers. The Colorado maduro gang was after his graft. He had only to change his politics, and stuff six figures in his inside pocket.

"Henry whispers to me and wants the pause in the programme interpreted. I whisper back: 'H. P. is up against a bribe, senator's size, and the coons have got him going.' I saw Mellinger's hand moving closer to the package. 'He's weakening,' I whispered to Henry. 'We'll remind him,' says Henry, 'of the peanut roaster on Thirty-fourth Street, New York.'

"Henry stooped and got a record from the basketful we'd brought, slid it in the phonograph, and started her off. It was a cornet solo, very neat and beautiful, and the name of it was 'Home, Sweet Home.' Not one of them fifty odd men in the room moved while it was playing, and the Governor man kept his eyes steady on Mellinger. I saw Mellinger's head go up little by little, and his hand came creeping away from the package. Not until the last note sounded did anybody stir. And then Homer P. Mellinger takes up the bundle of boodle and slams it in the Governor man's face.

" 'That's my answer,' says Mellinger, private secretary, 'and there'll be another in the morning. I have proofs of conspiracy against every man of you. The show is over, gentlemen.'

" 'There's one more act,' puts in the Governor man. 'You are a servant, I believe, employed by the President to copy letters and answer raps at the door. I

am Governor here. Señors, I call upon you in the
name of the cause to seize this man.'

"That brindled gang of conspirators shoved back
their chairs and advanced in force. I could see where
Mellinger had made a mistake in massing his enemy
so as to make a grand-stand play. I think he made
another one, too; but we can pass that, Mellinger's
idea of a graft and mine being different, according to
estimations and points of view.

"There was only one window and door in that
room, and they were in the front end. Here was fifty
odd Latin men coming in a bunch to obstruct the
legislation of Mellinger. You may say there were
three of us, for me and Henry, simultaneous, declared
New York City and the Cherokee Nation in sympathy
with the weaker party.

"Then it was that Henry Horsecollar rose to a
point of disorder and intervened, showing, admirable,
the advantages of education as applied to the American Indian's natural intellect and native refinement.
He stood up and smoothed back his hair on each side
with his hands as you have seen little girls do when
they play.

" 'Get behind me, both of you,' says Henry.

" 'What is it to be?' I asked.

" 'I'm going to buck centre,' says Henry, in his
football idioms. 'There isn't a tackle in the lot of
them. Keep close behind me and rush the game.'

"That cultured Red Man exhaled an arrangement
of sounds with his mouth that caused the Latin aggre-
gation to pause, with thoughtfulness and hesitations.

The matter of his proclamation seemed to be a co-operation of the Cherokee college yell with the Carlisle war-whoop. He went at the chocolate team like the flip of a little boy's nigger shooter. His right elbow laid out the Governor man on the gridiron, and he made a lane the length of the crowd that a woman could have carried a step-ladder through without striking anything. All me and Mellinger had to do was to follow.

"In five minutes we were out of that street and at the military headquarters, where Mellinger had things his own way.

"The next day Mellinger takes me and Henry to one side and begins to shed tens and twenties.

" 'I want to buy that phonograph,' he says. 'I liked that last tune it played. Now, you boys better go back home, for they'll give you trouble here before I get the screws put on 'em. If you happen to ever see Billy Renfrow again, tell him I'm coming back to New York as soon as I can make a stake— honest.'

" 'This is more money,' says I, 'than the machine is worth.'

" ' 'Tis government expense money,' says Mellinger, 'and the government's getting the tune grinder cheap.'

"Henry and I knew that pretty well, but we never let Homer P. Mellinger know that we had seen how near he came to losing his graft.

"We laid low until the day the steamer came back. When we saw the captain's boat on the beach me and

Henry went down and stood in the edge of the water.
The captain grinned when he saw us.

" 'I told you you'd be waiting,' he says.   'Where's
the Hamburger machine?'

" 'It stays behind,' I says, 'to play "Home, Sweet
Home." '

" 'I told you so,' says the captain again.   'Climb
in the boat.'

"And that," said Kirksy, "is the way me and Henry
Horsecollar introduced the phonograph in that Latin
country along about the vicinity of South America."

BROTHER RABBIT'S CRADLE

BY JOEL CHANDLER HARRIS

The names of few authors are so inextricably associated with one of their characters as that of Joel Chandler Harris (born at Eatontown, Ga., December 8, 1848) with his great creation, "Uncle Remus." This dear old negro story-teller was introduced to the world in 1880, in a book entitled "Uncle Remus, His Songs and His Sayings." And the delighted readers have compelled Mr. Harris to continue ever since adding to the collection. Mr. Harris is the editor of the Atlanta "Constitution." The present story first appeared in COLLIER'S WEEKLY for November 12, 1904.

BROTHER RABBIT'S CRADLE

BY JOEL CHANDLER HARRIS

"I WISH you'd tell me what you tote a hankcher fer," remarked Uncle Remus, after he had reflected over the matter a little while.

"Why, to keep my mouth clean," answered the little boy. Uncle Remus looked at the lad, and shook his head doubtfully. "Uh-uh!" he exclaimed. "You can't fool folks when dey git ez ol' ez what I is. I been watchin' you now mo' days dan I kin count, an' I ain't never see yo' mouf dirty 'nuff fer ter be wiped wid a hankcher. It's allers clean—too clean fer ter suit me. Dar's yo' pa, now; when he wuz a little chap like you, his mouf useter git dirty in de mornin' an' stay dirty plum twel night. Dey wa'n't sca'cely a day dat he didn't look like he been playin' wid de pigs in de stable lot. Ef he yever is tote a hankcher, he ain't never show it ter me."

"He carries one now," remarked the little boy with something like a triumphant look on his face.

"Tooby sho'," said Uncle Remus; "tooby sho' he do. He start ter totin' one when he tuck an' tuck a notion fer ter go a-courtin'. It had his name in one cornder, an' he useter sprinkle it wid stuff out'n a pepper-sauce bottle. It sho' wuz rank, dat stuff wuz; it smell so sweet it make you fergit whar you live at. I take notice dat you ain't got none on yone."

By permission of McClure, Phillips & Co.

"No; mother says that cologne or any kind of perfumery on your handkerchief makes you common."

Uncle Remus leaned his head back, closed his eyes, and permitted a heartrending groan to issue from his lips. The little boy showed enough anxiety to ask him what the matter was. "Nothin' much, honey; I wuz des tryin' fer ter count how many diffunt kinder people dey is in dis big worl', an' 'fo' I got mo' dan half done wid my countin', a pain struck me in my mizry, an' I had ter break off."

"I know what you mean," said the child. "You think mother is queer; grandmother thinks so too."

"How come you to be so wise, honey?" Uncle Remus inquired, opening his eyes wide with astonishment.

"I know by the way you talk, and by the way grandmother looks sometimes," answered the little boy.

Uncle Remus said nothing for some time. When he did speak, it was to lead the little boy to believe that he had been all the time engaged in thinking about something else. "Talkin' er dirty folks," he said, "you oughter seed yo' pa when he wuz a little bit er chap. Dey wuz long days when you couldn't tell ef he wuz black er white, he wuz dat dirty. He'd come out'n de big house in de mornin' ez clean ez a new pin, an' 'fo' ten er-clock you couldn't tell what kinder clof his cloze wuz made out'n. Many's de day when I've seed ol' Miss—dat's yo' great-gran'mammy—comb 'nuff trash out'n his head fer ter fill a basket."

The little boy laughed at the picture that Uncle Remus drew of his father. "He's very clean, now," said the lad loyally.

"Maybe he is an' maybe he ain't," remarked Uncle Remus, suggesting a doubt. "Dat's needer here ner dar. Is he any better off clean dan what he wuz when you couldn't put yo' han's on 'im widout havin' ter go an' wash um? Yo' gran'mammy useter call 'im a pig, an' clean ez he may be now, I take notice dat he makes mo' complaint er headache an' de heartburn dan what he done when he wuz runnin' roun' here half-naked an' full er mud. I hear tell dat some nights he can't git no sleep, but when he wuz little like you—no, suh, I'll not say dat, bekaze he wuz bigger dan what you is fum de time he kin toddle roun' widout nobody he'pin' him; but when he wuz ol' ez you an' twice ez big, dey ain't narry night dat he can't sleep—an' not only all night, but half de day ef dey'd 'a' let 'im. Ef dey'd let you run roun' here like he done, an' git dirty, you'd git big an' strong 'fo' you know it. Dey ain't nothin' mo' wholesomer dan a peck er two er clean dirt on a little chap like you."

There is no telling what comment the child would have made on this sincere tribute to clean dirt, for his attention was suddenly attracted to something that was gradually taking shape in the hands of Uncle Remus. At first it seemed to be hardly worthy of notice, for it had been only a thin piece of board. But now the one piece had become four pieces, two long and two short, and under the deft manipulations of Uncle Remus it soon assumed a boxlike shape.

The old man had reached the point in his work where silence was necessary to enable him to do it full justice. As he fitted the thin boards together, a whistling sound issued from his lips, as though he were letting off steam; but the singular noise was due to the fact that he was completely absorbed in his work. He continued to fit and trim, and trim and fit, until finally the little boy could no longer restrain his curiosity. "Uncle Remus, what are you making?" he asked plaintively.

"Larroes fer ter kech meddlers," was the prompt and blunt reply.

"Well, what are larroes to catch meddlers?" the child insisted.

"Nothin' much an' sump'n mo'. Dicky, Dicky, killt a chicky, an' fried it quicky, in de oven, like a sloven. Den ter his daddy's Sunday hat, he tuck 'n' hitched de ol' black cat. Now what you reckon make him do dat? Ef you can't tell me word fer word an' spellin' fer spellin' we'll go out an' come in an' take a walk."

He rose, grunting as he did so, thus paying an unintentional tribute to the efficacy of age as the partner of rheumatic aches and stiff joints. "You hear me gruntin'," he remarked—"well, dat's bekaze I ain't de chicky fried by Dicky, which he e't 'nuff fer ter make 'im sicky." As he went out the child took his hand, and went trotting along by his side, thus affording an interesting study for those who concern themselves with the extremes of life. Hand in hand the two went out into the fields, and thence into the great woods, where Uncle Remus, after searching about for some time, carefully deposited his oblong box, remarking: "Ef I don't make no mistakes, dis ain't so mighty fur fum de place whar de creeturs has der playgroun', an' dey ain't no tellin' but what one un um'll creep in dar when deyer playin' hidin', an' ef he do, he'll sho be our meat."

"Oh, it's a trap!" exclaimed the little boy, his face lighting up with enthusiasm.

"An' dey wa'n't nobody here fer ter tell you," Uncle Remus declared, astonishment in his tone. "Well, ef dat don't bang my time, I ain't no free nigger. Now, ef dat had 'a' been yo' pa at de same age, I'd 'a' had ter tell 'im forty-lev'm times, an' den he wouldn't 'a' b'lieved me twel he see sump'n in dar tryin' fer ter git out. Den he'd say it wuz a trap, but not befo'. I ain't blamin' 'im," Uncle Remus went on, "kaze 'tain't eve'y chap dat kin tell a trap time he see it, an' mo' dan dat, traps don' allers sketch what dey er sot fer."

He paused, looked all around, and up in the sky, where fleecy clouds were floating lazily along, and in the tops of the trees, where the foliage was swaying gently in the breeze. Then he looked at the little boy. "Ef I ain't gone an' got los'," he said, "we ain't so mighty fur fum de place whar Mr. Man, once 'pon a time—not yo' time ner yit my time, but some time —tuck'n' sot a trap for Brer Rabbit. In dem days, dey hadn't l'arnt how ter be kyarpenters, an' dish yer trap what I'm tellin' you 'bout wuz a great big contraption. Big ez Brer Rabbit wuz, it wuz lots too big fer him.

"Now, whiles Mr. Man wuz fixin' up dis trap, Mr. Rabbit wa'n't so mighty fur off. He hear de saw— er-rash! er-rash!—an' he hear de hammer—bang, bang, bang!—an' he ax hisse'f what all dis racket wuz

'bout. He see Mr. Man come out'n his yard totin'
sump'n, an' he got furder off; he see Mr. Man comin'
todes de bushes, an' he tuck ter de woods; he see 'im
comin' todes de woods, an' he tuck ter de bushes. Mr.
Man tote de trap so fur an' no furder. He put it down,
he did, an' Brer Rabbit watch 'im; he put in de bait,
an' Brer Rabbit watch 'im; he fix de trigger, an' still
Brer Rabbit watch 'im. Mr. Man look at de trap an'
it satchify him. He look at it an' laugh, an' when he
do dat, Brer Rabbit wunk one eye, an' wiggle his mustache, an' chaw his cud.

"An' dat ain't all he do, needer. He sot out in de
bushes, he did, an' study how ter git some game in
de trap. He study so hard, an' he got so errytated,
dat he thumped his behime foot on de groun' twel it
soun' like a cow dancin' out dar in de bushes, but
'twan't no cow, ner yit no calf—'twuz des Brer Rabbit
studyin'. Atter so long a time, he put out down de
road todes dat part er de country whar mos' er de
creeturs live at. Eve'y time he hear a fuss, he'd dodge
in de bushes, kaze he wanter see who comin'. He
keep on an' he keep on, an' bimeby he hear ol' Brer
Wolf trottin' down de road.

"It so happen dat Brer Wolf wuz de ve'y one what
Brer Rabbit wanter see. Dey wuz perlit ter one an'er,
but dey wan't no frien'ly feelin' 'twix um. Well, here
come ol' Brer Wolf, hongrier dan a chicken-hawk on a
frosty mornin', an' ez he come up he see Brer Rabbit
set by de side er de road lookin' like he done lose all
his fambly an' his friends terboot.

"Dey pass de time er day, an' den Brer Wolf kinder

grin an' say, 'Laws-a-massy, Brer Rabbit! what ail you? You look like you done had a spell er fever an' ague; what de trouble?' 'Trouble, Brer Wolf? You ain't never see no trouble twel you git whar I'm at. Maybe you wouldn't min' it like I does, kaze I ain't usen ter it. But I boun' you done seed me light-minded fer de las' time. I'm done—I'm plum wo' out,' sez Brer Rabbit, sezee. Dis make Brer Wolf open his eyes wide. He say, 'Dis de fus' time I ever is hear you talk dat-a-way, Brer Rabbit; take yo' time an' tell me 'bout it. I ain't had my brekkus yit, but dat don't make no diffunce, long ez youer in trouble. I'll he'p you out ef I kin, an' mo' dan dat, I'll put some heart in de work.' When he say dis, he grin an' show his tushes, an' Brer Rabbit kinder edge 'way fum 'im. He say, 'Tell me de trouble, Brer Rabbit, an' I'll do my level bes' fer ter he'p you out.'

"Wid dat, Brer Rabbit 'low dat Mr. Man done been had 'im hired fer ter take keer er his truck patch, an' keep out de minks, de mush-rats an' de weasels. He say dat he done so well settin' up night atter night, when he des might ez well been in bed, dat Mr. Man prommus 'im sump'n extry 'sides de mess er greens what he gun 'im eve'y day. Atter so long a time, he say, Mr. Man 'low dat he gwineter make 'im a present uv a cradle so he kin rock de little Rabs ter sleep when dey cry. So said, so done, he say. Mr. Man make de cradle an' tell Brer Rabbit he kin take it home wid 'im.

"He start out wid it, he say, but it got so heavy he hatter set it down in de woods, an' dat's de reason why Brer Wolf seed 'im settin' down by de side er de road, lookin' like he in deep trouble. Brer Wolf sot down, he did, an' study, an' bimeby he say he'd like mighty well fer ter have a cradle fer his chillun, long ez cradles wuz de style. Brer Rabbit say dey been de style fer de longest, an' ez fer Brer Wolf wantin' one, he say he kin have de one what Mr. Man make fer him, kaze it's lots too big fer his chillun. 'You know how folks is,' sez Brer Rabbit, sezee. 'Dey try ter do what dey dunner how ter do, an' dar's der house bigger dan a barn, an' dar's de fence wid mo' holes in it dan what dey is in a saine, an' kaze dey have great big chillun dey got de idee dat eve'y cradle what dey make mus' fit der own chillun. An' dat's how come I can't tote de cradle what Mr. Man make fer me mo' dan ten steps at a time.'

"Brer Wolf ax Brer Rabbit what he gwineter do fer a cradle, an' Brer Rabbit 'low he kin manage fer ter git 'long wid de ol' one twel he kin 'suade Mr. Man ter make 'im an'er one, an' he don't speck dat'll be so mighty hard ter do. Brer Wolf can't he'p but b'lieve dey's some trick in it, an' he say he ain't see de ol' cradle when las' he wuz at Brer Rabbit house. Wid dat, Brer Rabbit bust out laughin'. He say, 'Dat's been so long back, Brer Wolf, dat I done fergit all 'bout it; 'sides dat, ef dey wuz a cradle dar, I boun' you my ol' 'oman got better sense dan ter set de cradle in der parler, whar comp'ny comes'; an' he laugh so loud an' long dat he make Brer Wolf right shame er himse'f.

"He 'low, ol' Brer Wolf did, 'Come on, Brer Rabbit, an' show me whar de cradle is. Ef it's too big

fer yo' chillun, it'll des 'bout fit mine.' An' so off dey
put ter whar Mr. Man done sot his trap. 'Twa'n't so
mighty long 'fo' dey got whar dey wuz gwine, an'
Brer Rabbit say, 'Brer Wolf, dar yo' cradle, an' may
it do you mo' good dan it's yever done me!' Brer
Wolf walk all roun' de trap an' look at it like 'twuz
live. Brer Rabbit thump one er his behime foots on
de groun' an' Brer Wolf jump like some un done shot
a gun right at 'im. Dis make Brer Rabbit laugh twel
he can't laugh no mo'. Brer Wolf, he say he kinder
nervous 'bout dat time er de year, an' de leas' little bit
er noise 'll make 'im jump. He ax how he gwineter
git any purchis on de cradle, an' Brer Rabbit say he'll
hatter git inside an' walk wid it on his back, kaze dat
de way he done done.

"Brer Wolf ax what all dem contraptions on de
inside is, an' Brer Rabbit 'spon' dat dey er de rockers,
an' dey ain't no needs fer ter be skeer'd un um, kaze
dey ain't nothin' but plain wood. Brer Wolf say he
ain't 'zactly skeer'd, but he done got ter de p'int whar
he know dat you better look 'fo' you jump. Brer Rabbit 'low dat ef dey's any jumpin' fer ter be done, he de
one ter do it, an' he talk like he done fergit what dey
come fer. Brer Wolf, he fool an' fumble roun', but
bimeby he walk in de cradle, sprung de trigger, an'
dar he wuz! Brer Rabbit, he holler out, 'Come on,
Brer Wolf; des hump yo'se'f, an' I'll be wid you.'
But try ez he will an' grunt ez he may, Brer Wolf
can't budge dat trap. Bimeby Brer Rabbit git tired er
waitin', an' he say dat ef Brer Wolf ain't gwineter
come on he's gwine home. He 'low dat a frien' what

say he gwineter he'p you, an' den go in a cradle an'
drap off ter sleep, dat's all he wanter know 'bout um;
an' wid dat he made fer de bushes, an' he wa'n't a
minnit too soon, kaze here come Mr. Man fer ter see
ef his trap had been sprung. He look, he did, an', sho
'nuff, it 'uz sprung, an' dey wuz sump'n in dar, too,
kaze he kin hear it rustlin' roun' an' kickin' fer ter
git out.

"Mr. Man look thoo de crack, an' he see Brer Wolf,
which he wuz so skeer'd twel his eye look right green.
Mr. Man say, 'Aha! I got you, is I? Brer Wolf say,
'Who?' Mr. Man laugh twel he can't sca'cely talk, an'
still Brer Wolf say, 'Who? Who you think you got?'
Mr. Man 'low, 'I don't think, I knows. Youer ol' Brer
Rabbit, dat's who you is.' Brer Wolf say, 'Turn me
outer here, an' I'll show you who I is.' Mr. Man laugh
fit ter kill. He 'low, 'You neenter change yo' voice;
I'd know you ef I met you in de dark. Youer Brer
Rabbit, dat's who you is.' Brer Wolf say, 'I ain't not;
dat's what I'm not!'

"Mr. Man look thoo de crack ag'in, an' he see de
short years. He 'low, 'You done cut off yo' long
years, but still I knows you. Oh, yes! an' you done
sharpen yo' mouf an' put smut on it—but you can't
fool me.' Brer Wolf say, 'Nobody ain't tryin' fer ter
fool you. Look at my fine long bushy tail.' Mr. Man
'low, 'You done tied an'er tail on behime you, but you
can't fool me. Oh, no, Brer Rabbit! You can't fool
me.' Brer Wolf say, 'Look at de ha'r on my back;
do dat look like Brer Rabbit?' Mr. Man 'low, 'You
done wallered in de red san', but you can't fool me.'

"Brer Wolf say, 'Look at my long black legs; do dey look like Brer Rabbit?' Mr. Man 'low, 'You kin put an'er j'int in yo' legs, an' you kin smut um, but you can't fool me.' Brer Wolf say, 'Look at my tushes; does dey look like Brer Rabbit?' Mr. Man 'low, 'You done got new toofies, but you can't fool me.' Brer Wolf say, 'Look at my little eyes; does dey look like Brer Rabbit?' Mr. Man 'low, 'You kin squinch yo' eye-balls, but you can't fool me, Brer Rabbit.' Brer Wolf squall out, 'I ain't not Brer Rabbit, an' yo' better turn me out er dis place so I kin take hide an' ha'r off'n Brer Rabbit.' Mr. Man say, 'Ef bofe hide an' ha'r wuz off, I'd know you, kaze 'tain't in you fer ter fool me.' An' it hurt Brer Wolf feelin's so bad fer Mr. Man ter sput his word, dat he bust out inter a big boo-boo, an' dat's 'bout all I know."

"Did the man really and truly think that Brother Wolf was Brother Rabbit?" asked the little boy.

"When you pin me down dat-a-way," responded Uncle Remus, "I'm bleeze ter tell you dat I ain't too certain an' sho' 'bout dat. De tale come down fum my great-gran'daddy's great-gran'daddy; it come on down ter my daddy, an' des ez he gun it ter me, des dat-a-way I done gun it ter you."

THE TREE OF HEAVEN

BY ROBERT W. CHAMBERS

*Robert William Chambers (born in Brook-
lyn, N. Y., May 26, 1865) was an artist before he became an author, as might readily
be inferred from the rich beauty of his literary style. His "King in Yellow," published
in 1893, struck an absolutely new and original note in fiction. Like the aim of the best
work in pictorial art, its purpose was not so
much to "tell a story" as to present, as it
were, a color scheme—a fantasy vibrant
with imaginative quality, that would leave
a definite impression on the æsthetic sense
of the reader long after the specific characters and events of the novel had faded from
his mind. Since then Mr. Chambers has developed a chaster style, better adapted for
themes of a purer order of beauty than his
first work—tales of the arabesque rather
than of the grotesque, to use Poe's complemen-
tary divisions of imaginative fiction. This
the present selection illustrates admirably.*

THE TREE OF HEAVEN

BY ROBERT W. CHAMBERS

TIME, and the funeral of Time, alas!—and the Old Year's passing-bell! Whistles from city and river, deep horns sounding from the foggy docks; and under my window a voice and a song; ah! that young voice in the street below calling me through the falling snow!

. . . .

If it be true that Time makes all hurts well, I do not know; and a thousand years in Thy sight is but as yesterday when it is passed, and as a watch in the night; a thousand years! And this is also true; the flames of love make hot the furnace of Abaddon.

. . . .

We were in the gallery as usual, Geraldine and I —the gallery where the carpets of the East were hung along the shadowy walls. For lately it was my pleasure to acquire rare rugs, and it was my profession to furnish expert opinion upon the age and origin of Oriental carpets, and to read and interpret the histories of forgotten emperors and the mysteries of long-forgotten gods from the colors and intricate flowery labyrinths tied in silk or wool to the warps of some dead sultan's lustrous tapestry.

Here in the long sky-gallery hung my own rugs

Reprinted, by permission of the author, from "Harper's Weekly," Christmas number, 1904.

against the arabesque incrusted-ivory panels—Tabriz,
Shiraz, Sehna, and Saruk—a sombre blaze of color shot
with fire—all rare, some priceless; Turkish Kulah,
softly silky as a golden lion's hide; Persian Sehna,
shimmering with rose and violet lights; fiercely brilliant rugs from Samarkand, superbly flowered, secret-
ing deep in every floral thicket traceries of the ancient
Mongol conqueror; Feraghans glowing like jewel-
sewn velvets set with the Herati and the lotus—sym-
bols of Egypt or of China, as you please to interpret
the oldest pattern in the world.

Far in the gallery's amber-tinted gloom the red of
Ispahan dominated, subduing fiery vistas to smouldering harmony through which, like a vast sapphire
set in opals, glimmered the superb lost Persian
blue.

There was one other rug, an Eighur, the famous so-
called "Babilu," or "Carpet of Belshazzar"; but it
hung alone in imperial magnificence behind the locked
doors of a marble room, which it seemed to fill with
a soft lustre of its own, radiating from the mystic
"Tree of Heaven" woven in its centre.

．　．　．　．　．　．　．　．　．

We were, as I say, in this gallery; Geraldine poring
over an illuminated volume on cuneiform inscriptions,
I, with pad and pencil, idly shifting and reshifting the
Kufic key to the ancient cipher, which always left me
stranded where I had begun with the stately repetition:

> "King of Kings—
> King of Kings—
> King of Kings—"

As for Westover, my cousin, he was, as usual, in the laboratory fussing with his venomous extracts—an occupation which, to my dismay, he had taken up within the year, working, as he explained, on the theory that every poison has its antidote. Yet it seemed to me that he was more anxious to invent some new and subtle toxic than to devise the remedy.

From where I sat I could not see him, but the crystalline tinkle of his glass retorts and bottles distracted my attention from the penciled calculations. Without moving my head, I glanced across the room at Geraldine. She looked up immediately, raising her level eyebrows in mute inquiry as though I had moved or spoken; then, realizing that I had not, she bent above the book once more, the warm color stealing to her cheeks.

Within the year a wordless intimacy had grown up between us; we never understood it, never acknowledged it, and at times it disconcerted us.

I sat silent, tracing with my pencil series after series of futile Kufic combinations with the cuneiforms, but ever the first turn of the ancient key creaked in my ears,

> "King of Kings—
> King of Kings—"

until the triverbal reiteration wore on my nerves.

Geraldine leaned back abruptly, closing her book.

"I'm tired and nervous," she said. "You may wear out your eyes and temper if you choose—and you're doing the latter, for I'm as restless as an eel. Besides, I'm lonely, and I'm going back to the East—if you'll come too."

I laughed, understanding what she meant by the "East."

"Will you come with me?" she insisted.

"Yes," I said, "whenever you are ready."

She sprang to her feet, scattering the illuminated pages over the floor, and stood an instant facing me, tall, dark-eyed, smiling, brushing back the lustrous hair from her cheeks.

"Where is Jim?" she asked—although we both knew.

"In the laboratory," I replied, mechanically.

Still busy with her hair, she regarded me dreamily out of those dark, sweet eyes of hers.

"It would be wonderful," she mused, "if Jim should find an antidote to death; but I wish it were not necessary to kill so many little helpless creatures. Did you hear that pitiful sound in there yesterday? Was it something he was killing?"

"I don't know," I said. And after a silence, "What are you going to do?"

She shook her head vaguely and leaned against the window, looking out into the rain.

"Shall we go back to our inscriptions?" I suggested.

She shook her head again. After a while she turned away from the window, stifling a dainty yawn, and stretched out, languidly straightening up to the full height of her young body.

"I feel stupid," she said; "I'm tired of cryptograms and the pages of dusty books. I'm tired of the rain, too. The languor of April is in me. I'm homesick for lands I never knew. So come back to the East with me, Dick."

She held out her hand to me with a confident little smile; and knowing what she meant, I acquiesced in her caprice, and conducted her solemnly to the piano, leaving her before it.

She stood there for a space, musing, her lovely head bent; then, still standing, she struck a sequence of chords—chords pulsating with color; and through them flashed strange little trills like threads of tinsel.

"This is an Eighur carpet I am dreaming of," she murmured, as the music swelled, glowing as tints and hues glow in the old dyes of the East.

Wave on wave of color seemed to spread from the keys under her fingers; she looked back at me over her shoulder with a warning nod.

"I shall begin to weave very soon. Khiounnou horsemen may appear and frighten me for a moment—but I shall finish. Listen! I am at the loom."

Seating herself, she developed out of the flowing, sombre harmony a monotonous minor theme, suddenly checked by a distant rattle like the clatter of nomad lances on painted stirrups; then she picked up the thread of the melody again, dropped it, breathless for a moment's quivering silence, resumed it, twisting it into delicate arabesques, threading it across the dull, rich harmonies, at first slowly, then faster, faster, swift as the flying fingers of a nomad maid tying fretted silver in a Ghiordes knot. The whirring tempo was the cadence of the loom; soft feathery notes flew like carded wool; thicker, duller, softer grew the fabric, dense, silky, heavily lustrous.

Suddenly she broke the thread off short, the whole fabric falling with a muffled shock.

"Why did you do that?" I demanded, wrathfully.

"The rug is woven; the weaver is dead," she said.

"Oh, go on, Geraldine," I insisted; "don't stop half-way in a thing like that. It's the East—it's the real East, I tell you. How you do it—you who have never seen the East—Heaven only knows."

"*U Allah Aalem,*" she murmured; it's in me." Then she looked back at me, laughing. "Centuries ago you and I heard that music along the Arax—or I sang it among the Tcherkess roses for you, perhaps—perhaps in the gardens of Trebizond."

"That might explain it," I said, gravely. Lately she had found pleasure in a fancy that she and I had lived together in the East, centuries since, and that we were soon to return forever.

"You and I," she mused, touching the keys lightly—"and Jim, of course," she added.

"Of course," I said.

She dropped her head, striking chord on chord with nervous precision; and hanging in the wake of every ringing harmony a frail melody floated like the Chinese cloud-band in a Kirman tapestry.

"What's that air?" I asked, fascinated.

"I don't know; it sounds pagan, doesn't it?—like the wicked beauty of Babylon. Do you hear how it beats on and on like the rhythm of naked feet—little delicate naked feet ablaze with gems—the feet of Hero-

Robert W. Chambers

diade perhaps—thud—thud—tching!—don't you hear
them, Dick? And now listen to those silky, flowery
trills! They're Asiatic; ancient Cathay is awaking—
camel bells in the bazaar of the Golden Emperor!
Hark!—now you hear trumpets, don't you? Well, of
course that must be the Mongols marching with the
Prince of the Vanguard. Hark! How savagely the
brutal Afghan theme breaks in with its fierce
trampling and the staccato echo of Tekke drums!
It's frightening me out of the East. I think we
had better come home, Dick," she added, mis-
chievously running into the latest popular street
song.

"How on earth could you do that!" I exclaimed,
wrathfully. "You are a futile mixture of feather-
brain and genius!"

But where was the genius hidden under that laughing and exquisite mask confronting me? Suddenly
the delicate mask became grave.

"Let me laugh when I can, Dick," she said. "It
is not often I laugh."

I was silent.

"Of course you may be horrid if you choose," she
observed, with a shrug, running a brilliantly inane
series of trills from end to end of the keyboard. "But
it's no use scolding, for I won't study, I won't com-
pose, I won't try to do something, and I won't be
serious. I'm shallow, I'm frivolous, I've the soul of
a Trebizond dancing-girl, and I like it. Now what
are you going to do?"

"I'm going out," I said, ungraciously.

"Oh—alone?"

"Not if you'll come. It's stopped raining. Will you come? Oh, get your hat, Geraldine, and stop that torment of idiotic trills!"

"If Jim doesn't mind, I think I'll go and sit in the laboratory with him," she observed, carelessly.

I looked at her without comment.

"I have a curious idea," she continued, "that he might like to have me around to-day while he is working."

I stared at her, but there was no bitterness in her tranquil smile as she leaned forward, resting her elbows on the polished rosewood case.

"So I won't go with you, Dick," she said, slowly.

One of those intervals of restless silence which within the year we had learned to dread, menaced us now. Mute, motionless, I watched the soft color deepening in her face, then, impatient, roused myself and walked over to the laboratory. Westover looked up as I pushed aside the screen.

"Will you drive with us?" I asked. "The sun's out."

He declined, peering at me through his glass mask.

"Come on, Jim," I urged. "You've inhaled enough poison for one day. Take off your mask and wash your hands and drive us out to High Bridge. I'll telephone to the stable if you say the word, and they'll hook up the new four. Is it a go?"

"No," he said, coldly, and turned on his heel, lifting a test tube to the light.

He was more taciturn and a trifle uglier than usual. I watched him for a moment warming the test tube over a burner, then without further parley replaced the screen, closed the double glass doors, and walked back to Geraldine.

"Doesn't Jim care to come?" she asked.

I said that her husband appeared to be absorbed in his work.

"Very well," she said, with airy composure; "trot along, Dicky—and if you see a bunch of jonquils growing on Fifth Avenue, you may pick them for me—or for that pretty girl you met at Lakewood—"

"I'll send you a bunch as big as a bushel."

"A bushel of flowers is as compromising as a declaration," she said. "Send them to her."

"There's only one way to settle it," I said; "I'll send them to the loveliest girl in the world—shall I?"

She assented, laughing uncertainly.

"I think I'll pay Jim a little call," she said, rising from the piano and walking slowly toward the laboratory.

A few minutes later as I passed down the broad stairway I heard Westover's penetrating voice: "Let that glass tube alone, Geraldine! Why the devil can't you keep your hands off things when you come in here?"

I lingered for a while in the hallway, thinking that she might change her mind and come down, for she had left the laboratory to her husband, and I heard her moving about in her own apartment. She did

not come, and after a little while I left the house, a
sense of apprehension depressing me.

. . . .

The asphalt of Fifth Avenue was still wet with the
first warm rain of April, but the sun glittered on window and pavement and flashed along the polished
panels of carriages crowding the avenue from curb to
curb. A breath of spring had set the sparrows chattering and chirking; the movement of the throng, the
bright gowns, the fresh faces of young girls, and the
endless façades of glass reflecting it all were pleasant
to me—a man sensitive to impressions.

And so in the pale sunshine I sauntered on through
the throng, now idling curiously by some shop window
whither a display of jewels or curios attracted me, now
strolling on again content with the soft color in sky
and sunlight.

I found a florist whose shop windows were filled
with thickets of fragrant, fragile spring flowers; and
every little scented blossom that I touched, choosing
the freshest, nodded to the voiceless cadence of a name
repeated—and: "Geraldine! Geraldine!" they nodded,
so confidently, so sweetly, that what was I to do but
send them to her?

And so I sauntered on again, threading the throng,
half minded to turn back, yet ever tempted on by idleness, until above me the twin spires of the cathedral
glimmered, all silvered in the shimmering blue.

Halting, undecided, I presently became aware of an
old man, his withered hands crossed before him, standing quite patiently under the cathedral terrace. Be-

fore him on the sidewalk rested a basket draped with a brilliant rug or two and heaped with tawdry rubbish —scarlet fezzes, slippers of spangled leather, tasseled charms of gilt, flimsy striped fabrics—all the worthless flummery known as "Oriental" to the good people of the West.

Few stopped to look; no one bought. As I passed him his dimmed gaze met mine; all the wistfulness of the very poor, all the mystery of the very, very old, was in his eyes. Moved by impulse, perhaps, I spoke to him in a low voice, using the Turkish language.

A dull animation came into his misty eyes.

"*Allahou Ekber,*" he muttered, in a trembling voice; "it is sweet to hear your words, my son."

"Mussulman," I said, "who are you who recite the Tekbir here under the spires of a Roman church?"

"Is there harm in bearing witness to the glory of God here under the minarets of your cathedral?" he asked, humbly.

"Spire and minaret are one to Him," I said. "Who are you, Mussulman?"

"My name is Khassar," he said; "my nation Eighur; my Iort is the Issig-Kul; Baïon-Aoul my clan. I am an Eighur Turk, a Khodja; and I am able to write the Turkish language in Arabic and in Eighur-Mongol characters."

"Reverend father," I said, full of astonishment and pity, "how should a Khodja of the Baïon-Aoul come to this? Even the Tekrin horseman halts at the sea."

"It is written," he said, feebly, "that we belong to God and we return to Him."

Troubled, I stood there on the sidewalk, oblivious of the knot of idlers around us, curious to hear two men so different conversing in a common tongue.

I wished to give him something, yet did not venture to humiliate him without pretence of buying.

"Here is my card," I said, "on which is written my name and where I live. Bring me these rugs tonight, *ata*. I wish to buy."

"You do not desire them," he said, shaking his head. "You know the East; you understand these rugs; you know they are worthless, acid-washed, singed, rubbed with pumice, smoked—every vile Armenian practice used! You know the dyes are aniline; that they are loosely tied, hastily and flimsily woven by Armenian dogs and sons of dogs. You mean kindness; you have done me enough by speaking to me."

He passed his trembling hand over his ragged beard.

"You who know carpets and love them," he quavered, "listen attentively. I have a strip to show—not here—but I could bring it."

"Bring it," I said gently.

He fumbled in the pocket of his tattered coat and presently brought to light a scrap of paper on which was scrawled some Persian characters.

"It is such a carpet as I have never seen," he said; "there is nothing in our history or our traditions to teach us the meaning of this carpet—nothing save that it is an Eighur rug inscribed in Persian and in an unknown script. I have traced the characters in a single cartouche. Read, my son."

And I read, translating freely:

"Ten thousand thousand stars shine down on Babylon. The desert well reflects but one."

"I will bring the carpet," he said, after a silence. "I do not know its value; it has no beauty any longer; only the ghost of ancient splendor remains in the thin knots clinging to warp and weft. And it is old, my son, older than tradition. Upon it there is not one sign to teach us the mystery of its meaning."

He peered at me with his old, sad eyes, earnestly.

"I will bring it," he said. "Go with Ali, thou fair comrade of Hassan."

"May the Blessed Companions intervene for you," I said.

And so we parted, gravely and with circumstance, I to stroll homeward, touched, musing curiously upon this carpet of which a nomad Mussulman could make nothing. The Persian verse from the cartouche interested me too, the refrain lingering persistently in my memory:

"Ten thousand thousand stars shine down on Babylon. The desert well reflects but one."

Never before, save on the imperial carpet known as Belshazzar's Rug, had I encountered any inscription mentioning Babylon. So, at the first glance, the nomad's rug should have some value. But speculation was futile—surely I ought to have learned that if unnumbered disappointments could teach me anything.

Thinking of these things, I passed along the noble avenue, retracing my steps to the big dusky house standing alone, with two old trees to guard it—relics, like the mansion, of the great city's infancy—the last old dwelling left marooned amid the arid wastes of commerce. Here my cousin and his wife lived with me in winter; I with them at their Lenox home in summer.

A brougham or two at the curb before the house warned me of clients waiting or of visitors for Geraldine—doubtless the latter, for it was now past five.

Under the circumstances I went in to second Geraldine—for Westover never troubled himself to be civil to her friends.

There were people there, and tea—and a pretty wordless welcome from Geraldine.

The violet-tinted April dusk brought candle-light; people went away and others came; then, one by one, they left, and we were alone, Geraldine and I—and the new moon shining through the frail curtains. For a long time we talked together, aimlessly, of this and that which mattered nothing to anybody. A maid entered to draw the curtains. When she left, Geraldine laughed and picked up a cluster of yellow jonquils.

"Your courage failed you, after all," she said; "the loveliest woman in the world must go without my flowers to-night.

"She has them," I retorted.

"Do you mean me, Dick?" she said, under her breath.

"Did you doubt it?"

She bowed her head.   Silence, ever waiting to ensnare us, crept like a shadow in between us.   And I would not have it.

"An old man is to bring a rug to-night," I said, abruptly.

Geraldine stirred in her armchair, repeating in a low voice:

"Ten thousand, thousand stars shine down on Babylon: The desert well reflects but one.   Abaddon none."

Bolt upright in my chair I listened, incredulous of my own ears.

"Where on earth did you hear that?" I demanded.

"I read it on Belshazzar's Rug in cuneiform with the Kufic key," she answered, watching me.

"You—all alone—interpreted that?" I asked, astounded.

"Yes.   It is the cuneiform inscription in the gold cartouche."

Profound astonishment left me silent.   She lay back in her chair with a little laugh of pure excitement.

"After you went out," she said, "I was horribly lonely, and I thought of you, and then I thought about the work you loved—the cuneiforms—and—as Jim did not seem to need me in the laboratory—I thought to myself: 'Suppose—suppose by luck I could unravel the inscription on the gold cartouche!   Dick would be the happiest man in the world.   And then—your—your flowers came, and I sat for a while alone with them.   Then, on impulse, I jumped up and took the Kufic tables and all the combinations that you and I had tried together, and I slipped upstairs to the

marble room and knelt down before Belshazzar's Rug.
Oh, Dick! the Tree of Heaven seemed to quiver in
every jeweled branch and leaf!—it was only the
draught from the closing door that moved the rug,
but the mystic tree swayed there as the folds of the
carpet moved, and I seemed to feel the mystery of the
Prophet's Paradise stealing into me, penetrating me
like the incense of forbidden wine—and I—I felt very
Eastern and very pagan, kneeling there.

"It was strange, too; the intricate Kufic key seemed
to be falling into place of its own impulse, symbol after
symbol promising a linked symmetry of sense, until
almost before I was conscious of the miracle, it had
been wrought there in the marble room; and my eyes
were opened; and I, kneeling before the Tree of
Heaven, read quite clearly what is written in the gold
cartouche on the great carpet of Belshazzar.   Dick,
I prayed so hard that I might read it.   And I have read
it—for *you!*"

In the eloquence of her emotion she had risen, holding out both hands to me; I caught them, crushing
them to my lips.

Ominous pulsating silence grew between us; her
fingers relaxed and her hands fell from my lips.   The
stillness, intense, absolute, became a tension, a growing, resistless force pressing us apart, slowly, inexora-
bly driving me back step by step against the silk-
hung wall, which I reached for, groping, steadying
myself.

Never before had we been so swayed, so thrilled;
never before had we been so reckless of the peril.

Over us a magic snare had fallen, and we had evaded it; an unseen and delicate web, enmeshing us, drawing us together limb to limb, body to body, soul to soul, there on the kindling edges of destruction.

.   .   .   .

She sank back into the deep seat by the window, her white hands tightening on the gilded foliation of the chair's carved arms.   And I saw how pale her face was and how her dark eyes were fixed steadily upon the floor as though destruction was a pit whose edge lay at her feet.

Presently I became aware that the world outside the curtained windows was moving still—had perhaps never halted on its way to wail upon our fate.   And, crossing the room, I raised the shade and saw the new moon, low in the sky, kneeling amid the watching stars. Yellow rays from a street lamp illuminated the old tree's foliage, edging with palest fire the tracery of new-born leaves, tufting each stem and twig, exquisite, delicately formal as the leafy labyrinths of the Tree of Heaven spreading above the flowery field of Belshazzar's Rug.

.   .   .   .

Khassar the nomad had come and gone, and his rug hung in the marble room, pale as the tinted shadow cast by the great carpet of Belshazzar.

The nomad's rug was clean but very ancient, and so worn, so time-eaten to the very warp, that the Kherdeh was all but obliterated in the metnih.   But outside of that, between the outside band and the ara, or central line, there were traces of ancient glory and dimmed outlines of design; and I saw the twelve cartouches inscribed alternately in Persian and in cuneiform characters. There, too, were the worn remains of floral thickets haunted of beast and bird, intricate allegories, chronicles in color and symbol, every leaf, every blossom, every creature fraught with mystic meaning; and there also, still faintly to be made out, the shadowy foliage of the Tree of Heaven.

"How much did you pay for that ghost of a rug?" demanded Westover, who had followed me upstairs after dressing for dinner.

When I told him he shrugged his shoulders, but made no comment. A moment later Geraldine entered, and his small eyes, no longer furtive, became fixed and dull.

"They say in the East," I remarked, "that when all color is gone from an Eighur rug a lost soul takes it for its abode. Eighur women are supposed to have souls occasionally, and to lose them now and then."

"There are plenty of lost souls in town," observed Westover; "no doubt you'll have your choice of tenants for your carpet; or," he added, staring at space, "if you like I'll provide you."

I did not understand his remark, but it left a vaguely sinister impression. Geraldine, standing between us, her white fingers linked behind her, looked up at me very gravely.

"Do you know," she said, "that I am convinced that I wove that rug some centuries ago?"

"I have no doubt of it," I replied, smiling.

"Do you doubt it, Jim?" she asked, gayly.

He did not reply.

"As a matter of fact," I said, "it was always believed that a young girl who dared to weave the Tree of Heaven into an Eighur carpet died when her task was ended—her entire physical and spiritual vitality entering into the sacred tree and infusing it with mystic splendor."

"Oh, I died as you say," observed Geraldine, gravely.

"I don't see that you infused much physical or spiritual splendor into that rug," observed Westover.

"I must die again, you know, Jim, and bring its vanished beauty back," she said, gayly. "Shall I, Dick?—and leave you a priceless carpet as my bequest and monument?"

Westover turned on his heel, fidgeting with his collar. Recently his neck had grown fat behind the ears.

A few moments later dinner was announced.

We lingered late over dinner, I remember; Jim drank heavily—a habit which both Geraldine and I had long since left unnoticed, she shrinking from the sullen rebuff certain to follow even a playful protest, I understanding the utter hopelessness of interference. His mind, already shaken, would one day shatter, and the dreadful price be paid.

As he sat sousing walnuts in port, in his altered features and swollen hands I seemed to divine something malicious and patient and powerful—that indescribable physical menace one feels in the inert brooding eye of the mentally and spiritually crippled.

When Geraldine rose he stood up unsteadily. After she had gone he lighted a cigar and turned his bloodshot eyes on me.

"Is that wine expensive?" he demanded, pointing to Geraldine's half-empty glass.

"Rather," I said.

He picked up the glass, examined it, sniffing at the contents.

"It's poor claret," he said. "Taste it. It's pure poison, I tell you."

"I'm sorry," I said, indifferently.

Again he sniffed it. "Faugh!" he sneered, and threw it into the fireplace behind him. Then he got on his feet, heavily, muttering to himself, and stumbled off through the drawing-room.

For a while I sat there amid the shaded candles, staring at space. But I could not read the future pictured there amid the empty chairs and flowers, already drooping in each crystal vase.

When at length I roused myself and went up-stairs, passing her apartment, I heard her singing to herself, and I wondered that she could.

I paused on the gallery stairway to listen; and she could not have heard my footsteps on the thick deep carpeting, yet she came to the door and opened it, looking up at me where I stood.

"You are going to the marble room. May I come and help you?" she asked sweetly. And as I was silent, she said again: "Let me be happy, won't you, Dick? Let me be where you are."

"Have I ever avoided you, Geraldine?"

I descended the steps, she laid her hand lightly on my arm, and together we mounted the stairway toward the gallery.

"I was singing a Hillah tent-song when you passed," she said, "partly because I was lonely, and partly"—she hesitated, looking around at me—"partly because I've come to the conclusion, Dick, that I was once at Belshazzar's feast in Cadimirra—for there's a great deal of wickedness in me—you'd never believe it, would you?"

She smiled at me so innocently, so adorably, that I laughed outright.

"I've heard that the maids of Babilu-Ki had a bowing acquaintance with the devil," I said. "Even an Eighur girl nodded pleasantly to Erlik now and then —according to the chronicles of the Terkins."

"Oh, they surely did," she said. And, "Thank you, Dick," she added, as we reached the gallery; "when I am an old woman you must help me up the steep places."

"It is you who help me," I said, lightly.

She stood, resting her arm on the table while I gathered up the mass of papers containing our cuneiform combinations and the Kufic key.

"All that is useless," she said, suddenly. Her manner and smile had altered.

I looked up in surprise, and at the same instant she pushed the papers from beneath my hands.

"The memory of things forgotten centuries ago has returned to me," she said, feverishly. "I am a pagan again. It was Istar who first taught my hands to

weave and my fingers to tie the Sehna knot. I wove
that carpet; what I have woven there I can read.
Why do you laugh? Will you believe me if I translate the mystery of each inscription as easily as I read
the gold cartouche? Come; we shall never need those
papers again."

What new caprice was this? She was smiling,
almost fixedly, and I thought that there was something in her over-flushed face and in the starlike brilliancy of her eyes not quite normal. At the same
moment the electric lights in the laboratory went out.
Westover was evidently in there. I waited, expecting
him to appear, but he did not. Again I reached for
the papers, but Geraldine scattered them with a quick
sweep of her hand.

"Won't you believe me? Won't you let me try?"
she repeated, almost impatiently.

With a quick movement she bent forward past
me and shut off the lights in the gallery where we
stood. Another second, and the lights in the marble
room broke out fiercely; and there, full in the dazzling
glory, I saw the great carpet of Belshazzar hanging,
and beside it the Eighur rug—a pallid shadow on the
wall.

Geraldine, hands clasped to her scarlet mouth, dark
eyes fixed, moved forward slowly, opalescent tints
flashing on her smooth bare arms and shoulders, her
head a delicate silhouette against the glare.

I followed, pausing at her side, and we stood
silently before the miracle, the great folds gently stirring in some unfelt current; and I saw the upper

branches of the Tree of Heaven sway, and a thousand leaves, all glistening, quiver and subside.

"One can almost hear the rustling of the leaves, " I whispered.

"I hear more than that," she murmured. "I hear my soul bidding me good-by."

She smiled dreamily, turning to the faded Eighur carpet, and stepping back one pace, dropped her left arm, clasping my hand in hers.

"It was I who wove that carpet—I, maid of the Issig-Kul—and it was you, beloved of Hassan, who inspired it."

"What are you saying, Geraldine?" I began, uneasily; "where did you ever hear my name linked with the name of Hassan?"

Her palm was burning hot, her eyes, too, bright. The fever of caprice possessed her, and her imagination was running riot.

There was a silence, through which a distant sound penetrated—the faint ring of glass somewhere in the laboratory. Westover was tying on his crystal mask.

She heard it, too, and she turned, looking me full in the eyes.

"Dick," she said, "he has slain my body. My soul is bidding me good-by."

"It is my own that he is dragging to destruction, not yours," I muttered.

But she only clasped my hand tighter, the fixed smile stamped on her lips.

"Listen," she whispered, raising her arm. "This is

what is written in the rose cartouche on the Eighur carpet that I made:

> " 'Roses of Babylon; Ashes of Roses in Abaddon.'

"Love and its awful penalty, Dick—and the warning I wove, coffined in cryptogram! Listen again. The cartouche below was once topaz—for I wove it—I!

> " 'All Paradise the cost:
> Warp and weft for souls so lost.'

—Mine, Dick, mine!—lost in loving as I loved, centuries since. I have no soul; I have never had any since I lost it then. It is there, tenanting the phantom of an Eighur carpet. Do you not understand? There is my faded monument and refuge—that magic-woven sanctuary—that hiding-place from hell!"

Her little feverish fingers tightened convulsively in mine; the color flamed in her cheeks. Suddenly she crushed our clasped hands to her heart, and I felt it leaping madly.

"Geraldine," I stammered, "what is all this ghastly nonsense? Are you ill?"

"Listen! Listen!" she whispered; "the next cartouche was blue—the lost Persian blue! I know; why should I not know—I who wove it centuries ago? And thus it reads, O thou whom I loved to my destruction—thou whom I love:

> " 'Time and the Guest
> Shall meet me twice,—once East, once West.'

"Ah, prophetess was I by Istar's favor—seeing I died for love. Do you not understand, Dick? Time and the Guest!—the Guest is Death—the Guest we all must entertain one day—and I twice—once in the East, once here in the West—here, now!"

"Geraldine, are you mad?" I whispered; "look at me!—turn and look at me, I say!"

But she shivered in my arms, whispering that she was ransoming her soul and mine. A distant sound broke from the laboratory, and we listened.

"Hush, beloved," she said, breathlessly; "the last cartouche is black! And this is written there:

" 'Soul, lotus-sealed,
       Receive—thy—Paradise—' "

Her voice died out; a terrible pallor struck her face; she swayed where she stood, the smile frozen on her bloodless lips.

As I caught her to me, her head fell straight back and her body sank a dead weight in my arms. Then a dreadful thing occurred; the faded ancient tapestry glowed out like a live ember, kindling from end to end, brighter, fiercer, flaming into living fire; and the phantom Tree of Heaven, flashing, superbly jeweled, burst into magnificent florescence.

Blinded, almost stupefied, I staggered back, but the straining cry died in my throat as a voice is strangled in dreadful dreams. Again I strove to shout. The rug, glowing like a living cinder, slowly faded before my eyes. Suddenly the last spark went out in a shower of whitening ashes.

Again I strove to cry out: "Jim! Jim!" but my lips stiffened with horror as I listened. For he was somewhere there in the darkness, laughing.

"It was in her wine," he chuckled—"and I saw her

kiss the glass and look at you! and you, there, staring at nothing! Stare at it now!"

And again: "Do you think I have never watched her?—and you? Now she's in hell, and we'll race for her on even terms once more."

Silence; a low, insane laugh, cut by a report and the crash of glass as he fell, shattering his masked face upon the floor.

After a long while I spoke, listening intently. Then I took up my burden.

And there was no sound save the soft stirring of her silken gown as I bore her through the darkness, my cold lips pressed to hers.

END OF VOLUME FOUR